Chuck & Debbie

COLD LONELY COURAGE

Soren Paul Petrek

Black Rose Writing

www.blackrosewriting.com

Second printing

ISBN: 978-0-9825823-7-4

PUBLISHED BY BLACK ROSE WRITING

www.blackrosewriting.com

Printed in the United States of America

Cold Lonely Courage is printed in 12-point Times New Roman

Cover Art by Michael Morgan

Michael Morgan is a Member of the Royal Institute of Painters in Watercolour and a Founding Academician of the South West Academy of Fine Art in the United Kingdom. His extraordinary paintings are in private and public collections internationally.

For information concerning his original paintings and prints visit www.marinehouseatbeer.co.uk

For my parents, William and Sandra Petrek, my Rock of Gibraltar and my wife Renee, my sail on the horizon.

"I was responsible for recruiting women for the work, in the face of a good deal of opposition, I may say, from the powers that be. In my view, women were very much better than men for the work. Women, as you must know, have a far greater capacity for cool and lonely courage than men."

—Captain Selwyn Jepson, British Special Operations Executive Senior Recruiting Officer, World War Two.

CHAPTER **ONE**

Artillery shells roared through the sky, ripping apart the serenity of the late spring day. Their passing was an obscene display raining down death. The soldiers below clawed their way deeper into the trench, screaming in pain and terror. Men and equipment detonated, pieces of them falling into smoldering piles of dead and ruined bodies. The stench of scorched earth mixed with smoke choked the men and poisoned the air.

Yves Toche and the men in his unit watched as a sea of German uniforms and tanks came hurtling towards them from behind the bombardment. This was the German *blitzkrieg*, or "lightning war," that had seen Poland's million-man army fall within a month. The Germans pushed the French army back effortlessly as they poured out of Belgium into France.

The skies were full of German planes, relentlessly strafing and bombing the defenders. Yves watched as squadrons passed overhead, fanning out along the front to join the infantry and armor on the ground to crush the French troops before they had a chance to respond.

Yves peered over the top of the trench in front of him and shook his head. The French military was not prepared for something like this. They expected Germany to attack but it never seemed to come. Many had taken to calling it the phony war. War had been declared but there was no fighting. The French had placed their faith in the heavy guns directed at Germany and spaced along the mighty Maginot line. It was designed as an impenetrable fortress against invasion from the east. There were over 500 concrete and steel fortifications commanding gigantic firepower and hundreds of thousands of troops. The Germans feigned an attack along the line but then sent a million men and armor into the Netherlands and Belgium through the "impenetrable" Arden Forest. The natural and man-made barriers that were supposed to stop the enemy had failed. Germany had invented a mobile war machine and France simply wasn't prepared. Germany had learned from its mistakes in the trench battles following their loss in Yves' father's war. They didn't intend to make the same mistake twice.

Yves looked at the faces of the men in his group. They looked as scared as he felt. The troops descending on them were experienced and hardened. The Germans were emboldened by an expectation of easy victory. The French were paralyzed by the reality that every preparation they had made had failed completely. They were not fools; they expected a full-scale attack, but nothing like the avalanche crashing towards them. Yves saw a few men break and run, but most held their ground. Every muscle in his own body screamed at him to bolt. Instead he checked and rechecked his rifle. It seemed puny in the face of so much firepower, yet he held his position. The ground rumbled as the mass of men and machines came surging forward.

Yves heard the order to fire. He raised his rifle and shot wildly into the enemy line. Men to his left and right fired desperately. Behind Yves's position the French artillery was firing their cannons on the advancing Germans. It had little effect as the mass of men and machines charged forward. As he fired, Yves heard the terrifying scream of a Stuka dive-bomber falling down from the sky. He tried to scatter along with others but could only crouch at the last minute when the bomb hit. He was flung from his foxhole, cartwheeling through the air. For one wild moment events around him moved in slow motion. He was jarred back to consciousness when his body slammed into the ground. When he tried to move he felt impossibly heavy. He managed to control one of his hands long enough to reach up and feel the ruin of the right side of his face. He could not see out of his right eye, and could feel his mouth filling with blood. The terror of the implication of his wounds settled on him but couldn't penetrate the shock that enveloped his body. He knew that he was badly wounded and wondered why he hadn't been killed instantly. He could see a little out of his left eye but there was nothing left of the men that had been near him when the bomb exploded. They had been swept from the earth, swatted away by the terrible force unleashed from numerous explosions. His vision blurred, as he drifted into merciful unconsciousness.

Some time later, medics from an ambulance scooped Yves onto a stretcher and raced away towards the rear and a field hospital. Along with countless others, Yves's war had been cut brutally short.

CHAPTER **TWO**

"This is madness," Madeleine thought as she moved slowly down the hospital corridor, shrinking against the wall trying to avoid the dead and dying. A wounded soldier cried out as she slipped in a widening pool of blood pouring out of the torn remnants of his leg. Doctors and nurses rushed past, pulling her along in their wake as they flung themselves from patient to patient, trying to save what lives they could.

Madeleine turned as an orderly grabbed her by the arm and pulled her away from the triage area towards a desk stationed next to a set of double doors. A young doctor looked up from a chart, momentarily taken aback by her radiant beauty.

"Yves Toche, I'm looking for Yves Toche," Madeleine blurted out. "He was wounded and brought here."

The doctor gestured towards the double doors. "He's at the end of the ward," he said abruptly dropping his eyes and moving past her.

Madeleine saw a hint of hopelessness in the doctor's expression as he quickly looked away. A question died on her lips as she realized the meaning of the look on his face. Yves was severely wounded. There was no other explanation.

Madeleine hurried through the double doors and into the ward.

This ward was quiet and orderly. Madeleine realized at once that the men inside were dying and heavily sedated to ease their pain. She walked down the row of beds looking for her brother, her grief growing as she saw the extent of the trauma the young men had suffered. She clenched her hands, so overwhelmed by what she saw that she could not look away.

At the end of the room she approached the final bed. She

hardly recognized the young man beneath the bandages. His face and hands were tightly wrapped. A tube dripped into a needle in his arm. She quietly bent over him and whispered his name.

"Yves. It's Madeleine."

She watched as Yves came back from some far off place in his mind. He slowly responded to her voice. Finally his one eye widened as he looked at her. The cornflower blue was still there, but the life force behind it was distant behind a milky haze. Madeleine brushed away a few strands of golden curls that poked out from the bandages that were soaking through with the blood from his wounds. The bandages covering him were a mercy. She could barely stand thinking about the cruelty of the damage inflicted on him. Tears filled her eyes and she tried not to fall apart as she sobbed quietly.

"Madeleine. Is that you? I can't see," he said, his voice trailing off behind the drugs easing his suffering.

"Yes Yves, I'm here. Are you in pain? I can get the doctor," she said carefully, taking his hand into hers.

"No pain, medics and doctors worked on me already..."

Madeleine bent closer trying to hear as Yves whispered.

"Yves you can't leave us," Madeleine answered desperately.

"Have to go."

"You're breaking my heart," she cried as her tears streamed down her face, falling onto the bandages that held his mangled face together.

Madeleine held him until the last rasps of breath left his body.

It was long after he stopped breathing that she sat back and looked at him. The pain was gone and he seemed at peace. She prayed silently for him and her family. She asked nothing of God for herself. She was adrift. She could sense the room around her, but she wasn't there. Neither was Yves, just an empty shell that had once been the light to her dark, the day to her night. The enemy had taken that away without provocation. There had been an act of greed and revenge provoked by Germany's damaged pride, Madeleine thought. Both were mortal sins, evil in their implications.

Madeleine stared out the window behind Yves' hospital bed, trying to gather her wits. She knew that she couldn't sit next to Yves' bed and ignore the fact that German troops were rapidly overrunning all of France and would eventually overtake the hospital. She needed to get home and had many long miles to travel. There would be refugees everywhere, and the sooner she set out the better. She felt weak and alone in a way she had never experienced. She knew that she needed to get Yves back to La Ciotat. Her parents would be devastated. She would have to deliver the worst news a parent can get. She could not return without bringing him with her. At least his family could bury him.

Madeleine brushed the tears from her face. She stood up and kissed Yves on his cheek, the warmth of his body fading. She walked towards the front to get his remains released. She didn't intend to take no for an answer and didn't really expect any resistance. Life was for the living and a wounded man would need the bed. She felt strengthened by purpose and knew that somebody would answer for her brother's death. Germany would find France a hard trophy to hold, of that she was certain. The French people were long accustomed to controlling their own fate. Germany didn't have a monopoly on national pride. The French were renowned for it.

CHAPTER **THREE**

Madeleine looked from the train window and saw her parents waiting for her on the train platform. She squeezed her eyes closed; suddenly losing the resolve that she had mustered to deliver the terrible news. As she stepped from the train she saw them catch sight of her. She could not keep the anguish from her face. One look and they both knew. There would be explanations later but the message was conveyed. Her mother fell to the ground unable to move. Her father stood mute, crumpled by the blow. In his grief she saw his strength holding him together, his chin raised as he hobbled forward to embrace the child he had left.

"Soldiers die, Madeleine. We must honor Yves by living our own lives the best we can. The Boche has come before. When we defeat them this time we will destroy them utterly." Jean-Pierre said determination and coldness creeping into his voice. His eyes were distant, seeing something far away that only he could see.

Madeleine drew strength from his resolve; it was an anchor for her to hold onto. She knew her parents would not meekly accept the loss of their son, her brother. Revenge would be exacted.

As the terrible reality sank in and the German lines drew nearer, they clung to each other at every opportunity, afraid that if they let go they'd lose each other the way they'd lost Yves. Madeleine knew that they needed to open their restaurant and serve their customers. Families all over were quietly mourning, having lost young men at the front. Others had been captured and of them there was no news. France was falling rapidly and it seemed as if nothing could stop that now. The British had come to their aid but had been pushed back into the sea at Dunkirk, allowed to leave as Hitler permitted their escape. There would be no counter attack, and hope faded as a grim future unfolded.

Within a couple of weeks the Toches reopened their doors and continued the routine of managing their restaurant. Yves would have expected this. He had been born to run a restaurant. His easy manner with customers and his love and respect for the food that came out of the kitchen was obvious. When Madeleine served in the dining room or cleared tables, she lacked Yves' good-natured spirit. He had charmed everyone right down to the dour, unhappy people who thrived on complaint. They were no match for him. He shone like the sun with his easy smile and desire to please. Madeleine's reaction to customer complaint clearly indicated that she was a resteraunteur better suited to the back of the house.

Germany charged past the French defenses and took the country in little more than a month. Madeleine's father was silent as all of this transpired. Nobody knew what to expect or what to do. Eventually German troops established a presence in the town and more were garrisoned nearby. France surrendered and was broken down into two governing areas. A puppet government had been set up in the south in the city of Vichy. The fiction was that France was allowed self-government in the south. It meant little and was all the more insulting when Henri Petain, a national hero from the First World War, agreed to an armistice with Germany. He then took control of the Vichy government as its head. Her father said the world had gone mad. General Petain, a hero from the Great War, was now a collaborator with his old enemy. Madeleine watched as her parents aged before her eyes. The only normalcy was the routine of the restaurant as they tried to mask their grief through work.

Customers came to Chez Toche, but now they had a new clientele. German officers came in, and for the most part were at least cordial. A few were arrogant and boisterous, treating the French like servants to provide their every whim. The Toches did nothing to overtly antagonize the Germans.

Within a few months whisperings of a resistance movement began. Jean-Pierre said that whatever was to be done during the occupation would happen behind the scenes. The Toche family discussed the implications in secret, waiting and willing for an opportunity to do their part.

Madeleine was often the object of flirtations from the young officers. She came to realize that they weren't all Nazis. She never encouraged any of their comments or behavior. For the most part they were young men and boys far away from home, trying to live up to some romantic notion of fraternizing with beautiful French girls. A few glared at her in a way that concerned her but there was no one to whom she could complain. She did her work and moved ahead. She had no social life outside of the restaurant even though her parents tried to encourage her to see her friends. She simply told them that she wasn't ready, and they left it at that.

CHAPTER **FOUR**

Madeleine took over the duties of going to the market to purchase supplies for the restaurant. Because there were few restaurants in town they were able to obtain more rationed items than individual families. The strength of their cuisine made the restaurant a favorite dining spot among the German officers. Someone in a position of authority must have given orders to provide the restaurant with whatever was required. The sea and the countryside provided much of the menu. The Germans spent lavishly, and the Toches were able to buy better cheese and meat from the small farms. The fishermen in the port kept the supply of fish abundant and fresh. Wine in the region was plentiful and the restaurant kept their cellar well stocked.

Obtaining what they needed simply required more effort than before. Many Mondays when the restaurant was closed, Madeleine and her parents traveled around the countryside, gathering the wild thyme and rosemary that grew abundantly in the dry rocky terrain of the hills that rose up a few miles from the sea. Everything wild and edible was collected. The truffle hunters and their pigs went on providing the dark pungent fungus that could change an everyday meal into a gourmet feast. No one interfered with the truffle hunters. The magic of the ugly little fungus saw to that.

Madeleine loved the walks in the wilds of Provence, baking in the sun as she moved, collecting herbs or simply staring out to sea, breathing in the fine salt air as she walked along the *Callonques*, the narrow cliffs that surrounded small inlets from the sea. She felt that Provence was for the Provencal, the people of the region. They were happy to share their beauty and abundance, but on their own terms. The marriage of the land and the sea was the true secret to the magic of her home. The Germans had brutally violated that trust and had to be repelled. News came from other areas concerning resistance efforts. Madeleine knew that women were fighting alongside the men. She spoke quietly among her friends and acquaintances, those she felt she could trust. A strengthening desire grew in her as her patience with her own inaction became increasingly unbearable.

CHAPTER **FIVE**

On market day, Madeleine was returning from the bakery with a pushcart that she often took to accommodate larger orders. It was easy to maneuver it down the narrow streets and alleys behind the various establishments she frequented on restaurant business. She passed a few soldiers idly enjoying some time off. They touched their hats as they passed, taking the opportunity to look at her fully. Madeleine was used to men looking at her and was neither distracted nor upset by the attention. She took care with her appearance as the women of France do. The attention of men was simply a reassurance that she was both desirable and beautiful. It was a small measure of condolence in a world of uncertainty.

As she continued down the street an officer coming from the opposite direction glared at her like a piece of meat to be taken. He was the picture of Aryan arrogance. He was large and blond, with cruel blue eyes. His uniform carried the twin lightning bolts of the SS on his collar. Madeleine had heard rumors that some of the SS had been criminals or at least political zealots prior to the war. They preached an unwavering message of intolerance for any group deemed to be inferior. They believed that their destiny was to rule the world.

Madeleine felt dirty as she quickened her pace to distance herself from him. There was something threatening in his demeanor that suggested dangerous intentions. She looked away so as not to encourage any kind of encounter. She could feel his eyes following her, heavy with contempt and lust. He did nothing to disguise his feelings. Her skin crawled as they passed and she made a mental note to stay out of his way. She had come to learn that all the Germans were not alike. The *Schutzstaffel* or *Waffen-*SS were the feared military wing of the Nazi party. They were known for being both extraordinary soldiers and ruthless champions of the twisted racist beliefs of their party. They considered all non-Aryans inferior, a belief reinforced in their minds since childhood and strengthened by their group's formation in 1925 as Hitler's personal guard. How could a country allow such monsters to come to power? Their brutal treatment of the Jews, or anyone who opposed them, was legendary. The SS and the Gestapo rarely came to La Ciotat except when they were on leave, or so Madeleine suspected. War didn't lessen the draw of the south of France for those seeking to relax in the sun on her beaches.

Some days passed and Madeleine found herself walking the same route back from the baker. The family had an older car but only used it for longer trips or to transport larger items. Petrol was rationed and rarely available. Madeleine didn't mind the walk; it gave her some time to herself and her thoughts. She glanced down the narrow street and didn't see any other pedestrians. From time to time that happened and she thought little of it.

As Madeleine passed an old warehouse she suddenly felt a man strike from the shadows behind her. She was roughly grabbed, a hand clamping down over her mouth as she was lifted off her feet.

"Struggle and I will kill you," her assailant hissed in heavily accented French.

Madeleine felt the muzzle of a gun in the small of her back and smelled the heavy reek of drink on the man's breath. Faster than she thought possible, Madeleine was pulled inside a darkened room. She immediately recognized the man as the German officer she had encountered in the street. The look on his face gave away his intentions as he pushed her to the ground and towered over her. He seemed to enjoy the surprise and terror that flashed on her face as she made the connection.

He raised the gun to her head. "Oh yes, you remember me. Now stand up and take off your clothes," he said, lifting the back of her shirt with the barrel of his pistol.

Madeleine slowly complied. She knew that if she resisted he would either kill or severely injure her. He had the gun. As she undressed his eyes riveted on each part of her body as it was revealed. His excitement was obvious. She sensed it was his control over her and the violence of his actions that gave him the most pleasure.

"Turn around," he said, roughly grabbing her shoulder.

Madeleine closed her eyes as he pushed her roughly onto a table. She felt the gun pressed to the back of her head as the rapist thrust himself into her as violently as possible. She bit into her lip and was motionless as he rammed into her. Blood ran down the inside of her legs. He increased the force of his thrusting, excited more by the violence of his act than the sensation of it. He laughed and grunted when she tried to stifle her cries of pain.

Madeleine's mind left her body momentarily, disassociating herself from the cruelty of the man's violation. Her concentration shifted from pain and humiliation to survival. She watched dispassionately as if the assault was happening to someone else. She saw the savage zeal on his face in his reflection in a broken window leaning against a wall in front of the table. Spit and drool ran from his mouth as he grunted with the violence of each thrust. He finished and pushed her down into the dirt. He holstered his sidearm and straightened his clothing.

"Now, bitch, you have been with a real man. The next time I come to your restaurant you will personally serve me. If you tell anyone about this, I will carve your parents up in front of you after I have taken you and your mother in front of your father. You will be nice to me. You are a peasant, but a beautiful one. Once you understand that we Germans are your masters, you will come to seek out my affections. For now, I will take them until I tire of you."

Madeleine felt the blow of each word as physically as the man's assault. She hugged herself and prayed that he would leave her. She knew nothing she could say would do anything but feed his sadistic pleasure. A distant voice in her head said "patience" over and over again, like a tiny whisper from the bottom of a well. She knew it came from within herself and she clung to it with every shattered fragment of her will. Then suddenly he was gone, walking back into the street without the slightest hesitation or concern that his crime would be discovered.

Madeleine sat in the dirt for a long while, neither crying nor drifting into shock. She felt a growing anger seep into her. She saw her brother's shattered face and the horrible, psychopathic rapture on the face of her rapist flashing back and forth in her mind. The anger was sweet and seductive in its promise of revenge. At first, her own visions of the violence she would do to the rapist frightened her as vivid images of his mangled corpse came into focus in her mind. That fear gave way to rage. She allowed it to wash over her in a hot, cleansing torrent. She stood and began to arrange her clothes. The rawness of the ancient animal emotion gave her strength. She felt it course throughout her body, shimmering like molten metal. Her thoughts focused and the pure venom of it glowed in her mind. In the dirt and grime of her rape, she knelt down into the mixture of her own blood and the filth of the floor, and swore a quiet oath.

"I know what to do, Yves. Yes, I know what to do."

Madeleine walked back outside and picked up her cart of bread and headed back home. She held her head up. She would never walk around like a sheep again unless it helped her against these monsters. They would pay in blood and the German officer would be the first.

Madeleine walked her cart of groceries to the kitchen entrance in the alley behind the restaurant. She paused and collected herself, brushing dirt from her clothing and straightening her hair. She walked into the kitchen where her father was slicing vegetables into a large soup kettle.

"How were the prices today?" he asked without looking up from his cutting board. Madeleine pulled up a chair and sat down. When she didn't answer, Jean-Pierre paused and looked over at her. She was sitting very quietly and concentrating on her hands folded in her lap.

"Madeleine, what's happened?" he asked, setting down his paring knife and sliding into a seat next to her."

"I have something to tell you Papa, but you must promise to listen before you react."

"I promise," he answered with some hesitation.

Madeleine told him what the officer had done. She saw the rage in him build with each word.

"I will kill him, Madeleine. You point him out to me and he will die for his crime."

"No Papa, It must be me. He violated me. He and his kind killed Yves. I cannot stand it any longer. I must fight. The look on his face told the future of what lies ahead for France if we do not fight."

"No Madeleine, I cannot lose another child. You will be caught and killed. I have killed many men. One more won't make any difference when I go before God."

"Papa, if France is to be free then there will be a lot more killing to do. So I had better learn. The armies are defeated. It will be young men and women like myself who do the killing now. Besides, when you went to war against the Germans you were no older than I am now."

Madeleine held his eyes so completely that he felt the rage and courage charging through her. She had changed. The core of strength that he had always seen in her was now unclouded by her other emotions. He closed his eyes and slowly lowered his head as the truth took hold of him. There could be no other alternative. She would follow this path, the same path he remembered following as he went to the trenches full of youthful expectation and vigor, except she would go to her trenches filled with hate, determination and a calculating resourceful manner that he knew would serve her above all else.

"Then you need to know what it truly is you are running towards, Madeleine Toche. I will tell you what war is," he said, a hard edge entering his voice as he made up his mind. He was determined that she understand the extent of the horror of war.

"The first time you look into a person's eyes when you kill them will terrify you. After you have killed dozens or hundreds you will see their faces in your waking dreams because they will never leave you. You will walk on the edge of madness at times and it will only be your will to live that keeps you killing, listening to their screams as they beg for life and an end to their pain. You may make decisions that get innocent people killed, and still you must go on killing, because finally that is all you have left. And then one glorious day, the killing stops."

Madeleine slowly nodded her head. "Then tell me what I need to know, what I must know."

The two of them spoke late into the night, planning her revenge. It was then that he told her the stories that he had told no other. Stories of nights of despair and terror as the enemy shelling continued, pulverizing everything in its path. He told her how time and time again he and his friends had gone "over the top" and out of the trench when the commander's whistle blew. He told her how he knew that each time that whistle blew he would kill boys like himself and that some of his friends would not live to fight another day, and that he could receive a fatal wound and his terror would be over. He told her how he had felt the first time he had thrust his bayonet into a man, the look on the other's face as the man gargled and choked on his own blood. He spoke of how life began to mean nothing and how he and others used the bodies of dead soldiers to fortify their trenches for shelter from bombardment. He spoke of how the reasons for war became blurred and how it eventually broke down into a simple daily struggle for survival. He described the rats and the unspeakable food they were forced to eat to stave off starvation, and the vast number of men that died from the virulent diseases that took as many as the bullets and bombs of the enemy. He spoke quietly as he explained how each morning was spent collecting the dead, many killed by their own hand when they simply could not go on. Every day started by counting the living. Madeleine listened without interruption. He had lived such a long part of his young life in terror and misery, only to be rewarded with the loss of a leg and the death of so many of his comrades. He spoke to her as an equal and with great confidence, often times looking away as he saw things again that had been buried and covered by heavy mental scars that were best left undisturbed.

The next evening after the customers left, Jean-Pierre got up from the table and went down into the basement. "I have something for you," he said.

When he returned he laid a cloth-wrapped object down in front of Madeleine.

"If you mean what you say Madeleine, pick that up and unwrap it," he said, gesturing towards the object.

Madeleine's eyes were focused on the bundle. It was wrapped in a soft oiled cloth. She instinctively knew from her father's mannerisms what lay inside. She picked it up quickly and carefully pulled the cloth from around a small but wicked looking pistol. For its size it felt heavy in her hand. She did not hesitate and turned it over, snapping open the cylinder, closing it and pointing it evenly and smoothly towards the corner of the room. Jean-Pierre watched her handle the weapon; she had neither fear nor hesitation. He had never seen Madeleine handle any firearm before, and he felt her affinity towards it. The same way some people instinctively sail or play an instrument, some handle weapons as if they were an extension of their person. She was one of them.

Over the next few days they practiced at a deserted farm, far away from town. Jean-Pierre told her where to shoot a man to ensure a quick kill. As they spoke a plan developed between them. It was simple and precise. She would gain entry to the officer's rooms. Once he was asleep she would exact her revenge: she would wrap the small caliber pistol in a pillow, place it against his temple, and fire a shot into his brain. Madeleine made it very clear to Jean-Pierre that if the plan required allowing the man to violate her again, she would gladly do so with the knowledge that once he had completed the act she would kill him with no remorse.

Madeleine and Jean-Pierre said nothing to her mother. She would not understand and quite likely would try to kill the officer in rage when she learned of the rape of her daughter.

CHAPTER SIX

Madeleine and Jean-Pierre waited patiently. In less than a week the officer returned. He came through the door wearing his full SS uniform, swaggering and leading a small group of junior officers, his arrogance filling the room.

As soon as Madeleine saw him, she walked over to his table and spoke to him.

"Captain, how nice to see you again," she said convincingly.

He looked at her with some surprise. She made sure there was nothing hostile in her demeanor. Her eyes met his and were soft and compliant. He allowed his arrogance to explain her dismissal of the violence that he had visited upon her and answered cheerfully.

"You are as beautiful as ever tonight, mademoiselle. Please bring my men and me some of your best wine. I feel like celebrating."

As she turned to leave Madeleine intentionally brushed her hand against his shoulder being careful to make sure the other men at the table saw her do so. It had the intended result as she heard whispers from the men and some subdued laughing. Out of the corner of her eye she could see that the Captain was enjoying the attention. All the better to bring down his guard.

As the evening progressed and numerous large glasses of strong wine were consumed everything fell into place. He treated her like a favorite pet. She felt empowered as her control grew. She whispered into his ear from time to time as she manipulated him into the trap like Hansel and Gretel into the gingerbread house.

At the end of the evening, the restaurant closed and the soldiers rose to leave, staggering and holding onto one another as they stumbled and lurched towards the door. Madeleine placed a small bottle of cognac into the rapist's hands as he left and whispered to him that it was a gift, and that she would see him later. He drunkenly smiled and squeezed her backside as he veered towards the door. Tonight is the night I send you to hell, she thought as she smiled and walked back into the kitchen.

"They've left, Papa."

"Ready," he said. It was a statement and not a question. The implication was clear to her.

"Ready," she answered, retrieving the pistol from a cabinet drawer and securing it to the inside of her thigh, tucking it under an elastic strap.

Jean-Pierre embraced her quickly and led the way out the back door and into the night.

If everything went as planned it would be over quickly. They already knew where the officer's rooms were located and headed there directly. His night was over and the others would be sleeping off their drunks as well.

Madeleine and Jean-Pierre waited in the shadows and looked up at his rooms. They were located in a small conciergerie not far from the center of town. With a quick pat on her father's shoulder she walked up to the door and knocked without hesitation. She could hear heavy footsteps on the stairs and then someone fumbling with the latch. The door swung open.

"I knew you would come," the SS officer slurred, reaching for her as much out of lust as a means to hold himself up. His uniform was in complete disarray. He must have collapsed in it.

"Of course," she said quickly, kissing him and caressing his cheek as she stepped forward, closing the door behind her. They stumbled up the stairs. Madeleine's contempt for the man grew as she realized that he was completely defenseless. Well, so was I, she thought as they approached the door to his room.

Madeleine turned on the light and steered him towards the bed. He flopped down on his side and made little effort to right himself.

"I will be right back. I have to use the bathroom," she said.

His response was little more than a grunt.

Madeleine carefully opened the door and peeked out to make sure no one was up for a late night trip to the commode. She paused to ready herself. If she failed, her father would enter the building and shoot "any and all" Germans. He had said smiling. The remainder of the plan was simple. She would leave France immediately and try to make her way to England. If she was going to contribute to the war effort it would be at the direction of the British. Spain was a short distance away and, at least officially, a neutral country. Spain was a fascist state but had not joined Germany in her war against France and England. A fisherman friend would take her by boat to a small fishing village on the coast of Spain. With the help of some friends there, Madeleine would then find her way to Gibraltar and then on to England. If everything went according to plan she would escape long before the killing was discovered. Jean-Pierre would explain everything to her mother and bear the brunt of her panic. With Yves dead and Madeleine gone, their parents would only have each other to rely on until France was free and she could return.

Both Madeleine and her father were confident that France would eject her age-old enemy and reclaim her stature in the world once again. No matter how long it took, the French always defeated their invaders. In antiquity the Romans annexed Provence to its empire and they were gone. She was completely devoid of compassion for the rapist. Once the people of France woke up and saw what had happened they would retaliate. Jean-Pierre told her that he knew the Americans would come. They had been allies of France since the days of revolution almost two centuries ago when the British and Americans fought two wars. The French and Americans were brothers and sisters. Just as siblings rarely got along, so it was with the two countries. They squabbled and picked at one another, but when the call of freedom came they fought side by side. That is the way of liberty and freedom. The Americans would come.

Madeleine opened the door, holding the gun in the skirt she carried out of the bathroom. She checked the hall and walked boldly down it wearing a sleek negligee spirited out of her mother's drawer. She knew the man wouldn't notice the clothes in her hand when she appeared back in the room in the lingerie if he was capable of noticing anything at all.

When she returned to the room she carefully opened the door and slipped inside. The officer was still on the bed and snoring, his clothes and boots still on. Madeleine carefully put her clothes back on top of the lacy nightdress. She moved to the bed and removed a pillow, wrapping the gun inside. She knew the longer she hesitated the harder it would be. She pictured his violation of her in her mind, but it was the memory of her brother's disfigured dying face that gave her the strength to proceed. She leaned over and placed the pillow an inch away from the man's temple and pulled the trigger. The gun's report sounded like a small firecracker but to Madeleine it seemed deafening. Everyone in the neighborhood must have heard it, she thought. She froze waiting for someone to raise the alarm.

Several tense moments passed as Madeleine listened to every creek and moan the old building made. When nothing happen she realized that the room had largely contained the sound of the small caliber pistol. She turned and looked at the corpse, noticing a few feathers drifting down into the pooling blood beneath the man's head. She reached down feeling for his pulse and found nothing. She looked down at his lifeless eyes and knew the deed was done. She felt nothing for him and no revulsion for what she'd done. A feeling of satisfaction was there but it wasn't overwhelming. Madeleine was amazed how easy it had been to take a life under the circumstances of the man's crimes. She raised her skirt, tucking away the pistol.

Madeleine quickly checked the room making sure that she had left no trace of her presence. She walked to the door and turned out the light. No one in the small rooming house had stirred. Everything was silent. She walked down the stairs and back into the street, glancing quickly in both directions. The town was asleep as she made her way down to the docks through the shadows, keeping her face focused on the road so that anyone remembering a person passing would not be able to describe her accurately.

After a few minutes, the road opened into a broader market

area adjacent to the place where the smaller boats were moored for the night. She saw her father walk up and stand next to a string of fishing boats adjacent to the part of the port where the larger commercial ships docked. The dark water beckoned to her as it lapped languidly against the wooden posts supporting the dock. The fishermen's nets and their boats gave off a strong fish smell. It mingled with the familiar odors of the sea and a working port. The smell had a character all its own, personal to people that lived with it daily, depending on it for their livelihoods and identity. Madeleine savored it, wondering when she would be able to do so again as a free citizen of France.

"Well, soldier?" Jean-Pierre asked as he stepped out of the shadows, awkwardly limping with his false leg.

"He will rape no more," Madeleine said, embracing him fiercely.

"Always remember that he was an animal, Madeleine. There are more to kill, God's will be done," Jean-Pierre said, embracing her. Madeleine felt her voice catch in her throat, realizing that the hardest part of the plan had come. It was time for her to leave.

"I could hold you forever, Madeleine, but that would not be safe. It is time for you to leave and carry on the fight from wherever the English lead. They are a resolute and determined people. The men and women of that country would all rather die than be conquered."

Together they turned and Jean-Pierre led her a few steps down the dock, stopping in front of an open fishing boat. It was small but sturdy. A fisherman Madeleine recognized was readying the boat for casting off. He looked more weathered than the rough wooden boats of his trade. Without comment he took Madeleine's hand in his. She could feel the immense strength in his gnarled fingers as he gently helped her aboard.

"You know Jacques, Madeleine. He was on the sea long before I was born. He will see you safely off," Jean-Pierre said in a strained voice.

She reached over the side of the boat and hugged her father as he bent down to reach her. Both of them were in tears as he spoke.

"You are the warrior of the Toche family now," he said, struggling to bring his emotions under control. "Come back when Germany is gone from France. Your mother and I will breathe easier knowing you are in England."

With those words he turned and limped away, the sound of his sacrifice for France thudding dully against the wooden dock.

Madeleine went forward and quietly cried. The enormity of everything that had happened hit her at once. She was leaving everything behind she held dear for the emptiness of the unknown. Her mind raced as she clutched the hem of her skirt to her mouth and sobbed deeply into it. She searched her mind for the strength that had brought her this far, found an edge of it, and clung to it desperately. She knew her disappearance would do little to cast suspicion on her parents. Young people were being displaced constantly, many going to stay with family in other regions or being directed by their occupiers to relocate for work. Her rapist's crime had been done in secret as was his death. Time would heal that wound as well. He hadn't been an overly important man and now, she thought with satisfaction, he was only a dead one. She regretted leaving her homeland in secrecy and darkness. She drew comfort from the gentle rocking of the boat as it slipped from its moorings and the fisherman guided it out of the port. Madeleine let the motion of the boat calm her as she placed her trust and safety in the embrace of the sea.

CHAPTER SEVEN

From her position underwater, Madeleine could see the bright light of an overhead bulb shining on the surface a few inches above her nose and mouth. Her training told her to remain calm. She wanted a breath of air from the other side of the surface of the water more than anything she had ever wanted. Its closeness was maddening. Just inches away but she might as well have been at the bottom of a lake. She was inverted almost upside down in a tank of water. Her body was strapped to a board so that she could be easily lifted and dropped back down under the surface. Remembering her training, she controlled her panic as the sheer physical terror grew with her lack of oxygen. Suddenly she was lifted from the tank. Just as she gasped for air, she was punched in the stomach driving the air out of her lungs. She involuntarily choked and gasped and was immediately dunked back under the water. This time she had no control and couldn't remain calm. Her whole body screamed as she struggled not to open her mouth as she tried to gain control of her lungs. She had no choice, throwing herself at the straps pinning her to the board. She thrashed violently in an attempt to get her head up. Her struggles were worthless. It wasn't supposed to be like this, she thought. Her mouth opened in a desperate attempt to find oxygen. It was involuntary and she realized that she was going to die. Her helplessness enraged her. This death was pointless. She was desperate to survive. Her anger and hate kindled in her. There was no fear of death, just anger at the lost opportunity to fight the Germans and fulfill her promise of revenge. She could barely hear the pounding of her blood in her ears over her fury.

On the brink of unconsciousness, Madeleine was thrust up and out of the water. She sputtered and gasped, sucking in huge gulps of air. She had instantly been blasted into the light of the room and away from the point of despair. She choked uncontrollably, her body taking over as it raced back from near death. The door flew open and a tall officer stormed into the room.

"What the hell do you think you're doing, man? You almost killed her!" Captain Jack Teach yelled, moving quickly over to the board. His body was sleekly muscled from endless physical training and the harsh conditions of field operations. His blue eyes burned with anger, accusatory and enraged. He reached down to the slant board, slicing the straps that held Madeleine down with a knife that had materialized in his hand.

"Following orders mate. Keep them in until they break or pass out. SOE training, isn't it? She's a woman. There's your problem," Lieutenant Brian Fish answered in a swaggering, insolent tone, forgetting that the man he addressed outranked him.

"Get back, you bastard!" Teach screamed. Fish scoffed and moved a few paces back from the end of the tank. Madeleine stood slowly, bending as she retched water, holding onto the side of the tank to steady herself. As her coughing lessened, she turned her head slightly and peeked through the mass of wet hair covering her face. She saw a commando knife strapped to Fish's side. Without an instant of hesitation she grabbed the knife and plunged it towards his eye. At the last moment, Teach grabbed her hand and averted a very messy 'training accident.' Fish stood transfixed to the spot in terror, his body rigid with panic as he realized how close to death he had come. Teach slowly eased Madeleine's hand down. She did not struggle and released the knife. Fish, who was not a field man, was speechless.

Teach looked at him like a revolting insect. "Next time, I'm going to let it happen, you ghastly sadist. I'm of a mind to strap you to that board and let her have a go at you."

While the senior officer spoke, Madeleine raised her shirt to inspect the spot where she'd been hit. Teach glanced at what she was doing and saw the ugly bruising.

"I'll have you, you bastard," he roared and landed a giant right cross to Fish's jaw. Fish rag-dolled to the ground and Teach followed him down with the knife, clearly not through.

"Stop!" Madeleine yelled. "You can't kill a junior officer, Captain. Besides, this pig's not worth it," she added calmly.

Teach pulled himself back from the brink of violence, backing away slowly. Madeleine watched as his eyes cleared and the blood lust left them. It had been close. The training the recruits were under was full of knife-edged tension. The men who taught them were hard and brutal; Jack Teach was the hardest and most brutal of all. Madeleine was confused. Perhaps it was another of their endless tests designed to wash trainees out. She didn't know what to think. The intensity of the moment was still palpable in the room. Death had visited and had been momentarily cheated.

Without taking his eyes off of Fish, Teach said, "You're right, Toche. But I can recommend him for duty in North Africa. I believe he's an infantry man."

Unable to speak, Fish pulled himself up blubbering and wincing, his jaw broken in several places from a blow delivered by a man trained to inflict maximal damage.

"I bet you weren't bloody crying when you punched her, you coward. I mean what I said, it's combat for you. And by the way, when the 75mm shells come raining down on your position, you think about her. I wager she'll be waiting if you get back. As I'm sure you're aware, the casualty rating from Northern Africa is staggering. Now piss off, you bloody sadist. I hear one word about any of this and I'll cut you up into little pieces. I know London quite well. My people are down by the docks. My father is Robert Teach and a harder man you'll never meet. He'll know what to do with you."

By now Fish was not only panicked; he was terrified. Robert Teach was a known gangster, brutal and ruthless.

Fish all but threw himself out of the room as Teach turned to Madeleine.

"Toche, I can't have you killing my instructors," he said gently, brushing the hair back from her face. His touch was firm and purposeful. Her first reaction was to push his hand away and regain the stoic, almost mechanical demeanor that she had adopted during the training. There was no tenderness and mollycoddling in

Special Operations Executive training, just countless hours learning to kill in every manner known to man. When not in 'Kill School' there were codes and ciphers to master, as well as innumerable clandestine skills whose teaching suggested that their mastery was crucial. Madeleine had excelled at everything they had thrown at her.

After a fleeting moment Teach realized what was happening and pulled his hand away. It was a struggle as he looked at her savage beauty, made all the more alluring by the water soaked clothing that clung to her, dripping onto the floor. It was an awkward moment but neither of them moved apart. A dangerous passion sparked between them, raw with unbridled energy, the intense violence of the preceding moments kindling an equally physical need. Teach felt himself drawn towards a violation of duty as thoughts of her raced through his mind. He had never felt this way towards any other female recruit, and there were many young and beautiful ones each seeking to undertake the most dangerous of missions in the name of freedom. Madeleine was a breath away from reaching out and tearing his shirt open; she tingled as the delicious lure of lust began to overcome her.

"I thought I was dead, Captain. I must protest. It can't be wise to kill prospective field agents. Nobody will volunteer if they think they're going to die before they get a chance to kill Germans," Madeleine said, lifting her eyes up to his. In her mind she saw herself falling into his arms, her need was so great. She struggled to rationalize what was happening. She realized that whatever he wanted she would give without hesitation. All of her senses screamed at her to give in. One touch and the tiny thread holding them apart would break.

Suddenly Teach broke the trance, stepping back slightly.

"Well, right then. Time to get you back to the barracks and get you cleaned up. That's enough training for one day. Quite frankly Toche, I'm not sure there's much more we can teach you anyway," he said, his face breaking into an encompassing grin.

Madeleine relaxed as the promise of the moment faded. She was now convinced that what had happened had not been a hoax but instead a lack of restraint on the part of that bastard Fish.

She fervently hoped that he would show up on the casualty lists, a victim of Germany's Africa Corps.

Madeleine nodded, moving past Teach as she hurried into the hallway. As she made her way to the barracks she remembered once again that the training was designed to keep her confused, keep her guessing, forcing her to make decisions quickly. The training plus her physical attraction to Captain Teach kept her plenty confused, she mused. It would all come to an end soon enough. She would either be posted under cover in France or behind a desk in London.

Madeleine entered the women's barracks, suddenly wondering if her training was indeed over as Teach had suggested. She certainly wouldn't miss it, but she felt empowered by what she had learned and the physical training she had undergone. Everything from sleep deprivation to withholding water had been used. Clearly the simple things people took for granted could be utilized to torture them as well. Thirst had been the worst. By the end of that treat she would have endured nearly anything else for a swallow of water. Teach had been there for it all. Something about his presence encouraged her. Having him nearby made her feel strong in the face of the enforced deprivations. She found everything about him alluring. She knew that could have been an aspect of the training, another way to break her down or to test her. She allowed herself the fantasy of him as a man and walled it away in her mind, careful to give no indication of it. She knew that she had slipped in gesture or comment. Had he not seen it? These Englishmen. Even in the street they rarely looked at her. Was there something wrong with the way she looked? Wasn't she attractive? She couldn't understand the way they seemed to ignore her. Ever since she was fifteen or so, Frenchmen had always looked at her in an admiring way. Maybe these men didn't like French women. Still, Teach had acted ferociously in her defense and she had felt something radiate from him towards her that was overpowering. She sighed, knowing that once back in France she would probably never see him again. She laughed sharply, thinking that there it was, one more reason to hate the Nazis. Their damn war was taking her away from the most physically attractive and exciting man she had ever known. There just weren't that many men like Captain Jack Teach wandering around the world.

CHAPTER **EIGHT**

Over the next few days it became clear to Madeleine and the other trainees still in attendance that they had passed a milestone and that they would indeed be commissioned as field agents. They had been given their false identities and assignments. Now their days were spent sitting in makeshift classrooms and studying technical manuals as they perfected their individual cover stories. Madeleine was to join up with a fledgling Resistance group in the north, taking a job as a postal worker. Her posting would allow her to roam freely and obtain information through observation as she traveled throughout the region. She knew that the north was of special interest as a possible point of invasion. There was somewhat of a stalemate, as Germany couldn't wrest control of the skies from the RAF. A land invasion without air superiority would be madness. Hitler and his generals knew what that would cost.

Madeleine was listening to an instructor when Captain Teach walked into the room. The instructor paused as Teach pointed to Madeleine and gestured for her to follow him. Madeleine noticed a few of the women watching Teach as he turned and walked out.

Once in the hallway Teach spoke.

"I need to speak to you about additional training, Madeleine."

"Did I fail to meet the appropriate requirements, Captain?"

"Quite the contrary. You exceeded them all. Although you were not informed, you have been subjected to additional training beyond that of the standard field agent. It was necessary to determine the viability of your candidacy for a mission we must now discuss. I think it would be best to discuss this in my office and not in the hallway. It's quite important."

"If I may sir, are we on a first name basis now?"

"Oh, quite right. No, we call all of the trainees by their surnames. It's just a way to maintain discipline. Think of it as a reward for completing your training.

Teach gave her that huge smile again. The challenge behind his charismatic smile coupled with his startling blue eyes was arresting. Madeleine kicked herself as she realized that she was just standing there staring at him. He seemed even better looking now that the bitter challenge of training was past and the instructors took on a more congenial attitude. Perhaps it was because they knew what the new operatives were in for once they activated and were dropped into occupied territory.

"What assignment will I have, then?"

"That remains to be seen," Teach said with an air of mystery as they approached his door. He held it open for her as she brushed past him.

"Please sit down," Teach said, gesturing to a wooden chair facing his desk. The room was Spartan, consisting of a battered old desk, a telephone, and a second chair that didn't look any more comfortable than the one in which she sat.

"Madeleine, when you came to us you spoke of an assault and your killing of a German officer. I wish I could be more delicate with that information but our jobs simply do not allow for the delicacies of polite discourse. None of the other recruits have killed before. Do you follow me so far?"

"What is it you want of me Captain? If it involves killing Germans, I also want that. I do not want to deliver messages and make coffee for the real soldiers who fight. I am as capable as any."

"I am relieved to hear you say that Madeleine, because what the SOE is going to ask of you we can not order you to do. Quite frankly, it's a bit outside of the rules as they currently are."

"Rules? There are no rules for me. It is against the rules to attack a country and enslave its people without provocation. Now, what is it you want of me?"

"You seem almost eager. When you hear what I have to say, I fear you won't be quite so ready to jump into the fray."

"Then just say it," Madeleine said, firmly returning Teach's stare.

"We want you to be a killer, Madeleine. You will be an assassin. We need someone in each occupied country to kill the enemy directly. Demoralize the command structure; put the bloody fear of the long reach of the SOE into their guts. Make them look over their shoulders and kill them when they drop their guard. Can you do it?"

"Yes, I can kill for my country. Even though I wear the uniform of the British, I am a soldier of France as certainly as my brother and father before me. I will kill the enemy wherever he is until France is free. After that, I have a restaurant to run."

"Then you will continue your training, but it is a cold and lonely road you'll be going down. Your entire purpose will be to kill or, more specifically, to assassinate the enemy. Everyone else thinks the job needs to go to a man. I disagreed. I said the job should go to the most qualified candidate, the most likely to succeed. I went directly to the Prime Minister to argue my case. He was intrigued and authorized the balance of your training. Quite frankly, he was taken with the idea. He laughed and said, "Twas beauty killed the beast." Aside from the PM and I, everyone expects you to fail."

"I will not fail."

"I know you won't, Madeleine. You have a talent for violence but you need to control it. I know that gender is irrelevant to courage. I think you will be more successful than any man could be. You are a beautiful woman, highly intelligent and resourceful. You will blend in among your countrymen. You are French and won't have to pretend to be a native. You will be able to move freely into and out of communities under the guise of traveling to meet relatives or for employment. You will have no contact with any Resistance agent or SOE field operative. All of your instructions will come to you and only you from London. You will be permitted to choose your targets as you see fit. You will kill strategically advantageous targets, Gestapo, SS and command officers."

"When do I start?"

"Immediately." Teach said, clearly happy with her decision. "You will have only one instructor. I warn you though; he is not like other men. I have met him only once. I frankly don't believe there's any humanity left in the man. He's cold in a way that leaves no mistake as to his abilities. He is a German Jew. A decorated soldier and spy from Germany's World War One military regime. Germany no longer abides Jews, regardless of their previous contributions to their country. He was rewarded with internment and the disappearance of his wife and children. He believes them to be dead, as do we. We don't yet know the true extent of, or I should say, the result of the Nazi hatred of the Jews, but I fear we will discover true horror there when this is all said and done. He has spent the last few years revisiting old skills. Numerous high-ranking Nazis have disappeared. At first he did this on his own with no support, but he came to us when the war started. He has been watching you and the others for weeks. He has recommended you, Madeleine."

Madeleine looked at him and searched his eyes for a glimmer suggesting that he was exaggerating or having a joke with her. He was serious. Madeleine knew what she was being told wasn't simply idle information. It was a warning, and not made lightly. Clearly she had demonstrated the qualities Teach admired. Another part of her wished that he would see her as a woman. With the new training and assignment she knew that would remain impossible.

"When do I meet this man, Captain?"

"You are to go to a public place of your choosing tomorrow at two pm. He will contact you there."

"How will he know where I'm going to be?" Madeleine asked, somewhat confused.

"Don't worry. He'll know, Madeleine. He'll know," Teach said with finality.

Madeleine stood up and left the room. As she walked down the hall she felt a real fear of where she was headed. She couldn't help but think of the hypocrisy of it all. She was going to be taught to kill Germans by a German. The world had gone completely mad.

The next day Madeleine sat on a park bench in Piccadilly Circus. She loved the excitement and the freedom and bustle of the English, despite the fact that the *Luftwaffe* might rain bombs down on them at any moment. The Londoners and other city dwellers in Great Britain had suffered so much destruction during Hitler's *Blitz*. These were a solid, God-fearing people, stout and resolute. She questioned the propriety of the decision to wage an air war against this island nation. The Battle of Britain had been won through the sheer determination of England and her pilots. That, and a plane designed for combat, the Spitfire.

Madeleine kept a wary eye out all around her for the man she was to meet. As her training dictated, she positioned herself so that she could monitor her surroundings. People passed her in every direction. Women hurried by, carrying packages of rationed groceries. People were going about their daily obligations despite the war. Children were rarely seen, as so many of them had been sent to the countryside to avoid the bombing.

Madeleine knew she needed to be vigilant. Maybe he would wait until she left and surprise her from some dark corner. She decided to stay where she was, no matter how long it took. She was at a disadvantage, having no description of the man. Teach had been quite adamant that he would find her.

As the hours dragged on, she spent most of her time thinking about what lay ahead for her. She expected her assignment to be dangerous and involve killing. The Resistance movement was growing rapidly in France; disrupting the German war effort and creating maximum chaos were the two most important goals of the SOE. Winston Churchill's directive to them was to "set Europe ablaze!" That was clear enough for her.

As the afternoon wore on, Madeleine watched as the traffic thinned out and the people sought the shelter of their homes. There wasn't much nightlife near her, but she could hear some activity from a small pub tucked around the corner. Blackout conditions were in effect. People accepted the fact that they were at war. It had been thrust upon them in the most personal way. Civilians were bombed as indiscriminately as military targets.

Eventually, the street cleaners came out. Funny how even

in the midst of the chaos of war, the orderly and proper life of the British continued. She followed the progress of a lone dustman as he collected rubbish, moving away from where she sat.

"You are patient, I'll give you that," a hollow voice said to her. The words lacked any inflection; an icy finger of fear flickered down her spine.

Madeleine whirled her head around and saw a man standing behind her. He had materialized out of nowhere. She caught his eyes first and looked into a flat, bottomless pool. They seemed to lack any distinctive color as he regarded her. There was nothing distinguishing about him in any way except that he seemed aware of every sound and movement around him, as if he was part of the background and could disappear into it at will. Although he looked it, she instinctively knew that he was far from ordinary. He was not tall, short, thin, fat, or in any way distinctive. He did seem familiar, though. It was as if she had seen him just recently, if not today. So many people had passed her on the street; perhaps he had been one of them.

"Where did you come from, sir? I know I have seen you before, but at the same time I know that's impossible," Madeleine said, genuinely mystified.

"Do you not remember the kindly policeman that tipped his hat to you, or the drunken service man that stumbled into you and gave you a wolf whistle?"

"Those men were you?" Madeleine could scarcely believe it. Not only did he now look so different, the cop and the soldier couldn't have been the same man.

"Yes, *mademoiselle*. Those two and others. Hiding one's appearance just takes practice. You already have the greatest skill mastered. One that is very difficult to teach."

"What is that?"

"I have already told you. Patience. This business, I am to teach you requires little in the way of physical ability, but few have the mental strength necessary. Killing another human being is easy. After the first few it will be like turning off a light. The true art is in preparation and flawless execution. You cannot be caught. What you know is too valuable. Besides, it's not Cricket, as the

British say, to murder. 'Assassinate' is a nice word, but you will be a murderer. Your targets will have no chance to defend themselves, just like the people they themselves have tortured or killed. As I understand it, your targets will also be murderers. So perhaps you can take some solace in that."

"My solace comes from avenging the screams of my countrymen, the mangled corpse of my brother, and from God," Madeleine said in a dangerous voice.

A faint smile flashed across his face.

"Then they will have no one to pray to for protection from you. We will start tomorrow. Bring no weapon. First you learn to kill with your hands and all manner of ordinary objects. Remember, it is not skill that kills, it is knowledge. Skill comes with practice and can be useful. Learning never to hesitate is the most deadly lesson I will teach you. When I am finished with you, you will only fear two people ever again."

"Who?"

"Me," he said without the slightest hint of boast or bravado. "You see, long ago I crossed over to a place from which I cannot return. Madeleine nodded, following some of what the man said.

"And who else?" She asked.

"Yourself," he answered with a hint of sorrow as he walked away, disappearing into the night long before Madeleine should have lost sight of him. She sat transfixed to the bench, mulling over what the man had said. Teach was right: the man was terrifying.

Over the weeks that followed, Madeleine worked exclusively with the German. It became clear to her that she was learning from a master. He shared secrets with her that were truly frightening. She learned by example and constant reinforcement. She began to understand the mindset necessary to do the work that would be asked of her. It would be solitary and frightening. His lessons always came back to the core theme of preparation. The actual act was never technically difficult. It had to do with precise planning so that the assassin could get to the target. She learned that the more simple the details, the less chance for discovery. She began to understand why she had been chosen. It was for her courage and willingness to kill, but just as important was her understanding of the certainty of her own death. She fully expected to be killed in action. Her mentor explained that once agents accepted that fact they could operate with ruthlessness and precision without the hesitation caused by fear. Everyone in battle is afraid. Those who master it survive.

Madeleine was curious about the man's past. Teach had given her some information. She knew that he had been a highly decorated German soldier in the First World War but he was obviously much more than that. Little by little the man shared some of his personal secrets with her. He told her stories of kills that he had made so that she would understand the mistakes to avoid, mistakes that had nearly cost him his life.

As the weeks progressed, their fieldwork revealed Madeleine's gifts for disguise, guile, and deceit. She was placed in realistic training situations. Her orders were to avoid other agents trained to catch her. She was discovered twice, and only because the others had been tipped off to her description. In both instances, upon discovery she subdued her counterpart and escaped.

Her training was incessant and as realistic as possible. Many times Madeleine woke in the night with a trench knife held to her throat, the dead eyes of her mentor staring into hers. He forced her to adapt. She began sleeping in odd places and never in the same one twice. It didn't take her long to realize that her survival would require the same attention in the field. It became second nature, along with the physical and mental lessons that had become part of her. Weapons change over the millennia but little else. Madeleine learned that assassins struck from the shadows of their own making and that confusion and deceit would be her ally. She felt herself evolving into a weapon. She was changing, becoming harder mentally and physically.

Eventually, Madeleine sensed her instructor was expecting something from her that she had not yet accomplished. He found it increasingly difficult to find her at night and finally was unable to do so. She had taken to sleeping in remote places, sometimes out of doors. She learned to drop a tail instinctively, using many twists and turns and false trails to disappear.

Then, by happenstance she saw through her instructor's disguise as he attempted to follow her. He was dressed as a dustman and she knew she'd seen him before. He had made a mistake and she intended to capitalize on it. Madeleine ducked into a women's clothing shop and was able to hide in the toilet. Once inside she altered her appearance to give her an added advantage. She moved quickly back into the street and followed the dustman all the way to a small block of flats some distance from the SOE Baker Street offices. Dusk was falling and Madeleine noticed a light go on in a small second floor window just before the blackout curtains were closed.

Madeleine waited in an alley as the sun went down rapidly, the shadows of late afternoon becoming the darkness of night. She pulled off her street clothes, revealing dark trousers and a black knit top. She pulled her hair back, carefully, tying it so as not to obstruct her vision. She waited until the street was fully dark and she was sure that her quarry was in for the night. She checked the street and crossed over. Not pausing when she was in open view, she made her way around the side of the house and stopped near a black iron pipe dropping down from the roof. She grabbed it and in a matter of seconds reached the top and carefully lowered her body onto the tile. Her heart was pounding, not from the exertion of the climb but from adrenaline. She breathed slowly and evenly until she felt her limbs lose their rigidity and calmness seeped out from her core. She inched her way over the tile roof, moving silently with acrobatic grace. She kept her weight evenly distributed and tested each pressure point. She made no sound and moved towards the front window. She carefully lowered herself over the edge, finding a foothold on the window ledge as she focused her hearing toward the room. She'd learned that it was possible to focus one's hearing and ignore collateral sound. Eventually, she heard it: the even breathing of sleep emanating through the partially open window. Little by little, she folded herself into the room and moved silently towards the bed. She took notice of his body position and approached from his blind side, pulling a straight razor from a pocket sewn into the side of her jersey. She opened it and placed it against his neck.

"*Bonjour mon ami*," Madeleine said in conversational tone.

"I am glad you are my friend, Madeleine," he answered after a brief pause. He had been asleep and unaware of her entrance. "I have so few."

Madeleine pulled the razor away and returned it to her pocket as he sat up and swung his legs over the side of the bed.

"I was wondering when you'd get around to finding me, Madeleine," he said as he turned on a small lamp next to the bed.

"To be honest, it was the first time I ever noticed you tailing me."

"My mistake?" He questioned.

"The dustman. The same from the first day."

"My God, how foolish of me," he said, shaking his head, an honest smile crossing his features. "Well, Madeleine, there will be no more testing, only work from here on out."

"Do you think I am ready?"

"You have been since the day I first met you. You will remember that I talked to you about the difference between acting without hesitation and utilizing skills. We have been working on skills. You have shown innumerable times your inherent ability to act. Now you must do so."

"Will my instructions come from you?"

"No, only from the SOE. They will discuss that with you. I expect that I will hear of your work. Like all of the people who do this work, you will develop a signature. At first only I will recognize it. But in time, others will as well. I trained you, therefore it makes sense that I will recognize it first. Besides, I have work to do back in Germany. Many Germans have not lost their humanity and need help fighting the Nazis from within."

"Is there anything else I need to know?"

"Trust no one. You have taken steps down a road you may be able to leave some day but it will always be there, expecting your return. Governments like assassins until they are no longer useful; then they send someone, usually a person of trust, to eliminate their concern for what you might disclose. I have chosen to be your insurance policy. I have told them that if you survive the war and they excise you out of some sense of necessity, I will kill everyone I know to be associated with this project."

Madeleine was thunderstruck. At that very moment she swore to herself that she would never understand men. One moment they were brusque and full of masculine bravado and the next capable of the deepest concern.

"Have you made that commitment for your other trainees?" Madeleine asked, not knowing what else to say.

"There have been no others."

"Then why do it for me?"

"I know that you were recruited because you have already killed. I have no one. My family is dead. My blood and the blood of my Jewish brothers who fought in the Great War was spilled as willingly as the next man's. My wife and daughters disappeared when I was away. When they needed me most, I was gone. I should have left Germany with them long ago, but my foolish pride and belief in my country has cost them their lives. I do not know where they've been taken. We Jews are being slaughtered with an unbridled hatred. Madeleine, the Nazis are evil. Kill as many as you can. You must be the hand of God."

As he spoke, a flood of pain filled his eyes. It was the first strong emotion she had ever seen in the man. It was so overpowering that she reached out and embraced him. It was a strange humanity between killers. She had already killed and she would do so many times again or die in the attempt. The lessons that he imparted to her were the most honest and frightening she had ever experienced, and she knew she would draw on them time and again for her survival. The German clutched at her arm and held on as his veneer of hate and death slid away for the briefest of moments.

"I will," Madeleine said firmly.

The man smiled and shook his head, coming back from the private hell he held in his heart.

"Then we are done. Be careful. Trust no intelligence. Know before you act."

"May I know your name?" Madeleine said needing to take something from the man other than the cruel lessons of death he'd imparted.

"I am Berthold Hartmann," he answered slightly raising his chin.

"And your profession?" Madeleine continued.

"I was an attorney in Wiesbaden, but my practice is on hold just now."

"Of course," Madeleine replied picturing the stone killer in a courtroom arguing a case, and reminding herself never to underestimate anyone ever again.

Madeleine rose and left the room, this time by the stairs. She wondered if she would ever see him again.

His words were both a comfort and a sentence. They gave her hope that she would be successful and help to defeat the enemy. It also meant that she would be completely alone, walking through the terrors that would be constantly there until her job was finished or she was killed. She remembered that faith had carried so many before her through impossible odds. She resolved not to be alone. She too would draw strength from faith.

CHAPTER **NINE**

The night air was alive around her as Madeleine placed a powerful explosive charge under a railroad track, pushing rocks and debris around it. It was primed and hidden, one of two that when detonated would derail even the largest locomotive. A silenced pistol lay near her hand, an extension of her consciousness.

She glanced a short distance down the track, seeing Teach working silently to place additional explosives to ensure maximum destruction and derailment of the munitions train. He felt her eyes on him, flashed her a quick thumbs up of encouragement, and returned to his task. She knew this was one of many missions that he had successfully completed. This was her first. She reluctantly pulled her eyes away from him and rechecked the bomb's wiring to make sure it would trigger with a slight delay once the train traveled a short distance over it. Her thoughts were a jumble of fear and excitement, not only for the mission but for being in the field with Captain Teach.

Once her final training had been completed Madeleine was put into action immediately. Under cover of darkness Madeleine and Teach were flown to a temporary airfield and deposited not far from their target. They were far too valuable to risk injury during a parachute drop. Both were trained to jump but preferred the safer, more reliable Lysander aircraft. It flew under the radar and could take off with little runway.

As she stood, she was aware of everything around her. The night had its own pulse and being. She smelled the dampness from the light rain that had fallen earlier leaving a mist through which there was only a hint of a town in the distance. The train would pick up speed here and most of it would be over the blast zone when it arrived. She felt alive being back in France and in action.

The simple things around her energized her; the road signs in French along the meandering roads and the architecture. She was not in her native Provence, but she was home.

"Charges set and timed?" Teach whispered, motioning her into the shadows along the side of the track. His face was close to hers and she felt his alert ease and confidence as she moved closer.

Teach sensed Madeleine was in her element. His faith in her skills and courage were being rewarded and he was there to see it. Her cool demeanor was remarkable, as this was her first time in the field. Her additional training had given her a fluidity of movement. There was no indecisiveness on her part. Teach almost felt like he was in her way. There was also a new, frightening aspect about her that came from the training she'd had with Hartmann. Even in the gloom he could sense the fierce strength she commanded. Although petite and feminine, she was born for this work. He had seen it first in training and now it was confirmed. Although he had been in combat and on many missions he felt himself strengthened by her presence and confidence. As he thought of her, he was cautious not to allow his mind to wander too deeply into the other qualities he admired in her. His physical attraction to her was consuming. She was a true beauty, dark and lithe, smoldering with sexuality. She seemed to regard her looks as a tool or an asset but in no way a definition of herself. Experience had taught him how to focus on the mission and ignore the jumble of emotions running through his mind. He had struggled with thoughts of her since the first day of SOE training. He tried to ignore them but it didn't help in the least. He knew few people could do this work and it had little to do with physical ability. What was most important was focus. Everyone was afraid of what might happen or what could go wrong. He had learned to concentrate on what was happening. Worry was for the planning stages and had no place in mission execution.

"Charges are set, Captain. Everything is on schedule." Madeleine whispered, glancing at the luminous dial of her watch. Just as she did so the darkness was split as a match was struck. A German sentry extended the match as a second leaned in to light his cigarette.

"*Danke,*" the soldier said quietly as he moved away from the match.

The two soldiers separated and began walking towards Madeleine, Teach, and the explosives. They seemed to be paying particular attention to the ground in front of them, glancing around repeatedly as they moved forward. Teach could tell from their manner that they were not green recruits. These men had walked point in combat, perhaps countless times. They would find the explosives.

Teach made an instant decision. He made eye contact with Madeleine, pointed to himself and the guard on the far side of the track. Madeleine then touched herself and pointed to the other. Teach nodded firmly and slid farther back into the shadows and several yards farther up the track. Madeleine moved back and to her right, slowly raising her pistol and training it on her soldier. Her focus was razor sharp. While her mind saw the other sentry, everything else went away as she concentrated. As he passed she silently stood, taking measured steps towards the track and fired into the middle of the man's back. Two more steps and she fired a second round into his brain. She heard the almost simultaneous double spit of Teach's gun and the clatter of the sentry's gun as he fell. She walked up and grabbed her soldier by the feet and dragged him off the track and into the darkness. Teach did the same. They both quickly returned to the track and scanned it for debris. Together they pulled the soldiers farther back into the woods along the track, covering them with a quick layer of forest debris, moving silently off into the dark, away from the train tracks. The entire operation had taken a few long minutes.

Madeleine and Teach began a loping trot through the darkness and towards safety. They moved as one, two parts of a dangerous animal seeking the safety of its lair after a kill.

As they ran, Madeleine allowed a little of what had happened to enter her mind. She had killed a soldier in combat. It was different than killing the SS officer who had raped her those many months ago. She was taking revenge then. Now, it was offensive and not defensive in nature and she preferred it this way, like so many soldiers in ambush throughout the ages. Her father's words came to her as she ran. Soldiers die. After enough killing of their own, they come to expect it. He knew of what he spoke. She had seen the memories of Verdun in his eyes. They told the story of a place where the innocence of his youth died in mud and horror.

They slowed as they approached a small car. It was parked to the side of a cart path under the branches of hedge, hidden in gloom. Teach got behind the wheel and Madeleine slid into the passenger seat. The car looked old but when Teach hit the starter it immediately roared to life. The engine had been lovingly maintained and improved by a sympathetic mechanic somewhere along the line. Both Madeleine and Teach eased a little as the little car pulled forward and moved them out of the immediate danger zone. Teach carefully drove by moonlight down the grassy track, thankful for the way the woods deadened the sound of their passing.

After a few moments, Teach allowed a surge of excitement to build in him as he realized that, absent an explosives malfunction, they had pulled off a very dangerous operation. He turned and grinned at Madeleine and playfully slapped her knee in camaraderie. She took his hand and squeezed it in return, holding it in both of her hands, living the moment of their success to the fullest. He glanced at her, expecting her to release his hand quickly. When she did not he relaxed and held her hand firmly, not daring to hope that her gesture was anything other than a product of their comradeship in arms. He fought the urge to turn and look at her. There were so many reasons that he should have pulled his hand away, all of them very military and reasonable. He ignored them. He felt the importance of this moment more strongly than anything he'd ever felt before. Everything else in his mind shimmered away. She was the fiercest and most beautiful woman he had ever known. There was an unspoken acknowledgment between the two that they had transcended some boundary as elusive to some as it is magical. It was the gift of love, at least on his part. The magnitude of it filled him with a new courage and understanding for why he fought. It was so that nothing be allowed to destroy the good in the world, manifested in the simplest of gestures of love between people, holding hands against the dark.

Teach and Madeleine drove through the night, keeping to secondary roads, some not much more than a trail through meadows and farm fields. The first sunlight glowed in the east as they pulled up to a dilapidated barn, almost completely obscured by a tangle of trees and shrubbery shielding it from a nearby country lane. They had been traveling west and had covered several hundred kilometers during the night. Now they were only a short distance from Spain, a quick sprint out to the sea, and a fast boat ride back to England.

"We'll be here for the night and then you're on your own, Madeleine," Teach said as they approached the barn door. There was an unmistakable reluctance in his voice. Madeleine said nothing and nodded as he spoke. He tried to read her expression but it was clouded and set. Her brow was furrowed and she avoided making eye contact.

They walked to the barn and swung open the door. Teach went back to the car and pushed it inside as Madeleine closed the door. They looked around the interior of the barn. It had been out of use for a long time. Dust and straw littered the floor, but it was clean. It must not have held any livestock for sometime. There was a small room off to the side, separated from the barn by a door. Perhaps the room had served as a living area for the farmer or his helpers during the harvest or as the family's shelter while their permanent home was built. It was rustic, but it would keep the wind and the rain out and some heat in if they could get a fire going. The area was remote enough that a small fire wouldn't attract any attention.

"If there's food, I could make us something to eat," Madeleine offered.

"There had better be. There were strict instructions to the local *Maquis* group to provision this location."

"Have the *Maquis* here seen much action?" Madeleine asked. "There's never much news about the armed groups taking the fight to the enemy."

"We can't afford any continuity yet. We must keep these groups individual and secret so that when the invasion comes we can hit them from everywhere at once."

"When the invasion comes. There will be a hard road for France and her people before that day," Madeleine said quietly.

"I think your road will be the hardest, Madeleine," Teach said gently as he put his hand on her shoulder. Madeleine moved in closer to him and leaned against his tall, spare frame. Her hands at her side, she leaned her head against his chest, seeking shelter against the enormity of it all. Teach put his arms around her and held her quietly. It didn't seem like a time for words and he was afraid the embrace would end if he spoke. He marveled at her control. There were no tears or sighs. He could feel the force of her in her small body. She had a center like iron and yet there was nothing inflexible about her. He worried for her as she went forward. He knew that she would probably be safer without him, as she would blend in and move among her people easily. Her looks were disarming. Although she was clearly a woman, her youth lingered in her features everywhere but her eyes. He had absolute confidence in her abilities. He remembered the machine-like efficiency with which she had killed. No emotion, no remorse. She was magnificently formidable, like a seemingly frail flower masking the most deadly poison.

"We should eat," Madeleine said without breaking the embrace. She was here now and didn't want to be the one to pull away. As if by some unspoken command they parted and moved toward a table and a small stove.

"At least we won't have to freeze," Teach said. "Hopefully there's something to eat."

Madeleine looked into the small room off to the side, cluttered with tack for the animals that had once sheltered in the barn and found a weathered, gray wooden crate that looked promising. She pried back one of the panels and saw several jars inside and pulled them out.

"We are in luck," Madeleine said. "Someone prepared a meal and preserved it for later use. There are peaches, vegetables and a stew." She pried the top off of one jar and smelled it. "It's lamb," she said with delight.

"How do you know?" Teach said casually as he inspected the stove and pushed some tinder into the firebox from a small pile left at the side of the stove. When she didn't immediately answer he glanced at her. The expression on her face was priceless. She was looking at him as if he had just said the most ridiculous thing in the world.

"What did I say?" Teach laughed, grinning helplessly.

"You should know better than to question the French about food. We invented cuisine. And never question a Toche. We are legendary cooks, and that is something in a nation where everyone knows food." For a moment he saw Madeleine as she was, before war and death had invaded her soul. He felt a joy come into him like an unquenchable light. The weight of struggle and worry lifted from him. He knew that he should be confused but he wasn't. His experience of the love for his family and friends was but a glimpse into this. He knew this was the type of love that once felt could never be burned from a person's soul.

Madeleine looked at Teach and saw the way he looked at her. He couldn't be more beautiful. He shone with an inner light that was barely contained. His confidence and character was the mortar that held him together. She felt a raw fire building out of the smoldering physical attraction she had always felt for him. She brushed past him to set the jars on the counter. He made no move to get out of her way. Every part of her making contact with him screamed as it passed along his body. She set the jars down, her hands shaking with physical need. She turned and burst upon him like a wave, pulling his face down to hers as they desperately threw themselves together. Nothing was tentative, nothing held back. Together they took from each other with a fury that was without control. Madeleine pushed the table out of the way as they collapsed to the floor into each other. There were no sweet kisses or tender caresses as their pent up lust crashed together and raged. Their clothes were torn as they struggled becoming one, their breath ragged and snatched between their gasps and moans. They gave in completely, raw and base as they fed their desire trapped in a madness of hunger. For a moment nothing else existed. Their fears and the hopelessness of the world vanished.

It was a long time before Teach stood and helped Madeleine from the floor. He moved towards the stove and started to open the jars of food. She came up next to him and took them from his hands and walked him over to the table and sat him down in a chair.

"Let me," Madeleine said in way that told him she wanted to do this simple thing for him.

Again he felt the urge to speak, but listened instead as she spoke of the food and how it must have been prepared. She served him first and then came with her bowl and sat very near him. The room was fragrant with the thyme and rosemary the lamb was cooked in, spices pulled from the rough terrain over which the sheep grazed.

"The food is very good, Madeleine, Thank you."

"The people of this region have a fascinating cuisine that is both Spanish and French. Flavorful and abundant, but it is not Provencal," she said, raising her chin involuntarily with pride, letting the name of her home glide off her lips with the satisfaction of certainty.

"Some day we will eat together near the sea *en Provence*," she promised them both.

"It will taste all the better knowing that the Nazis are out of France forever. I cannot wait to stand with you on the beach in a free France," he said, holding her eyes. As she looked at the magnificent blue of his eyes, she saw the sea. Although he was from London she believed that the people of Great Britain all have the sea in their eyes. As an island people, the British were held in its embrace. More so than ever, the sea and the pilots of England had shown the timelessness of the marriage of the people to their protector, a rough and raw stretch of the North Sea.

"France will be free again. People will not abide the Nazi yoke of hate much longer," Madeleine said, reaching out to touch his hand. He took hers and held it against his chest.

"Madeleine, I don't have much experience with women and feel like I'm not much more than a boy just out of school. But I am not confused or uncertain about you. I love you. Not just because of this tonight. My feelings for you have been growing since you first came for training. I could not leave without telling you. I hope you have feelings for me. This war doesn't give us much time for a courtship, but I would like to be with you when this is all over. Will you give me that chance?"

"I love you too, Jack. So much of me died along with my brother. I never thought I could find any happiness again. I cannot imagine a person so uncomplicated and caring as you. Neither of us knows what is going to happen. But, if we make it through the war, you had better come looking for me. I will not worry if you stray, as long as you come running back," she said, straddling the chair he was sitting in, her beautiful body entwining itself in his.

"You're joking," he blurted, lost in disbelief.

"No, I am French. And by the way, you're no schoolboy, Jack Teach," she said, her eyes burning with black fire as she raised her mouth to his.

The next morning came all too quickly. They ate a meal of canned peaches and the leftover stew. Neither of them said much but touched almost constantly. Finally Jack looked at his watch.

"I have to leave, Madeleine. I have to meet my contact well into the foothills and have many miles to go into Spain."

"Funny how you have to escape from fascists through another fascist country."

"Spain will not be fascist forever. We have many friends among the loyalists. Many have come to fight the fascists among the Resistance groups here. They have known war longer than we and hate the Germans for helping the fascists during their civil war."

"The fight must continue until this plague of fascism is gone from Europe," Madeleine agreed.

Teach smiled and said, "You sound like a communist."

"I don't understand politics, nor care to at this point. The French people will decide the future for France. That and revenge will be enough for me."

With that Teach kissed her and walked out the door. Madeleine watched him walking away with powerful strides towards the hills that lay just behind the house, and then he was gone. She went back inside the barn, covered her face in her hands, and sobbed silently as the war demanded sacrifice from her again.

As Teach made his way carefully through the jutting rocks and boulders of the frontier, tears ran freely down his face. He clenched his teeth and kept his chin firmly locked against the pain in his heart as it ached and screamed at him to turn around. He forced his feet forward, on the path that would bring him back to her. It would be a long, impossible road, but like his countrymen, he would never surrender.

CHAPTER **TEN**

More than three years later, Madeleine pushed her bicycle slowly down an alley towards the front entrance of a police station. She was acting on very recent intelligence and swift action was required. She didn't like having to expose herself to enemy eyes, but the situation dictated it. She wore no disguise. She needed to appear as normal as possible and for the men to focus on her body, not her face. She could not disguise her beauty, and tried to utilize it to her advantage. There were too few clothes to choose from and the ones she'd chosen were worn and threadbare. Although the garments were loose, her looks captured the attention of the police officers loitering around the entrance. She hoped that the last thing the men would look at was her face. She made sure that the clothing didn't obscure her curves completely, positioning her body to ensure that they did not. She leaned the bicycle against a lamppost and collected a few loaves of bread and a wheel of cheese from the basket behind the seat. The loaves were irregular in shape but were mostly baguettes, partially wrapped in paper with the top halves sticking out. She moved uncertainly, seemingly confused and frightened, trying to appear subservient and nonthreatening. The men showed no concern for security, despite the fact that two of their more important masters were inside the station on an inspection.

"*Bonjour, mademoiselle*, you are new. Where is Marc today?" The closest of the officers called to her as she moved towards the door.

"My uncle is ill today and cannot make his rounds," She answered, making only brief eye contact with the policeman and smiling demurely, shrinking slightly into herself.

This is a shy one, the man thought. With looks like that

perhaps she will not always be so. He admired her openly, and inwardly bemoaned his own lack of success with women. Half of them seemed to be afraid of him because of his position as a police officer working with the enemy, the Vichy government. It wasn't his fault France had fallen so quickly. In his mind, one did the best they could under the circumstances and followed orders. His situation had been vastly improved by his cooperation. He was better off now than before the war. His food and clothing were more than adequate. He was thriving under the occupation. He felt that reporting illegal activity was his duty. After all, he was a police officer and the Resistance were terrorists and subversives. They made life harder for everyone else. The war couldn't last forever, and it didn't seem like the Germans were going to leave France. He sighed inwardly as he looked at her. In passing he thought about searching the bundle of bread and the small package the girl carried, but she seemed so young and insecure, she'd probably collapse in fright if he did so.

"Let me get the door for you. I hope Marc remains ill for a while so that we may enjoy your company again." The man smiled and looked over at his fellow officers who were only interested in Madeleine's feminine charms. They made no move to search her deliveries.

"Thank you *monsieur*, I will be sure to tell my uncle of your kindness," She almost whispered as she slid past him and into the hallway of the police station.

As she entered she saw two leather overcoats hanging in the hallway. They bore the insignia of the Gestapo. The intelligence had been correct. A routine visit by the hated German secret police was underway. As soon as she was out of sight of the men at the front of the building, the transformation in her demeanor was instant. She seemed to grow and harden, her limpidness replaced with iron. She moved swiftly towards the back of the building where the small kitchen was located. She walked past two offices along the corridor and heard voices coming from the one closest to the kitchen. They were distinctly German. As she unloaded the bread onto a table she listened to see if a third voice came from the room. She moved slowly and with patience, knowing that for what she intended to do, patience and nerve beat bravado and recklessness every time. The men in the room were smoking, and thus would have at least one of their hands occupied. She could detect different odors of tobacco. One of them had a pipe. Their conversation was languid and unhurried. There was no excitement in their voices. Given the time of day, it was likely that these officers had eaten a good meal. Their movements would be slow.

Madeleine worked with her hands as she kept an eye on the front. She was aware of everything around her. Her senses heightened and became acute. She selected one of the thicker baguettes and tore open one end, revealing a small metal cylinder. She raised her skirt and took out a pistol that was bound to the inside of her thigh, a location few men felt comfortable searching under fairly routine circumstances. She quickly screwed the silencer into the end and tucked the gun under the bread paper and carried it over to the office door behind which she heard the steady cadence of the men's conversation. She paused briefly, then gently pushed the door open and walked into the room holding the silenced weapon along her side so that it wouldn't instantly be noticed. The officer seated at the desk turned only after she was fully into the room. Without hesitation she shot him squarely in the forehead. The other officer seated in front of the desk didn't have time to register surprise. She turned and put a bullet through his throat and face in instant succession. Turning back to the first officer, she shot him a second time so there would be no mistake. Although the room smelled of gunpowder, the silencer had done its job. Both men remained slumped in their chairs, surprise etched on their faces. Madeleine moved swiftly out of the room and closed the door behind her. With practiced efficiency she unscrewed the silencer and tucked it away inside her sweater. She placed the gun in her pocket. She moved back to the kitchen, opened a window and dropped a short distance to the pavement below. It was a market day, and although many things were scarce, the street was getting crowded. She was well into the crowd and away before she heard the first shriek of a police whistle.

CHAPTER **ELEVEN**

Madeleine sat next to a small campfire at the entrance of a cave at the top of a hard hike along a forgotten path through scree and boulders on the side of a mountain. It was a semi-regular hiding place that only she knew of. She had discovered it months ago while moving from one area of southern France to the next. The smells of wild herbs and the breeze off the sea comforted her. Living wild wasn't by choice. Although she generally used safe houses, someone other than she knew of their existence. She could never stay with one of the Resistance groups. Not even for a short while. The risk was too great. Her exploits had reached legendary status and the reward for her capture or death was high enough to make the most resolute consider treason to the Resistance. In the beginning she had brief encounters with Resistance members. Little by little, it was clear that they feared her as well. They were cordial but always in a hurry to distance themselves from, "*L'ange de la mort*" as she had come to be called by both civilians and the Germans.

Madeleine worked alone, receiving her missions in code from London. It was no longer safe for her to associate with any of the scattered individual Resistance groups. They had to operate autonomously with little or no association. That meant that the capture of one group would not lead to the capture of all. They all knew that the Gestapo used torture and were good at it. One could tolerate physical pain to a degree, but the torture of others, especially loved ones, was impossible to withstand. There was no humanity in torture and the Gestapo encouraged sadists to do the dirty work. Their enjoyment increased with the intensity of their victim's pain. They were the people Madeleine targeted for execution. There was no question of guilt. She rationalized that they were truly evil and that she was protecting the innocent from the enemies of all people.

She cut a piece of bread and placed it along with a lump of lard into a small frying pan that she kept buried in the back of the cave. This time she had scrounged a piece of hard goat cheese. She broke off a piece to nibble on and crumble onto the bread when heated. She sighed and thought about Provence in the days before the occupation, when cheese was so abundant and so varied that you could eat the freshest, only days old, or the drier and older aged pieces that burst with flavor as they melted slowly in your mouth. Funny how much she thought about food and how important it was to her. She wasn't quite sure that the cheese she had was intended for the longer aging process, but she didn't care. It was cheese. She also had a skin of wine and intended to drink all of it. The cave was the safest place in her world, except perhaps for England. She fingered the cyanide capsule she always kept on her person. At least she wouldn't need it tonight. Still, she knew she'd probably never use it. If trapped, she intended to die in a gunfight or at least with her hands around the throat of the enemy.

Madeleine's thoughts turned to Teach. He was constantly with her. She didn't allow herself any doubt that she would be with him again. She thought that he might have other women. She remembered telling him as they parted that if he did, she would understand, as he was a man. She smiled, remembering the shock on his young face, his looking at her like a dangerous animal, wanting her but afraid of being bitten. She laughed out loud. It was these tiny moments of joy that kept her sane and pushed her forward. Her life had been an endless path of death. She had to make it through.

Outside the cave the day quieted into twilight as she tended her cooking and drank from the skin. The wine was good and she felt it warm her spirits. She was elated that she had performed her mission so well and knew that her "uncle Marc," a member of a Resistance group from outside the area, had probably reached safety by now. His mission had been to deliver bread and other foods from the bakery around town.

Marc, like so many of the other men of his generation, was a veteran of the First World War. His hatred for the Germans reached a level beyond even Madeleine's comprehension, born of gas attacks in the night in a blasted land. He was a soldier, not an assassin. He thought of war in a conventional manner that included rules of engagement. In Madeleine's mind, the monsters had forfeited the game. She was bound by nothing. Not even the directives of London. She freelanced when she saw the need.

Madeleine opened the pages of the leading Resistance paper, "Combat." They weren't easy for her to come by. She picked them up during the brief contacts she had with Resistance groups. She realized that the Gestapo knew something of what she looked like, although she varied her appearance slightly each time. Sometimes it was eye wear or baggy clothing. She also used variations in hairstyle or accent.

America was in the war now, and everyone was expecting invasion. It seemed that it would never come. She was tired of running and hiding and fear. Her only goals were to live to see France free again and to find Jack. It was hard to believe that it had been more than three years. She had had no news of him. There was no way for her to get any. She knew that he was alive. She had not had a premonition of tragedy, which were common to the women in her family. Their feelings were so acute that people had long ago stopped discounting them. The premonitions were both an asset and a curse, and so overwhelming as to be shattering in their psychological effect. Madeleine and her mother had known the instant her grandmother had passed away. It bordered on telepathy and, some said, clairvoyance. Madeleine relied upon her ability to know that Jack was alive and well.

The last three years had been a jumble of killing and hiding. Madeleine was able to rest from time to time in one of several remote safe houses. Even though the British SOE maintained them, she felt like a noose was slowly tightening around her neck. She had been very lucky so far, but it seemed the Germans were never far behind and were always getting closer. Little by little the mood in France turned toward the anticipation of invasion. It would come. The bombers flew over towards

Germany in ever-increasing numbers, and the resistance to them seemed to dwindle. Now the German people suffered and she was happy for it. She felt no empathy except for the children. The German people did not hold their leader or the military accountable for any atrocity. So she did. The day of reckoning was coming. She expected the call to come any day, encoded in a BBC broadcast.

Madeleine's orders came in a code singular to her. She was the hand of retribution, a source of terror among those that feared the Resistance. The Germans saw the Resistance as terrorists. The notion that one can be a terrorist in one's own conquered and occupied country made no sense to her. Wouldn't the German people fight an oppressor? Their nationalistic pride and the yoke of servitude after their defeat in the First World War had been the tinder that allowed a monster like Hitler and his henchmen to come to power. She knew the SS and the Gestapo, Hitler's elite, regarded anyone not of pure Aryan race as sheep to be slaughtered at will, without compunction. No, the planes and bombs were just. If that was what it took to eradicate the evil that was Nazi Germany, then the German people had called it down upon themselves.

Madeleine spread out the remnants of the fire and covered them with dirt, making sure there was no trace left. She took her blanket and walked to the rear of the cave where she had discovered the entrance to another, much larger chamber. She squeezed through the opening and lowered herself onto a bed of grass that she had accumulated over the times she'd visited. A man, especially one with a gun, would have one hell of a time getting to her. She could stay inside and shoot many Germans if they tried it. If they used grenades then they'd probably end up sealing the entrance anyway. If that happened she hoped there was another way out. She was provisioned and there was a natural spring farther back. As she drifted off to sleep she found herself dreaming of home and her parents. She wondered what other desperate souls over the centuries had used the cave as a sanctuary. She said a quiet prayer and went to sleep.

CHAPTER **TWELVE**

Horst Stenger stood inside the office and stared down at the two corpses of the Nazi Gestapo officers. He was a regular army major and a criminal investigator. His authority was all but autonomous as Berlin's fear of insurgency increased in every quarter. He was often called in to look into such matters, and lately there seemed to be more work. He sighed as he thought of his civilian job before the war in Berlin, working in an organized police force as a detective with a solid reputation for solving difficult crimes. Vichy had called him in to avoid the Gestapo simply rounding up a bunch of civilians and shooting them. His first order of business was to declare this an outside professional assassination and not the work of any local Resistance group. That would be easy. He knew who had done this. As soon as the police officers had described the young girl who had mysteriously disappeared he had known who he was after. In his circles, she was known as the Angel of Death. An apt name, he thought, as she seemed to target the Gestapo and SS almost exclusively. He smiled inwardly as he thought of the religious analogies of the whole thing. You butcher innocents and God sends down one of his less compassionate angels to straighten things out. The description was usually the same: a young beautiful girl, on the petite side. She was undoubtedly the type of girl that would blind recollection with her beauty. It was an odd notion, but men were men. They simply acted differently in the presence of a dramatically beautiful woman. But this one never seemed to be described in exactly the same way. Nor did she always follow the same procedure. Most of the time she wasn't seen. Still, when he read the reports, he knew it was her. Many people are killers, but few are surgical assassins of her caliber. He shuddered a bit at the notion that one so young could be so deadly.

He hoped that her work was a reaction to some atrocity and not a fondness for killing. He worried that she would extend her killing to those less deserving of it. Therefore, he needed to stop her.

His attention turned to the hysterical screaming directed his way by Major Gunter Von Schmelling, a particularly annoying Aryan superman who was in charge of the SS in this portion of southern France. At least the man had some sense: he yelled from a distance. Stenger was a war hero, and a harder man than blond boy Schmelling. He'd personally punched more than one Gestapo officer. He hated the perversion of his army the SS represented. They were maniacal in their belief of their racial superiority. Their reputation was as tough and determined soldiers. The SS deployed on the Russian front had killed thousands of civilians with no compassion. They had a well-deserved reputation for ruthlessness. Clearly the most dangerous patients had gained control of the asylum. How had his country allowed this to happen? What had been a movement of national pride had become a wave of brutality, blind to anything but devotion to a poisoned cause.

He sighed and thought of the angel of death, the assassin the French called *L'ange de la mort.* She's probably my daughter's age, he thought. How many young men and women in Germany would come running to defend their families and homes? All of them, he hoped. When he was her age, he'd been at the Marne, a ghastly horrible memory of screaming and death. Germany, England, and the Americans had sacrificed a generation to move their trenches inches at a time. These Gestapo were the criminals from his civilian past, set loose to satisfy the whims of a dictator. He wasn't surprised at the tenacity of the French Resistance. These were the sons and daughters of the men he'd fought against. They were as hard as nails, and patriotic. France had been taken because France was still tired of war. Hitler's *Blitzkrieg* came from careful planning and the pride of the defeated. They had destroyed two armies, the Polish and the French, each with more than a million men. Apparently, surprise worked well. He thought of the Japanese and Pearl Harbor. That was a mistake. He remembered the courage of the doughboys. They were farmers just like those in the large family he came from. They were probably his cousins. Americans, when angered, are the sum of their people. They were industrious and driven. And they were on their way.

He took two steps towards Von Schmelling and said, "Major, you are standing in my crime scene. I do not care what you want me to do. I know my duty and have done it well, long before you tortured your first pet. You raise your voice to me again and we will meet on the field of honor."

Dueling had been a thing of the past for some time in Europe, but Von Schmelling knew what the detective meant. In addition to his skills in investigation, Stenger had been a marksman in the first war and was known to practice every day. Von Schmelling hated the old warriors he couldn't intimidate, especially the ones he feared.

"If you can't catch this bitch, then we'll just start shooting these sheep, Stenger!" Von Schmelling was well past hysterical. The other soldiers looked at him, wondering if he was going to pop.

"Well, Major, you could. But then the Field Marshall would undoubtedly have me arrest you. I would, of course, have to detain you while your appeal made its way through channels. Cherblinka would be a fine place for your stay. Say in the general population," Stenger said, poking Von Schmelling with his threat. A flicker of bowel-chilling panic passed through Von Schmelling's eyes. He knew this crazy bastard would do it. Put him in with the Jews in the worst concentration camp in the region. They would eat him alive, slowly.

"Just do your job! Berlin will sort you out in time!"

"Before or after the Americans come back to France? You see, they've been here before. I can assure you that they do not like to pay for the same real estate twice. I am sure you SS boys will have every opportunity to show your worth in the face of allied armor," he said, his voice dancing with sarcasm. Like most men his age, Stenger knew he'd already won the exchange. His silence was more painful than any further comment he might offer.

Over to Stenger's right his second in command, Captain Willi Peterson covered his mouth with a gloved hand. Where

Stenger was tall and lean, Willi was smaller and compact with dark hair and short balanced limbs. He held himself with an easy fluid grace. He had the look of a prizefighter who won more than he lost. He stifled a laugh and tried to keep from shaking. He chided himself for laughing at the image of Stenger casually raising his pistol and shooting Von Schmelling. There was nothing overtly humorous about that, but he just couldn't help it as he pictured Stenger dropping the idiot like a cow on a kill floor. As he got himself under control, he decided it was best not to mention this particular mental picture to anyone but Stenger. Willi had been with Stenger in the trenches and knew he would shoot Von Schmelling without hesitation.

The SS major spun on his heels and stormed off. Some of the other officers in the area smirked as he left. It was a pity, Stenger thought, that these fools were leading the new German army. We could have retaken some land and been strong. All the rest was arrogance and madness. He glanced around the room and knew he'd find nothing. Catching the Angel would be about anticipation. Be that as it may, was it a good idea to chase a female panther in the dark?

Von Schmelling was in a foul mood after his run-in with Stenger. Fool, he thought, the Reich will never be defeated. We will rule for a thousand years. Von Schmelling was a true believer. After a childhood filled with bullying and anti-Semitic poison fed to him by his aristocratic parents, he was a natural for the SS. His family name and blond Aryan looks assured him a meteoric rise to the top. His superiors liked his results and supported the murder and torture he used to obtain information. He rarely tortured directly, choosing to observe instead. He was fastidious about his appearance and didn't want to dirty himself by touching an inferior being.

"Take me to the interrogation center," Von Schmelling shouted to his driver. He loved to have soldiers at his command. These two were like robots and did precisely what he told them, when he told them, without pause or compassion. He had chosen them for their pure Aryan lineage and ruthless nature.

Occasionally as a treat he gave them prisoners to do with as they pleased, as long as they disposed of their bodies when finished. Generally there was little left for disposal.

The major's staff car drove up to an imposing building that looked like a castle but was, in fact an ornate mansion, formerly owned by a well-to-do French family who had been permitted to relocate to a summer residence until Germany no longer had a need for their home. To the Germans aristocracy commanded respect and it was usually afforded. By all accounts they did not create any problems and had provided some assistance to their conquerors in exchange for assurances that their wealth would not be plundered in their absence.

Von Schmelling strode quickly through the front door and paused only long enough for a valet to take his outer wear and hat.

"Bring Gaston Marcher to his wife's cell immediately, sergeant," Von Schmelling said, almost pleasantly.

A brutish SS sergeant snapped his heels together and smirked in anticipation of some sport. As he lumbered out of the room he had to turn slightly to get his shoulders and back through the narrow doorway. It was a wonder his knuckles didn't drag on the floor when he walked.

Von Schmelling descended a flight of stairs that led to a vast cellar that had been converted to a number of cells and rooms that neither saw the light of day nor allowed any sound to escape. Von Schmelling stopped in front of a cell and gestured for a uniformed guard to open the door. A small light bulb illuminated the room and showed a young woman huddled in the corner, sitting on a filthy mat and shaking with fear. Von Schmelling knew she had already been tortured because he had ordered it, along with strict instructions not to damage her appearance unduly. That usually meant having the jailers strap her to a slant board and then drop her head into a trough of water in ever-increasing duration, all but drowning their victim each time. Other times a carefully placed needle did the trick. "Bring me a chair," he said, as a chair materialized beneath him.

"Ready to cooperate, madam?" He said conversationally.

"My husband and I are school teachers, we know nothing,"

her exhausted voice heavy with submission. She was almost ready, Von Schmelling thought as he observed her like a laboratory specimen.

"No, you are terrorists plotting against your benevolent occupiers, but, more importantly, against your countrymen."

"We are not," she wailed, a breath away from complete psychological breakdown.

Two guards brought in a young man and threw him onto the floor. He had already been beaten severely. He smelled of burnt flesh. The burns were in areas that were covered by the rags of clothing left on his body. Electrodes had been affixed to his testicles. It was one of Von Schmelling's favorite pastimes. It made him violently aroused. Following those sessions he had a female prisoner brought to his study above for some personal attention. They were so much more fun than the Teutonic bitch his parents had arranged for him to marry. Wealth and privilege had its burdens and rewards, he thought. Well, she's home in Dresden torturing the domestic staff in her own way. God, I hope the war lasts, or that I can get a permanent foreign posting, he mused.

The unfortunate man on the ground moaned and the woman crawled over to him. One of the guards was about to beat her back, but Von Schmelling waved him off. He wanted her to get a good look at her husband.

Finally he said, "Enough. Stand Mr. Marcher up and tie his hands to the ceiling bolt." Involuntarily the woman's eyes looked up to see an iron ring attached to the ceiling. Marcher's shackles were hooked to the ring and he hung there with just the tips of his feet touching the floor.

"So, madam, your bath didn't loosen your tongue, perhaps this will." He motioned to the brutish sergeant who smiled and slammed a ham-sized fist into Marcher's kidneys. Despite his almost unconscious state, the hanging man screamed under the massive blow.

"No, Major!" Mademoiselle Marcher screamed.

"A few to the ribs I think, Joseph. Now, his terrorist balls." Soon Marcher began to cough blood.

"I will do anything, sign anything, just stop," the woman

was past hysterical.

"I know you will, mademoiselle," Von Schmelling said, clearly communicating his sadistic intent. Von Schmelling waived a scented handkerchief gesturing to have the victim taken down. Marcher poured down to the floor, lacking any control over his body.

"Take him out," Von Schmelling sighed. Two guards roughly grabbed Marcher and dragged him from the room. "Clean her up and bring her to my study. Find her some decent clothing. Till we meet again, Fraulein." Von Schmelling smiled and strode from the room, a spring in his step. Even the toughest couldn't stand seeing their loved ones tortured, he thought. He always saved that for last. He didn't like them talking too soon.

CHAPTER THIRTEEN

The sky roared by the window just a few feet in front of a group of paratroopers flying over the English countryside. John Trunce stood in the middle of the row of men preparing to jump. The man behind him checked his gear as he checked the man in front of him. It was another training exercise. He was getting tired of them. He was one of the 82nd Airborne currently stationed in England. He and his friends had seen action in Italy, and while their constant training kept them on their toes, it did nothing to quell their urgency to get back at it and bring the war to a conclusion.

It had been many months since John left home. Everyone knew the invasion was coming. Command was waiting for the optimum conditions to assault "Fortress Europe." While he was apprehensive about the unknown, he had the impatience and sense of indestructibility that came with his young age. At nineteen he felt like a caged animal, in too big a hurry to get back into combat. This time they would be facing Germany's best general, Erwin Rommel, a man widely respected on both sides of the channel. Rommel believed in armor and he led from the front. He'd be there to meet the invasion head on.

John focused on his strong sense of duty and defense of his country. Pearl Harbor had shown everyone that America wasn't isolated. Just like most of his friends, he joined up and chose the paratroopers because they were the best. He thought fighting with the best might improve his chances of survival. It made practical sense to him, but he knew nobody would really know until they were in combat. He'd been with his buddies in combat and there wasn't a coward among them. Like them, his biggest fear was letting anyone down. So he listened to orders and focused. He instinctively knew that this was probably going to be the most important thing he did in his life. This was not the time or the place to screw up.

John's thoughts were interrupted by the flashing green light and the jumpmaster's signal to move. As the stick moved forward, John shuffled towards the door, jumped out, and was caught in the prop blast and pulled out into the heavens. He loved it. He felt like he was flying. If he survived the war he was going to learn to fly. He just knew he'd never be able to give it up completely.

CHAPTER **FOURTEEN**

Stenger sat back at a wooden desk, feet up, hands behind his head, smoking and staring at the ceiling. Willi sat in a chair on the other side of the desk and rested his ankles on the corner nearest him. Stenger smiled and thought, these Aryans think they look German? Hah! Willi looked German. Strong features, dark hair and a rugged build. He always looked relaxed. People were often mistaken about Willi until they saw him in action. Then, they were wary of him, and rightfully so. His was a tough old farm family that was passionate about boxing. Willi grew up sparring with his older, bigger brothers. They had shown him no mercy. So he improved his own skills until he could turn the tables on them, which he reportedly did with great relish. His skills were a source of pride to his father, who characteristically showed little emotion towards his children, but who loved the fight in Willi and told him so.

Stenger looked around the orderly little room. Once they removed the dead Gestapo agents he moved right in. Most of the blood had been cleaned up, but it didn't matter to Stenger and Willi. They were well past that. Yes, he liked this police station; not too much clutter and only one phone which to his great joy rarely worked. He preferred to work alone with Willi. Their minds worked differently but when necessary they could anticipate one another's thoughts.

"Well Horsty, how are you going to catch this femme fatale?" Willi said, pulling a pack of cigarettes from his pocket.

"I'm not so sure I really want to, Willi, but I'd deny it."

"I think your secret is safe with me, Horsty. I've been keeping your secrets for years now." Willi said, lighting his cigarette, a twinkle in his eye.

"That you have, Willi. How is it possible that you and I find ourselves in another damn war?"

"Our soaring national pride, I guess. At least this time we're out of the trench and away from the front."

"Before this is over Willi, the same countries that fought for the same little pieces of land that we bled over will be back here again."

"Just think of the poor bastards that are our ages, pulled back onto the line trying to hold back the Allies again."

"Well, when they come through, I'm staying on this side," Stenger said. "I've already moved my family to Switzerland. The wife and daughters are there already, permanently visiting my wife's sister. I find it so hard to believe that our magnificent leaders expected to take this much territory and hold it, and then go and piss off the Russian bear. Every sane military leader knows you can't fight a war on two fronts forever."

"That's why bachelorhood is so desirable, Horsty. My brothers are scattered all over and my parents are far away from the cities on the farm. So don't worry, I'll be right behind you when the Americans come," Willi said with a wry grin.

Stenger laughed. Willi was the furthest thing from a coward a man could be. He remembered going over the top of the trench with Willi countless times. Each time he would shrug, clap him on the shoulder, and say, "Who knows Horsty, maybe they got a four star trench over there." Stenger knew Willi felt the horror. How couldn't he? Often times their dead were stacked up like cord wood, used to shore up the trench. A frozen body makes pretty good timber. Willi dealt with things with humor. He came from a hard farm life, his father stern but caring. Other members of his family were hard working brew masters. One side grew the hops and the other processed them into one of the tastiest beers around. Willi learned how to cope and squeeze some measure of happiness out of any situation. When Horst had left the military, he encouraged Willi to go into the police force with him. Willi was smart but not ambitious. He didn't need to be, Horst thought. He's with me and I wouldn't have it any other way.

"Well, Willi, I have to get her out of circulation. When the invasion comes and the French are left to their own devices, there will be a lot of killing of collaborators and folks deemed to have collaborated. To her, killing is like tying your shoes. We can't have her as judge, jury, and executioner. There will be retribution. People are good that way. You'll see, the ranks of the Resistance will swell as the true danger passes. Everyone will want to seem to have been fighting us all along. The real fighters like our friend here will want to return to their families and their homes to forget about war," Stenger said, tapping on the thick file he kept of the assassins' known activities.

"Do you think this one will? She's killed a lot of people."

"Bad people and traitors exclusively, it seems. Gestapo, SS, you know, Hitler's henchmen. Who would have thought one Bohemian corporal could cause so much trouble?"

"I'd like to shoot a few of them myself," Willi said, wistfully blowing a smoke ring towards the ceiling."

"We'll leave that to the professionals. We're just policemen trying to catch a killer."

"So how do we do that, *Mon commandant*?" Willi asked, with an exaggerated French accent.

"We use Von Schmelling as bait, of course," Horst said with a huge smile.

"Maybe she'll get him in the process," Willi chuckled.

"That's what I love about you, my friend, always the optimist."

Suddenly there was shouting in the street and the sound of several vehicles stopping abruptly in front of the police station.

"Now, what?" Stenger said, walking to the front room of the police station. He pulled aside the curtain on the front window and looked out into the street. There were a dozen or so people being herded into the back of a waiting truck. At least two families with small children were being forced by SS soldiers into the back of the vehicle.

"Jews being arrested?" Willi said.

"Yes, I think so. Let's go see."

Stenger and Willi walked out into the street and approached one of the SS soldiers standing to the side shouting orders.

"What's going on, sergeant?" Stenger asked.

The sergeant turned in annoyance. His attitude changed when he saw that Stenger was a Major in the military police. He almost fell over himself snapping to attention and saluting.

"*Heil Hitler*!" were the first words out of the sergeant's mouth.

"Yes, good, right," Stenger said, returning his salute half-heartedly. "Now I asked you a question soldier. For what offense are these people being arrested?"

"Jews, sir. They are being transported out of the country."

"No criminal offense aside from that? Surely the children haven't committed any crime," Stenger asked evenly, already fully aware of the answer.

"No, sir," the sergeant answered looking at Stenger a little quizzically. To the SS being a Jew was as significant a crime as one could commit.

"Of course, but you never know with these people," Stenger said in a conspiratorial tone putting the man at ease. "Where is the truck headed?"

It worked. The sergeant didn't appear to be uneasy in the least. "Down to the train station, *Herr Major.* We are rounding up several hundred from throughout the area."

"Good, good," Stenger said encouragingly. He patted the sergeant on the back and pulled out a pack of cigarettes, offering him one. "We can't have them running around loose, now can we?"

The sergeant smiled, enjoying the praise of a major. Stenger looked as Aryan as a man could. He was tall and blue eyed, a poster boy for the master race. Willi stood to the side expressionless. The only thing that gave away any hint that he was silently enjoying Stenger's charade was the merriment dancing in his eyes. He knew Stenger was about as far from being a willing member of the master race as a rabbi.

The truck was loaded and the sergeant and his detail jumped in the back with the families. Stenger caught the stare of one father as he held his young children close. There was panic in his eyes as the man looked at Stenger. Stenger held his gaze and just as the canvas was dropped over the back of the truck, Stenger gave the man the slightest of nods. A flash of surprise showed in the man's face. He was clearly unsure of what Stenger's gesture meant.

As the truck pulled away, Willi walked over to Stenger. "Now what, Horsty? You have that look in your eye," Willi teased, wagging a finger at him.

"Now I go down to the train station and figure out how to get those people off that train and onto another one headed some place safe."

"Good, let's go."

"I can't ask you to follow me every time I go crusading, Willi," Stenger replied.

"What, and miss some real fun? How unsporting of you, Horsty. By the way, what's your plan?"

"No plan. I'll make one up as I go along."

"Well, for once, I have a plan."

"I am all ears, Willi."

"We'll join the Gestapo for an hour or so."

Stenger looked at Willi quizzically. "How, my friend?"

"With these," Willi said, pulling out the two leather Gestapo coats that had been hanging in the hallway when they arrived at the crime scene.

"Tell me you have their hats, too, Willi?" Stenger said reaching for one of the coats.

"In a drawer in the kitchen," Willi said, smiling.

"Any particular reason you collected these garments, Willi?"

"Do you have any idea how easy it is to pick up women on leave when I'm back home in one of these?" Willi said, sliding into one of the long leather coats as the two walked over towards the police station.

"Willi, Willi, what am I going to do with you?" Stenger chuckled, walking out the front door of the station.

An hour later Stenger and Willi arrived at the train station in time to see the last of a group of Jewish families being loaded into boxcars.

Stenger walked over to one of the conductors, a Frenchman holding a clipboard. He was perusing a schedule as Stenger walked up.

"Good afternoon. Are you the stationmaster here?" Stenger asked in his most authoritarian manner. He threw in a little contempt for good measure.

The second the stationmaster saw Stenger's searing blue eyes burning into him he blanched. Stenger snapped a pair of leather gloves he found in the coat pocket into his hand for effect.

"Yes," was all the terrified stationmaster could manage as he took in the rest of Stenger's costume, the leather coat complimenting the officious sneering expression.

"Where is that train headed?" Stenger said, gesturing to the train on the opposite track from the one loaded with the Jewish families.

"Spain, sir."

"When do the Jews depart?"

"Not for several hours sir."

Stenger bit back his initial inclination to explode. The families crammed into the locked boxcars would be trapped in the heat as the sun beat down for the remainder of the day while other unfortunate souls were being collected. Stenger knew the people wouldn't be given water or food, much less any facilities for relieving themselves.

"And that one?" Stenger said, gesturing to the train bound for Spain.

"One hour sir," the man replied, shakily checking his clipboard.

"No. It leaves when I say it leaves."

"But sir, the schedule," the man replied without thinking.

Stenger took two steps closer to the stationmaster and backed him into a nearby wall.

"I want to go to Spain, my French friend. Perhaps you would like to join me for a little ride. We can enjoy the sights together for awhile," Stenger hissed through clenched teeth, his eyes wild, as if his grip on sanity was just for show.

The stationmaster could barely breathe. He had visions of

Stenger tossing him from the train and shooting him as he ran. Stenger thought the man might actually wet his pants as he stood and shook.

"When you say so. Yes sir."

"Excellent!" Stenger said, instantly stepping back from the man, reaching over to straightening his lapels and patting him affectionately on the cheek. He was all smiles and handshakes for the terrified stationmaster.

"May I go and see to it, sir?" The man said, sliding towards his office.

"Yes, go. But I warn you this is top-secret Gestapo business. We are following strict orders from Berlin. I wouldn't make any phone calls just yet," Stenger said, as if scolding a young child.

"Oh, no sir. No sir."

"Fine then, off with you," Stenger said, dismissing the man with a wave of his gloves.

"Nice work," Willi said walking up to Stenger.

"What do you think, Willi? You take the guards on this side on a wild goose chase. How about some vital Gestapo business while I move the people onto the train bound for Spain."

"Maybe I should take the guards down to the bar and buy them some drinks?" Willi said, gesturing around the corner.

"Don't let them see your face too much, Willi."

"Nobody ever looks the Gestapo in the face. All they see are black coats and jack boots. Don't worry. I'll excuse myself right after I get them seated and set a couple rounds of drinks in front of them. So be fast, Horsty."

"I'll move them the second I see you go."

"What about the stationmaster?"

"Oh, he gets a bump on the head."

"Once a cop, always a cop," Willi said as he turned and walked towards the two regular army soldiers guarding the boxcars.

Hours later, Willi and Stenger were two hundred kilometers away from the train station, riding in a *Kubelwagen* taking an impromptu temporary leave of absence.

"So how does this little side trip fit into our current investigation, Horsty?" Willi asked, his feet up on the dash as he leaned back, enjoying the last rays of sunlight.

"We are following leads, Willi. You know that. The game is afoot, as old Sherlock would say."

Both men laughed as they drove west into the sunset.

Several hundred kilometers to the west a man peered through the open door of the westbound train, looking for an opportunity to get off.

"We have to jump." One man said, scanning the terrain for a safe landing spot.

"Right after we cross the Spanish frontier," another answered. He was the man who had seen Stenger at the police station and again at the train station. He was able to see a very familiar looking Gestapo agent shouting at the stationmaster through a small crack in the side of the boxcar. He caught another glimpse as the same man moved the families onto the other train.

"Get everyone ready. Hold onto the children and roll as you land," the first man said as he threw open the door as the train passed into Spain. It was an express, coming from Italy. It wouldn't stop now until it got to Barcelona.

Hundreds of people flung themselves out into the twilight, flying momentarily and then landing along the side of a grass-covered embankment.

Once he landed, the man collected his wife and children.

"Who set us free?" The man's youngest son asked.

"A policeman, *mon fils*," he answered, smiling at his son and silently thanking Stenger as he and his little family stole away into the night.

CHAPTER FIFTEEN

Günter Von Schmelling stood in front of a full-length mirror, admiring his finely tailored suit. The hours he spent in the saddle kept him lean, along with calisthenics he had performed regularly since his youth. He was from a wealthy old German family and had enjoyed privilege his entire life.

"I wonder what Father would think of me now?" He muttered towards the mirror, absently ignoring the tailor who stood demurely behind him, awaiting any instructions.

"What do you think, *Monsieur* Leblanc?" Schmelling said.

"You look splendid Major. The *demoiselles* will be duly impressed."

"Yes, you have outdone yourself, Leblanc. I will need two more uniforms and two casual jackets. I will of course pay in advance for the material to be ordered from Paris as before."

"Yes, Major."

"You are a good Frenchman, Leblanc. I wish all of your countrymen would accept defeat as easily, unlike those terrorists in the Resistance."

"Thank you, Major," Leblanc said. He had been a merchant for a long time and the customer was always right. In his mind he would make all the tailored uniforms this SS clown wanted. He secretly hoped Von Schmelling would be buried in one of them.

"I am off then, Leblanc. I will be back in two weeks for a fitting. Put it in your calendar."

"Just as you wish, Major."

Von Schmelling turned smartly on his heel and was followed out of the building by his two SS guards. He jumped into an open officer's car and signaled the driver to proceed. The driver careened out into traffic, heedless of the pedestrians scurrying to get out of his way.

Horst and Willi sat unobtrusively in a small café across the street, having followed Von Schmelling to the spot.

"How much for one of those suits, do you think, Horsty?"

"Too little. Having to touch Von Schmelling, much less fit him for a suit, would be nasty indeed."

"Think he'll be back?"

"Well, let's go find out."

The two men left coins for their coffee, such as it was during these times of occupation. The French struggled under the yoke of the invader, required to foot the cost of the occupation. The financial burden, coupled with the deportation of millions of French men and women to work in German factories was crippling, and another reason that the ranks of the Resistance grew daily.

Stenger walked into the tailor shop, looking as much like a policeman as possible. Willi at his side, giving Leblanc his old soldier's thousand yard stare.

"How can I help you, gentlemen?" Leblanc asked, clearly afraid of the two.

"We are from the investigation unit of the army police force."

"Not Gestapo?" Leblanc said clearly relieved.

"No, my friend. We are working men like you, following up a lead on a fairly routine black market matter."

"I do no business with those people. My customers order their material through me from Paris and other regional suppliers. I myself keep little in the way of stock on hand."

"Then you will have receipts for those purchases."

"Yes of course, officer. I keep them in the back. You are welcome to see them. I have nothing to hide."

"Yes, I will do so then," Stenger said, sounding officious. "Captain, watch the front of the store so that we may review the records without interruption." While Stenger addressed Willi he glanced meaningfully at the scheduling calendar on the counter next to him. He put his hand lightly on Leblanc and steered him towards the back to avoid having him collect the calendar.

Willi carefully spun the open calendar around and determined the date that Von Schmelling was scheduled to return. He quickly returned the calendar to its original position.

Stenger looked through the receipts that Leblanc had carefully catalogued pausing here and there for effect.

“I compliment you on your thoroughness, sir. Everything is in order.”

Leblanc was visibly relieved. He followed Stenger back towards the front of the shop.

“Captain, everything in order?”

“Yes, sir,” Willi said, nodding his head slightly.

“Thank you, *monsieur.* We will leave you to your craft. Your work is quite beautiful,” Stenger said.

“Thank you, Major,” Leblanc said, beaming.

“Perhaps I will visit you from Germany when the war is over and have a suit made.”

“I hope that will be soon, sir.”

“As do I, my friend,” Stenger said as he and Willi turned and walked through the shop door.

Once outside Stenger and Willi walked back over to the café for an early lunch.

“Did you get it, Willi?”

“Two weeks on the dot, Horsty. Now how do we get that information to our friend the Angel of Death? Such a lovely name. Do you think Von Schmelling will like meeting her?

“Von Schmelling ought to be able to take care of his jackbooted self. But we will be there to arrest her if she does take the bait.

“It doesn't sound like you really believe that.”

“Her confirmed kills number more than two hundred, Willi. I am sure she’s responsible for twice that. No doubt she’s formidable, but Von Schmelling might get lucky and capture her. Naturally, he'll want to torture her. She will kill herself if faced with that. She will not surrender if she is given the option. We must take her completely by surprise.”

“You admire her, Horst.” Willi had dropped the informal address he usually directed towards Stenger. Willi could become dead serious instantly. His statement wasn't a reproach or a question. He didn't even seem to expect a response, he was simply voicing an important fact regarding the operation they were to undertake.

"Yes, Willi, I do. I hate what Germany has produced in these monsters. If some of us don't stand up and represent the good people of Germany our country will be lost to the ages. The Nazi party controls Germany, but it is not Germany. I am a policeman and a German. I know what is right and wrong. This woman must be captured for the safety of the French and herself. I see her as a soldier. She does not prey on the innocent, at least not yet. The last chapter of the atrocities of Hitler's thugs has not yet been written. When the Americans and British invade, the SS and Gestapo will take a terrible revenge on the French. These men are the worst of the criminal element that we dealt with at home. I have actually seen names among the SS that were documented psychopaths prior to the war. You can't get normal, God-fearing people to do what they have done to the people of Europe. Some, but not all, will be brought to justice after this is over."

"Are we going to help the enemy round them up after the war, Horst?"

"I will, Willi."

"Then we will, Horsty."

Stenger smiled and picked up the menu.

"You still haven't told me how we're going to pull this off."

"We give the information to our friendly local double agent, of course."

"Pardon my ignorance, but who might that be?"

"A piggy little butcher over in Toulouse. He's making big money selling meat on the black market. Clever bastard. He hasn't been discovered yet. He profits by selling information to both sides. We discovered his activities and used him to feed disinformation to the British.

"So what happens to him if the Resistance discovers his disloyalty to France?"

"He'll end up in a pork sausage hanging in his window, no doubt."

Their lunch came and the conversation turned to thoughts of home, people they knew in common, and the cases they had worked together. For a brief moment the war was forgotten and they were just policemen trying to do what was right.

CHAPTER SIXTEEN

Many miles away in the basement of an old factory used to store useless rubbish from a more prosperous time, Madeleine pondered the message that she received over the wireless. It provided the details of another hit, an SS Major this time. She sat in a small apartment, hidden behind a wall in the corner of a greasy common room, where employees had stored their belongings for decades when the factory was in service. The factory was fire damaged and closed. Nobody ever entered it. If they had, they would have discovered nothing. Madeleine heated up a pot of soup on a small electric burner and considered the message. There was something about the fact that her controller had guaranteed the presence of the target that bothered her. That was something new. Whether the intelligence was that good or if there was some other reason, she didn't know. She knew from experience that intelligence sent to an agent or soldier on the ground was only good upon confirmation. Countless times she had received directives that were scanty or downright wrong. The Gestapo in particular wanted to capture her. She treated each of these situations first as a trap and then as an opportunity. This one seemed too good to be true. During her years of operating alone, she had plenty of time for contemplative thought. The old maxims like "if it sounds too good to be true, it is" were sound advice. This one required maximum scrutiny. She needed to see the layout of the killing ground. Until then she labeled it a trap and planned accordingly.

Madeleine finished her soup and heated up some hot water for a bath. She was accustomed to bathing in a smaller metal tub. She didn't mind it. She remembered how as a child her mother would bathe her brother and her on Sundays in the back yard, soaping them up and rinsing them off with the cold water from a small garden hose. Her father would often chase them around the little courtyard spraying them with the icy water as they squealed with delight and pretended to run away, always stopping if he couldn't keep up on his peg leg. Suddenly, she burst into tears at the intensity of the memory. She saw her brother, her beautiful twin, torn to pieces. She would never forgive or forget. The image blazed in her mind as she held herself against her loneliness.

Slowly her sobbing subsided as she tried to push back the memory of her brother's death. The best way was to concentrate on a happy memory. She did not have to choose: she thought of Jack. She thought of his spirit and the traits of character that she so admired in him. As she soaped her body in the warm water she couldn't help but think of the feel of his strong hands on her and the force of his need. She let herself be pulled into the sensuality of the memory, if only somewhat keeping one foot on the floor of the reality of the situation. She rinsed with cold water and allowed the air in the room to dry her. Summer was here. Late May in the south of France is just a hint of what's to come. The mighty Mistral wind had subsided and the blaze of summer was just behind it. Madeleine stood, and as the water evaporated off her skin she felt clean and cool. She sighed as she forced herself to put on her clothes. At least they were clean and fit reasonably well. Too bad she couldn't sit around naked and think about her lover a little more.

She laughed at the thought and finally said to the empty room, "You better be ready when I see you again, Jack Teach; the next time will make the first time seem like a tender first kiss."

She never doubted that he would be there, alive and ready for her. It was her beacon of light at the end of the tunnel. It seemed closer now. Every day she listened for news of the invasion. She could sense that something was changing. The Resistance had mobilized and was causing problems for the Germans all over the country. She resolved to continue to do her part. Given her skills she could have disappeared for good and waited out the rest of the war, sitting on the laurels of her work to date. She knew that Jack would fight to the end and therefore so would she.

CHAPTER **SEVENTEEN**

Madeleine hid in the attic of the building adjoining the tailor's shop in Nice. She had been there for almost twelve hours and was sure that she had not been seen. She knew that if the operation was a trap, the military police or soldiers would have the perimeter of the shop covered and would expect her to enter in a clandestine but conventional manner. They would not expect her to be in the perimeter already. She had experience far beyond their training. They could not stop her. If everything wasn't right, she would back off and come at the target again later. Her caution had served her well many times before.

It seemed to Madeleine that she spent most of her time watching and waiting. It was a lonely way to fight, but it was the way she had chosen. Her courage had to hold at all times. There was never any relief from danger in her solitude, no chance to step back and rely on others. She knew it wouldn't last forever, but it seemed as if she had never known anything else. If today was a trap her escape route was already determined. She had walked it already. She had also walked the most direct route to the kill. It consisted of a short path along the parapet between the roofs of the buildings, through a small door and down a flight of stairs. She would then be able to enter the tailor's fitting room from a small adjoining room, and strike. She didn't much care if the tailor was present or not. He wasn't a known collaborator, and death and killing was a daily occurrence during war. All he was going to see was her back walking away, if he saw anything at all.

Madeleine watched from a small window high above the street; she did not see any activity. No policemen arrived. The tailor came and opened his shop and busied himself preparing for the day's customers. Madeleine could hear the activity next door plainly, and it seemed to be business as usual. Customers came and went and nothing seemed out of the ordinary. Madeleine never took her eyes off the entrance or the surrounding rooftops. There was no back door to the small shop as the necessary deliveries were carried in through the front door. She was extremely careful to make sure that the people who entered also left.

The scheduled hour of the SS officer's appointment came and went. Madeleine was about to consider the mission aborted and leave the building when a large staff car came driving down the center of the street, scattering pedestrians and vehicles alike. A tall, arrogant looking SS Major stepped out of the back as one of his two escorts opened the door for him. The escorts moved as one towards the front door and positioned themselves as sentries outside. Both men carried machine guns and looked well versed in using them. Stay outside, Madeleine thought as she watched to ensure there wouldn't be any other arrivals. She doubted whether there would be any more casual traffic into the store with a giant staff car parked out front flying the Nazi insignia and SS markings. She moved slowly, deliberately affixing a silencer to her pistol. She checked her back up weapons and felt confident to proceed. This time she was dressed in well-worn street clothes with a scarf for her head, which would help to hide her features. More than likely all the tailor would remember would be the gun in her hand. She made one final check of her escape route and the back of the building, and then moved out of the attic and across the parapet.

"I don't know, Horsty, no nasty killer so far," Willi said, looking out from the back room where Stenger had glanced at the tailor's receipts two weeks ago. He leaned against the counter and smoked a hand-rolled cigarette, completely at ease even though they were waiting for a notorious assassin. Willi looked like he was casually waiting for drinks to be served.

"With the two goons out front she'd have to have steel nerve to come in that way. But she has done it before. I guess she just doesn't come across as a threat." Stenger motioned with two fingers asking for a cigarette. Willi slid a tin and some rolling papers towards him.

"I'll check the street for anyone fitting her description,"

Willi mentioned.

"What description? A young beautiful girl, never looking quite the same? France is full of beautiful young women. Besides, she's very good at what she does. She might just materialize out of thin air and shoot the bastard."

"Clearly, we're not here to protect Herr Schmelling."

"We're policemen, not body guards, Willi. Besides, Major Von Schmelling is an SS superman with two more out front. That's three supermen verses one little girl. Besides, he is an arrogant ass and would screw up this surveillance if he knew the plan."

"Still, if she got through and we missed her, somebody will want to know if we told Von Schmelling."

"Correct me if I'm wrong, Willi, but if he's dead, who's to say we didn't tell him?"

Willi just chuckled and smiled, clearly in agreement.

"Peek in up there, Willi, but don't let Von Schmelling see you."

Willi started up the stairs, trying not to make too much noise.

Von Schmelling admired himself in the full-length mirror as the tailor made some last minute adjustments to his sleeves. The Major was completely engrossed in his image and failed to notice Madeleine enter the room through the door and approach him from his blind side. Leblanc was focused on the items of clothing on a small side table as Madeleine moved boldly up behind both men. She raised the silenced pistol in one fluid movement as she entered the room. At the last second Von Schmelling caught movement out of the corner of his eye, spinning around in disgust, a reproachful retort on his lips. Madeleine paused just long enough for the fear to show in his eyes. He needed to suffer a glimpse into the terror that he so easily inflicted on others. Before Von Schelling could react, Madeleine fired two bullets directly into his chest and throat. Von Schmelling clutched his throat, blood spurting profusely through his fingers. He flailed around trying to find something to hold himself up. Leblanc moved away from Von Schmelling, clearly unwilling to help him in any way. Madeleine shot Von

Schmelling again through his right eye and turned immediately to leave the room. As she did so Von Schmelling crumpled to the floor, and his head struck the floorboards with a solid thud. Leblanc was motionless, his face and eyes hidden by his arms. He didn't want to see anything, much less the killer turning the gun on him.

As Madeleine approached the doorway she heard faint steps on the stairs. She knew that there was no time to cross the landing at the top and get away. Madeleine ducked behind the door and waited for the man to enter the room. She assumed that once he saw Von Schmelling he would run over to the body and then she could slip away. Madeleine wanted to avoid a confrontation knowing that she had made a mistake. Someone had been in the building already, waiting just like she had done next door.

Stenger watched as Willi walked up the stairs until he lost sight of him. It was then that he heard the thud from above. A couple of seconds elapsed before a wave of realization hit him. It was instinct coupled with confirmation of fact. Someone had hit the floor. He pulled his side arm and sprang for the stairs.

"Willi! Watch out!"

Willi walked through the door just as Stenger yelled. Madeleine simultaneously stepped out from behind the door and held the silenced gun to Willi's head, keeping herself behind him.

"Either of you move, this man is dead," Madeleine said in German.

Willi stopped dead in his tracks.

"Hands up," she said to Willi as she nudged his head with the silencer. She knew that even if she got the man in front of her, there was no telling how the man on the stairs was armed. Willi looked regular army, not SS or Gestapo. She did not want to kill him unless necessary.

"Don't shoot him," Stenger immediately responded in French. "We can work this out. Nobody has to die."

"No such luck for the SS Major. He had to die," Madeleine said.

"You know mademoiselle, I really don't care about him at all. You've done the world a favor." Stenger's words sounded tired and hopeless. He really did care for the man on the other end of her gun.

"Then you're not SS or Gestapo?" Madeleine asked. Willi snorted spontaneously.

"I am Horst Stenger. I am a police officer and a detective."

"What next, detective?"

"I don't suppose you'll just give up? It would make my life a lot easier."

"And be turned over to the tender mercies of torturers? I think not. Maybe I shoot him and then you and I shoot each other."

"You can't."

"Why not?"

"He's my friend, my brother. Just don't do it. He's a good man."

"He's a German soldier killing my countrymen and occupying France."

"No, he is not! Stenger said loudly, now angry, He is a detective in the Berlin police force and a hero. He saves lives, he does not take them!"

Madeleine did not waver with indecision. There was something in this man's voice, and the fact that the man in front of her was calm and unafraid. She needed to get out. She thought of Jack and knew that this situation was pivotal. Die here and never see him again.

"I am leaving, Officer Stenger. Your friend will kneel on the ground with his hands behind his head. You back down the stairs and around the corner. I see you even out of the corner of my eye and I will put one in his ear."

"I will do as you say."

"There's one more condition."

"What?"

"I want a five minute head start."

"You'll get more than that. I've got a slight problem. I never told the Colonel up there that we were setting a trap for you. Willi and I are definitely leaving. The SS twins in the front are going to have to deal with this."

"You wanted me so desperately and now you let me go? Why?"

"You're not the person I thought you were."

"Maybe I'm not completely the person I thought I was either."

"Willi, get down," Stenger said.

Willi slowly sank to his knees and Stenger backed out of the stairwell and into the front room. Madeleine immediately moved from behind Willi, with only a quick glance down the stairwell. She was across the parapet into the adjacent building. Two steps from the back door, a storm drain was ajar. A filthy packing crate covered it. She pushed it aside and pulled the crate back into position. She turned and disappeared down the tunnel.

"Willi, you okay?" Stenger yelled, coming up the stairs. As he did so he saw Leblanc slumped in a chair, stunned.

"Yes, my brother," Willi said laughing. "Shit, Horsty, that was bad. Seemed like a walk in the park for her."

"Mr. Leblanc. We weren't here. It's integral to the investigation. Besides, if she thinks you're giving any information to the SS, well, I'm sure she'll pay you a visit." Stenger said with certainty. The look on Leblanc's face was enough for Stenger to know he'd never say a word.

Stenger and Willi walked across the stairs and into the adjacent building.

"I'm not so sure. She is an enigma. She must just go after the real bad guys, not regular grunts like us," Stenger said.

"Maybe it's because we're policemen. She could have an uncle or a family member that has the same damn thankless job we do."

"It's not all thankless, Willi. Sometimes when policemen are off duty they can drink beer together."

"You get to buy the beer, Horsty. I'm going to need several to soothe my frazzled nerves. That was like holding a poisonous snake in your hands when you're too petrified to move. There was no doubt in her. She would have shot me without a flicker of remorse."

"You're right, Willi. She's a killer. Some people can just

do it. You remember the men from our old unit who were like that."

"Glad we're not like that, Horsty. Fighting like a soldier is one thing, but to do what she does, you have to sell your soul to the devil."

"I've read the file. She goes out of her way to not harm others. She doesn't bomb indiscriminately, although I'm sure that that would be effective. Granted, I'm sure she's been involved in other matters where regular soldiers have been killed, but it's war. Every time there's an Allied bombing raid, civilians die. She seems to have made a conscious choice to avoid that. I do not believe she enjoys killing at all. I think she sees it as her duty, perhaps to God. If that is so, she is more formidable than I realized at first. Makes you think, doesn't it, Willi? How would God punish the wicked? He can go Sodom and Gomorrah on them, or he could send a Golem like the Hebrews believe. Golems can't be stopped until their purpose is fulfilled."

"Beer, Horsty. No more lovely, scary bedtime stories for poor Willi."

"Here we go, Willi," Stenger said, walking out into the alley behind the tailor's shop, just as they heard Von Schmelling's bodyguards yelling at the discovery of the body.

CHAPTER **EIGHTEEN**

Madeleine was back in the storage facility, miles away from the kill site. Tonight she would stay here and then move on. She hoped never to return. She sat on the small cot with her back against the wall, thinking and smoking. The old can next to her had several butts in it; she had been winding down for a while. She shook her head slowly as she considered how close she had come to capture. She was lucky to run into a real cop, not a Gestapo or SS goon. There would have been a fight. She and several of the enemy would be dead. Must be a guardian angel looking out for me, she thought smiling at the notion and thinking how ironic it was that her nickname was "the Angel of Death." With no effort on her part her legend had grown. London was careful to move her around the country so that she wasn't pinned down regionally. Travel was the most dangerous part of her job. The killing had become so organized and habitual that the act itself was a relief. She remembered the words of the ghostly German who told her never to become complacent. He told her to expect capture, and to relish each escape from it as a victory. She forced herself to plan to the point where her actions were like a dance or a story, with a beginning, middle, and an end. Each part was as important as the others.

Madeleine moved from the bed to the small stove and opened another container in a seemingly endless parade of prepared food. Generally it was edible and designed for maximum nutrition and energy. She longed for the days prior to the war when she and her family would often discuss the meals of the day to come, what they would eat, who would prepare what, which new wines were available. To her family, food was life. She longed for the days when her family sat on their veranda overlooking the town and ate their meals together. They watched their friends and neighbors pass by and observed the comings and goings at the beach a few blocks away. They worked hard, but play was just outside the door. They did everything you could in a beach town. On Mondays, when the restaurant was closed, the family would take their small sailboat to one of the hidden callongues. The little inlet knifed in from the sea, and its waters were clear and cool, protected by the sheer rock cliffs that formed its sides. They would anchor the boat and swim until it was time to eat. They always had a cold lunch, washed down with a white wine from the nearby village of Cassis. Her father would lower a bottle down beneath the boat to cool and heighten its perfectly crisp, dry bite. When she thought of it, she could taste each sliver of melon and pulled chicken splashed by the fruit of the wine's flavor. By the end of summer the Toche's had the deep tans of their Provencal heritage, Yves's set off magnificently by his blond hair and blue eyes and hers married beautifully with her mane of wild black curls.

Chez Toche prospered because of the family's attention to the quality of their food and the loyalty of their patrons. She physically felt the loss of not being there working a Sunday afternoon meal. She worried about her parents and how they would cope without her and, sadly, Yves. He had been gifted. He had been so serious about the restaurant and the food from such a young age. Madeleine could cook; her mother and grandparents had taught her how. Yves just knew how. He was an artist born to the kitchen. He could watch one preparation, taste it, and improve it. He could look at herbs and other seasonings and invent dishes and entire meals of many courses as vehicles for their flavors and nuances. She allowed a little happiness into her grief as she thought of him. She knew that when the thoughts faded she would feel that slow sink back into melancholy and despair. It was a mire of pain from which she could only extract herself for short periods. Lately, there seemed to be an increasing glimmer of hope. Some promise of happiness to come. She knew the allies would invade soon. She was privy to information that came directly from the premier espionage service in the world. Her organization knew the military secrets before the military knew them.

Madeleine always speculated that Prime Minister Churchill had something to do with that. There was a man, she mused. What were the Germans thinking, taking on the Brits with him as their leader? He was born for conflict. Not only that, he was half American, his mother having been from the States. Madeleine was Churchill's dagger at the throat of the enemy. He had insisted that she be assigned the task. She had met him only once, but remembered the occasion vividly. He had simply asked if she was capable of the job. She remembered the two of them holding one another's eyes for a long pause after his question. She had pulled all emotion into herself and allowed his piercing gaze to be absorbed into the empty hole in her soul. It was the place where her happiness had once been. Then the great man had laughed, pushed a brandy into her hand and talked about everything but the war. Too soon other duties called him away, but she carried his confidence every day as a bolster to her courage and against the loneliness of her heart. It was that confidence that allowed her to hope that she would be with Teach again, with the miseries of this life behind her forever.

CHAPTER NINETEEN

Stenger sat with his feet up on the desk, pushing around a few files. Willi was in his customary position; hat tilted back, unabashedly snoozing. Stenger smiled, knowing Willi purposefully cultivated his laid back manner. It must be nice to have that kind of contentment. I just don't have it, he thought. Every time I try to sit still, I get more restless. Out of curiosity, he picked up a file with SS markings. He opened the file and noted that it was a theft case. Finally he had something where the culprit might have exercised a little ingenuity and not just wanton violence or unplanned killing. During his time in the civilian police force, murders were the exception, not the norm. Financial crimes and large-scale thefts with intricate planning and execution, now those were the crimes Stenger liked to investigate. They were truly cat and mouse. Often he didn't even dislike the thieves he tried to catch. They seemed to consider their work an occupation, just like the traditional jobs that people went to every day. The illegality and the prison time associated with getting caught were just part of the equation. Many times when he'd apprehended a major criminal, they seemed to be madder at themselves for getting caught than with him for catching them. He did his job well. Catching them was one thing, convicting them was another. These men and women didn't just give up when apprehended. Few confessed and when they did, only to the bare minimum.

This case was a priority for the SS. Apparently, varying amounts of gold had been disappearing with some regularity in the Limoges region in the western part of the country. With Hitler shooting generals with little compunction, nobody was above suspicion. It seemed that with the threat of invasion and increased Resistance activity, there were few resources for an in-depth investigation. It seemed that nobody had interviewed the commanding general in the region, General Heinz Lammerding. In fact, nobody seemed interested in questioning anyone from the General's SS division. Stenger read on to find out some more about the *Das Reich* Division. They had seen some of the bloodiest and most vicious combat along the eastern front fighting the Russians. Stenger knew from personal knowledge that the Russian civilians were tortured and killed indiscriminately. Whole villages were decimated. The Russians retaliated in kind. Some of these atrocities took place within sight of both enemy forces, like some horrible tit-for-tat game of death with women and children and helpless civilians used as fodder. Presently, *Das Reich* were regrouping and resting up in the Limoges region, apparently in anticipation of the invasion. He shook his head. I certainly hope that the allied generals don't think the invasion will be easy. With soldiers like *Das Reich*, killing is like eating or sleeping. You send men with no combat experience up against those kinds of troops and you will see hell. He paused while he looked down into the depths of the file in front of him. His memory went back to the terror of battle and the knowledge of how effective seasoned troops could be. These were men with the stare that never seemed to settle on anything but was aware of everything. He had it and Willi had it. It never really left. He had heard it called the thousand-yard stare; the one searching for the enemy, knowing they were coming.

Stenger's silence alerted Willi, who glanced up and saw the look in his partner's eyes. Willi said nothing and closed his eyes again, knowing that Horsty would work through whatever demons were creeping into his mind, just as he did when they came to him. When they did discuss war, they talked of the fond memories of comrades and episodes of mirth in a morass of darkness, fear, and death. They did not speak of battles, except in passing or to accentuate a point. They knew that they could rely on one another implicitly, and that was all the discussion they needed. Willi shook his head thinking how their lives as young men had been defined by war and how their lives after it had seemed false after the crushing reality of death and destruction. Their survival together bonded them more closely to each other than to their families. After the magnitude of war everything else seemed transparent and not quite real. They were each other's strength and anchor in the world. Willi was thankful for it every day. Regardless, it wasn't something they expressed with words. They were far beyond the need for them.

Stenger shook the cobwebs out and pulled back from a walled-off place in the recesses of his mind. He looked back down and started reading where he'd left off. Apparently, a large amount of gold that had been seized from the civilian populace had disappeared. Nobody seemed to know anything about it. He smiled; it seemed that the SS could commit any act of depravity against mankind, but if you stole from the Reich, that was a different matter, one that could get you shot. The perfunctory investigation had thus far revealed nothing, and suggested that the Resistance might have intercepted the gold and hidden it away. The report mentioned a few SS officers of varying capacities, but was careful not to cast any suspicion their way. Stenger liked the idea of looking into the matter. He expected no help from the SS, and it seemed to him that the best way to get the SS off his back was to investigate them. He would proceed with caution and considered the fact that this new investigation might turn out to be his last of the war. He and Willi would casually look into it, and when *Das Reich* ran off to quell the invasion he and Willi would sit quietly in a police station and surrender peacefully when the allies came. Either that or take a side trip to Spain and wait the war out there. He just wasn't going to shoot any more young men for the Fatherland. Willi was with him on that. The investigation would take them out of the area, which was an added bonus due to a question or two thrown their way concerning Von Schmelling's assassination.

Stenger had closed the book on chasing the Angel now that he'd put a face to the assassin. She wasn't a random, out of control killer. She was precise and measured. Stenger instinctively felt that she would have done anything to avoid shooting Willi. His instincts had served him well in the first war and throughout his police career. He would not abandon them now. Willi had previously suggested, albeit after several large beers, that she didn't need catching. Willi was quick to point out that it wasn't because she was terrifying; it was because for some reason, the entire time she held the gun to his head, he felt safe. Willi didn't have to say that he trusted Stenger not to do something stupid and get him killed; the possibility of that happening was left on the battlefield decades ago. Now, the feeling had come from her and he just couldn't explain it.

"Willi, how about a trip to Limoges?"

"How's the food?"

"Wonderful, like everywhere else in France. Don't you want to know what we'll be doing there?"

"As long as it doesn't involve assassins and guns in my ear, I don't care, Horsty."

"Gold, Willi!"

"Do we get any?" Willi asked now fully awake.

"You know, Willi, ordinarily I'd say no. But now, who knows? Sounds like some of it might be German gold and it would be our patriotic duty not to allow all of it to fall into enemy hands. Besides, if we open a *Hoffbrau* after the war we'll need capital."

"What? The intrepid Detective Horst Stenger will put down his magnifying glass?"

"Consultation or private work, Willi. No more day in and day out."

"Sounds good to me. Where do we put the Hoffbrau?"

"Right in the middle of Munich. When the city is rebuilt we'll build right next to everything. Your family makes the beer; we sell it and give them a cut."

"On one condition, Horsty. I get to hire the beer maids."

"Who better, Willi? Who better?"

CHAPTER **TWENTY**

John Trunce lay on his cot and tried to concentrate on a long letter from home. Everyone in his family added a page or two and he got all kinds of news, sometimes the same news from different perspectives. It never failed to be entertaining. He loved his family and his home in Missouri. He relied on these lifelines, and usually devoured them, rereading them many times. Today, he just couldn't concentrate. The whole mood of the base had changed. None of the officers said anything, but the troopers could sense apprehension in their officers. They knew something, and the activity level had increased dramatically. Everyone from the guys in his stick down to the cooks and the boys in the motor pool felt something was up. Nobody asked. The sergeants hadn't said a word, and there was no guarantee they knew anything anyway. Some of them were the quietest of all. They knew that on the ground their jobs would be among the hardest, keeping the men alive. Everyone was anxious to get going and get this thing over with. John felt that way. He hated feeling so tense. He felt like he was part of a huge body of water penned in behind a dam that was creaking and groaning under the strain. He knew that had to be the plan. This wasn't going to be some little push. It was going to be a tidal wave, a long time coming. Men and supplies were amassed all over southern England. He'd seen plenty of it during the training missions. He figured the generals decided not to try breaking the door down with some carefully placed kicks. They were going to run through the door with everything they had. John felt good about that. He thought an all-out assault would overwhelm the enemy and save lives. The Germans on the other side of that thin strip of water had years of combat experience. Most of the American army would have to get on the job training, but he was confident that they would win the day.

He rolled over and saw a line starting to form by the mess tent. He folded the letter and shoved it under his pillow. He left the tent and walked towards the chow line. The orders could come at any time, and he thought it would be better to go into battle with a full stomach. Besides, even though he was as skinny as a rail he was always hungry. Once it started he had no idea when he'd be able to expect food again. He smiled as he looked at the line. That's one thing paratroopers can do, and that's line up, he thought.

CHAPTER **TWENTY-ONE**

Hundreds of miles away in the middle of western France, Gabrielle Richard glanced out the window and into the courtyard of her neat little home. She was keeping an eye on Antoinette, her wandering three-year-old. Gabrielle smiled, thinking how precocious the little girl was. She was so cute with her jumble of curly blond hair and blue eyes. She was always talking and laughing. Antoinette was a village favorite. She was curious and warmed up to people right away. She would often take neighbors by the hand and lead them around her yard, showing them her latest discoveries. She was beautiful in every way.

Gabrielle cut some root vegetables from last year's garden. Soon enough, she thought her backyard garden would give them a supply for the coming winter. Her husband Marcel was off working. He was a short train ride away but would be home for the evening meal. Gabrielle sighed and felt fortunate. Day to day life in Oradour sur Glane was much the same as it had been before the war. She had been a newlywed then. Marcel had mild hearing loss from a childhood malady that kept him out of military service. The only German soldiers Gabrielle had seen drove through as part of a convoy headed somewhere else. That was exactly what Oradour sur Glane was, a town on the way to somewhere else.

More than once Gabrielle thought about life outside of Oradour. She had traveled as a girl. Her cousin and her family lived in the south. Gabrielle visited Madeleine, her younger cousin, several times. They were a few years apart and Gabrielle had taken it upon herself to teach her about the ways of the world, the ways of boys and men in particular. While Madeleine was dark with sculpted features and a somewhat reserved personality, Gabrielle was blond, with the bold open features of the outdoor rural life. The two complimented each other perfectly. Gabrielle saw the way men looked at Madeleine from an early age and decided that Madeleine needed a little schooling in the art of flirtation and manipulation of men. Gabrielle sighed and regretted that she had lost touch with Madeleine. Letters from the Toche family had abruptly stopped after Gabrielle was informed of the death of Yves, when the Germans invaded. She mourned his loss but knew his death must have been devastating for Madeleine. Madeleine and Yves had been so close.

Soon, this war will all be over, Gabrielle thought as she dropped slices of carrot into the stock she was preparing from last night's chicken. There were shortages everywhere, but in the rural farm areas a little bartering could get you most of the staples. Sugar and coffee were almost impossible to find and were reserved for special occasions. Perhaps the rationing would be over soon. The townspeople spoke about the coming invasion with increasing frequency. That would be a special occasion. Everyone expected it, but had no idea where or when it would happen. She heard that more German troops were being moved into the coastal areas near Normandy, a possible landing area for the Allies. Others thought the Calais area would be the target, or the south of France across from the allied controlled areas of Africa. She wondered if the fighting would ever come to her little town. It held no strategic importance whatsoever. That's fine with me, she thought. Not even the Resistance groups did anything in Oradour sur Glane. As far as she knew, there was no *Maquis* group functioning within, or even related to the town. She supposed some men might be active but word gets around and there had been no talk of any such activity. It was as if there had been an unspoken understanding among the townspeople to stay out of the Resistance and hope the Germans would continue to ignore their little village.

Spring was turning to summer and perhaps all of this would be past soon enough. Gabrielle vowed to visit the Toche family as soon as the Germans were gone and it was safe to travel. It had been almost five years. What a beauty Madeleine must be now. Who knows, maybe she has a young man. She could even be married for all she knew.

C H A P T E R **TWENTY-TWO**

Teach was covered in black from head to toe. His face was smeared with grease to hide his pale complexion from the sentries on the beach and elsewhere. He glanced around at the men with him. These were British commandos and their peerless reputation as soldiers preceded them. He had been on a couple of missions with this group, and after some skirmishes with the Germans he had been accepted. He was an outsider, though, from SOE and not regular army. He sensed the men viewed him with some distrust, knowing that he was some kind of intelligence officer. As in all wars, men on the ground often thought intelligence men were suspect and untrustworthy. Perhaps there were too many stories of double agents and spies to engender much faith. Additionally, more times than not the information that they supplied was incomplete or downright wrong and got men killed. Teach was different. He kept his head in combat and showed true courage. He fought alongside them and kept his end up. They knew that once upon a time he had been regular army and that was good enough.

Teach moved silently into the shadows as the remainder of the team buried the small rubber raft that had carried them from the submarine offshore. He knew this was a mission of vital importance. His team was scouting drop zones for the Paratroops and making contact with a few select indigenous Resistance groups. Their jobs would be crucial before the invasion. Their objective was to frustrate the enemy response as much as possible and then to fight openly when the time came. He knew that Madeleine would not be among them, not even by a chance encounter. She was not a *Maquis* soldier. He felt the hollow place inside him tug at his feelings. He hadn't known what to expect of his emotions when he left Madeleine those long months ago. This was all new to him. He had relationships in the past, one quite serious that had simply dwindled as the heat of passion went out. This was completely different. If anything, his longing for Madeleine increased with each day. It grew with the promise that perhaps the war would be over soon and they would be reunited. He didn't entertain the thought that she would forget him. He didn't care. They were in love, a love born during dark and dangerous times. If it could survive the war, it would survive forever.

Teach checked his gear and motioned to the men to do a weapons check. Caution and care flashed through his mind. He winced involuntarily when he thought of the dressing down he had just received from Colonel Jones on just that very issue. His last mission had been quite hairy and he and his men had narrowly escaped. Teach had carried one of his wounded for miles to meet the raft they used to escape from France. Clearly, he had been careless. His Colonel had put his face an inch away from Teach's so that their noses almost touched. The lambasting he had received was right out of the, "Hard Case Guide to British Military Discipline." The last words echoed in his mind.

"Do you understand, Captain? You put yourself and your men in a position to be discovered again, and I will personally make it my life's unending task to make yours a hell on the earth." His Colonel was shaking with rage, spit flying from his mouth.

"Yes, sir!"

The Colonel moved back a pace or two and the instant Teach spoke he was right back in his face.

"Do not speak! When I want to hear your voice, I'll tell you, Laddie! Now get out."

Teach saluted, spun smartly on his heel, and marched from the room.

Teach was ashamed and searched his mind for a reason for the near failure of the mission. After a few days rest and early briefing on his current mission, Teach learned that his Colonel had put him in for a citation and a field promotion. He heard the news with disbelief. He was a major now, and when the Colonel pinned his new insignia on his uniform he said loudly to all assembled,

"Major Teach, your King and country are proud of you and I am proud of you." His words had given Teach a glimpse into the difficulties of command. He understood the anguish that some commanders felt, sending men to fight, often sending them into certain death. The anguish was beyond description. He understood the harsh words and silently vowed not to let his Colonel or his men down. The thought of death paled in comparison to the horror of making mistakes and getting men killed.

Teach brought his mind back to the task at hand. I will be patient, he promised himself. I can't single handedly win the war so that I can get back to Madeleine sooner. For a brief instant he wondered what would be left of her after so much killing. He didn't know many specifics, but her success was common knowledge among the ranking staff at SOE. He smiled. She was amazing. He had seen it immediately, and apparently she saw something in him. His doubts were only for himself and not her, but he would be damned if he let another man have her.

Teach glanced down the beach in both directions. He signaled his men and they silently ghosted over the small dunes and disappeared into the night.

CHAPTER **TWENTY-THREE**

General Heinz Lammerding held his head in his hands as he shuffled reports around on the antique desk. All bad news, he thought as he slowly shook his head. He pawed through a couple of sheets, catching a phrase or word here and there. It didn't help. The bad news remained the same. He finally gave in to the inevitability of it all. He grabbed a cigarette from a wooden box on the desk, lighting it from an ornate crystal desk lighter. He spun in his chair and looked out the tall windows behind his desk and out onto the manicured lawns. He would miss the beautiful Chateau he had commandeered upon his arrival in France. A regular army Colonel moved out without a word of protest. After all, he was a general and led the infamous *Das Reich* division. Its status was legendary. Which made carrying out his plan for the future that much easier.

He'd known for a long time, starting during his posting at the Russian front, that there would be no victory in this war. Once the Nazi advance had been stalled, there seemed to be an ever-increasing number of Russian soldiers pushing them back towards Germany. His troops had endured months of cold stalemate punctuated by periods of absolute chaos. Both sides had committed atrocities in plain view of the opposing forces. His men were hard and callous and saw little distinction between combatants and civilians. One of his elite regiments, *der Fuhrer*, was particularly savage. Things were different on the Russian front, desperate and brutal. There were no rules of war and people died. He hoped that the relocation from the front would calm his men's frazzled nerves and restore at least part of them to a more civilized state. He didn't envy the Allied generals preparing to throw green men into the Atlantic wall against seasoned veterans.

His *Das Reich* SS would chew into them like the starving wolves of winter they were.

His memory went back to the heady days at the beginning of the war and how the German *Blitzkrieg* onslaught overpowered their enemies. They conquered at will. Initially he had been in favor of at least repatriating German lands sacrificed in the armistice following the First World War. He supported some acquisition of additional territories, but knew it was arrogant and disastrous to have attacked Russia. Hitler had been intoxicated with victory and believed his own propaganda. The disorganized rabble that had been the Russian army melded into an astonishingly brutal and determined steel-hard wall of hate. It pushed relentlessly to drive Germany from Russian soil. Stalin spent any number of men to achieve victory. His generals carried out his commands with religious fervor. Their sheer numbers would ensure victory. Even women served and fought. Many were the best snipers Stalin commanded.

On the other side of the channel the indomitable British, now fortified by the United States, prepared for invasion. Field Marshal Ernst Rommel had personally seen to the fortification of the Atlantic wall. His preparations were so awe inspiring that they led to the term, 'Fortress Europe'. The defenses were impressive but Lammerding knew they couldn't hold forever. He had seen first hand the courage of American soldiers in the first war. They were coming, these sons of the men he had fought at the Marne. In addition to their bravery, they fought with a conviction that they could not be defeated. American courage always flirted with reckless abandonment. They were well provisioned and believed in the cause of freedom. It would be one hell of a fight, and the pivotal battle of the Twentieth Century.

Lammerding stood and walked over to a sideboard and poured himself a cup of coffee, glancing into the mirror on the wall. It was an act of reassurance and a justification for his criminal behavior. He had managed, with the help of a couple of his most trusted officers, to divert some gold headed for the coffers of the Third Reich. He didn't care that it had been stolen from the French people; to the victors went the spoils. It had been that way since Roman times, the adage attributed to Rome's conquering legions. There had been such large scale looting throughout the war that his little nest egg seemed modest in comparison. How many others had fortunes waiting in Swiss accounts to ease their disappointment at the prospect of the loss of another war? He didn't care as long as he had some. His stash had grown to approximately half a ton. His orders had been to use whatever means necessary to disrupt Resistance efforts. He knew that meant the terror tactics he employed without compunction. The orders had given him a free hand to collect as many valuables as possible and he preferred gold. Gold, you could spend anywhere. Jewels required appraisals and questions and negotiations. Gold was worth what the world market dictated. Eventually he was satisfied with what he had collected. He had committed no crime in his eyes. His fellow SS officers had been hedging their bets all over the European theater. There was hidden gold, precious art and antiquities everywhere. His would be hidden where he could easily get to it, not at the bottom of some lake or the Mediterranean. The deed was done. All he had to do now was get the gold to Zurich. All of the necessary arrangements had been made. Capture meant summary execution, although he was confident punishment would be forestalled until after the invasion. He smiled at the thought. He couldn't claim that the gold had fallen into enemy hands or had been lost during battle. His actions would be clear. His excuse would be that he had moved the gold to Switzerland for safekeeping. Of course he should have moved it to Germany, where he was sure it would be "redirected" into the hands of others, meaning that he'd keep none. It was worth the risk involved. He had lived with the specter of death in two wars, and now as a General commanded by a lunatic. Besides, he told Hitler what he wanted to hear and avoided any contact with those who conspired against the madman. No, he would not be caught. His junior officers would never reveal anything. More than likely, if anyone got too close or suspected the truth, they would be killed. He felt a little like Roman generals of old, operating with a degree of impunity afforded by the command and loyalty of thousands of soldiers.

He remembered all too well the deep wounds Germany suffered at the hands of the victors following the first war, the scarcity of money, the inflation, and the suffering of the people. What better breeding ground for the kind of fascist takeover Hitler had orchestrated? The people thirsted for revenge and blindly followed the man that promised it to them.

Lammerding paced around the ornate room, his mind shifting from issue to issue. The real question was, how to move the gold? The old tactician in him knew that the time to do so was when the invasion started. Everyone would be moving at top speed towards the fighting. That would be a perfect time to send his gold in the other direction. He and his men would stay and fight while one of his officers transported the gold to the railroad station and sent it to Switzerland disguised as documents. His agents in Switzerland would offload the gold and spirit it away into the impenetrable darkness of the Swiss banking system. His assistants would be well compensated with more than enough for a life of ease after this madness was over. He intended to fight until surrender to the United States was unavoidable. He would make sure that he and his men were as far away from Russian troops as possible. His retirement didn't include torture and an indefinite stay in a Russian Gulag. He would slip away just prior to surrender and make his way to South America, beyond the reach of extradition or discovery. He would be comfortable with his young wife and his gold. He had been making careful preparations for her departure. Planning was one of his strengths. All he had to do now was wait. Patience was another strength learned in the trenches and in the snow of the Russian front. Never be in a hurry when you could avoid it. Haste usually meant mistakes. There could be no mistakes now. He picked up the phone and put the plan into action.

At the other end of the line, Major Kampfe listened intently to his general's instructions. He simply answered yes when asked if he understood. He had taken orders from this man for so long that he followed them without hesitation or question. He had an additional motivation for following the general's orders but would have carried them out whether he got a cut of the gold or not. The pay was a bonus, the general had privately explained, and he had assured the major that he would certainly earn it when the Americans came.

Kampfe smiled ruefully as he placed the phone back in its cradle. He knew he was getting the assignment because the General trusted him, he who had collected much of the gold at his direction. He came upon several of the bars of gold while looting and harassing the French. Other amounts were discovered through systematic pillaging taken from civilian homes, businesses, and in some instances, banks themselves. It was an effective tactic to keep people in line and the fear of assisting the Resistance very real in their minds. Any infraction was met with execution in as public a manner as possible. He felt justified to do whatever was necessary in the furtherance of the Nazi cause. He had recently intensified his efforts at the direction of the General and collected even more gold. Every soldier expected invasion soon and the window of opportunity was closing daily. The General confided in him that he was in possession of additional gold that was given to him for safekeeping. He had wondered if that had been the General's biased version of events, but Kampfe didn't care; he would share in the spoils. Besides, who was going to question the motives of the commander of an entire division with the reputation *Das Reich* enjoyed? Their real weapons were brutality and fear. He scoffed; this was nothing compared to what had happened in Russia. He wasn't about to fight every dirty French peasant with a pitchfork that got a dose of bravery once the Allies invaded. He felt contempt for them. They were like sheep, conquered and subject to the will of the Third Reich. He had personally overseen the execution of any who had offered even the slightest resistance. He felt no remorse killing young or old. Fear was his ally and he would exploit it to its greatest advantage.

Sitting in the small room that served as his office, Kampfe considered what the General had told him. The plan was simple, mark the gold containers as 'records' and put them on the convoy headed towards the front, then spirit them away at the opportune moment to a nearby railroad station and put them on a train bound for Zurich. As for his role, a more important part of the plan was to survive the battle and live to enjoy his share. He wondered whether he should tell his friend, Major Diekmann, about the specifics of the general's plans. No, he thought. If the General wanted Diekmann to know he would tell him personally. Diekmann was his friend and a man of unwavering loyalty to the Reich. He was a member of the elite *der Fuhrer* regiment. Diekmann was brutal to the enemy, civilian and soldier alike, but brave and resolute when it came to the concerns of the Division. Kampfe had shared with Diekmann many a leave and uncounted bottles of whatever was handy. Perhaps Diekmann liked his drink a little more than was appropriate but it had never interfered with his command duties.

CHAPTER **TWENTY-FOUR**

"The *der Fuhrer* regiment, Horsty? You think they have something to do with stolen gold?" Willi asked, flicking the ash from his cigarette as Stenger drove along the steep winding road.

"Willi, it doesn't matter who. We are definitely not going to solve this one anyway." Stenger smiled at his friend.

"Now, that's an investigation I can sink my teeth into sir," Willi said as he laughed and threw Stenger a partial salute about waist high.

"We ask a few questions. Demonstrate monumental investigative incompetence and stay out of the damn way when the dough boys hit the beach."

"Is there much Resistance activity in the area?"

"Not much that I've heard about. But once the invasion begins, everyone will claim to be a Resistance fighter. Many may actually join the fight."

Willi was quiet for a moment and then quietly said, "Think she'll be there, Horst?"

Stenger was surprised by Willi's shift from his usual carefree attitude to the serious way he asked the question. The episode with the beautiful assassin had more of an affect than Willi let on.

"I don't know, Willi. I don't know what to say. She is not what she seems. Granted, she is a killer of the highest skill. But she is not a murderer. These Nazis are bad. Although we try not to speak about it, we have both always known that to be true."

"I know it's best not to talk about it, even when we're alone, but we have interfered with the Gestapo and the French Vichy *Milice* police squads and their wholesale internment of Jews. Anyone finds out and we get shot," Willi said with a hint of uncharacteristic concern.

"So we redirected a few trains and took custody of some Jewish "criminals" out of their hands. Anyone with any compassion at all would have done the same thing."

"There's that and warning Jewish families ahead of time. But I guess we got away with it, Horsty. Just like I avoided the Angel's bullet. That was undoubtedly the strangest experience of my life. I was completely helpless. It felt like I was being judged and I passed the test."

"I think that was exactly what happened. I guess you're not such a bad man after all. Besides, I have always said, any man whose cousins own a brewery can't be all bad."

"I hope it's all there after the war."

"Pilots don't bomb breweries. That is a known fact."

Willi laughed and smiled, happy as always to be with Stenger. He was as smart as they came. Horst would see the two of them through this war as well. He had been happy to participate in Stenger's humanitarian efforts. They had tacitly agreed that saving one innocent life was more important than catching a thousand criminals. Stenger was a policeman through and through. He truly believed his responsibility was to protect and serve the people, all people.

CHAPTER **TWENTY-FIVE**

Madeleine sat next to a radio in a small weathered shack. The building barely held together as the bleached boards of the walls settled with the incessant beating of the sun and the winter snows. It was probably an old shepherd's hut, working its way into a pile of useless lumber. She rarely came to this location. She knew it was the impending invasion that drew her away from the south and towards the north. Still, the location was remote and the countryside beautiful in spring. This was her favorite time of the year. It was the time of the rebirth and renewal of the land and a reminder that all things change.

Madeleine had been directed to the region. It was within striking point of numerous reserve German troop divisions. Only a very few among the Allied command knew the exact location of the invasion. She had her own ideas but tried to stay as close to the middle of the country as possible so that she could react and go towards the main invasion wherever it came. It could happen on any of the coasts, but logistics favored the north. She already knew her orders. They were to create as much chaos as possible. She would target the movement of troops and supplies.

She turned the dial to the appropriate setting and listened. Her attention to her orders was always intense, but now she was waiting for an announcement of the impending invasion. Thousands in the Resistance waited anxiously for the coded messages specific to their individual groups. Only she knew her code. She listened at the same time each day and grew increasingly tense when the message didn't come. Madeleine realized that a great part of her frustration came from knowing that the invasion would mark the beginning of the end of the exile between her and Jack. She reminded herself that others were in greater need than she for the arrival of the allied troops. There were untold numbers of civilians, Jews and 'undesirables' waiting in concentration camps of unspeakable horror, along with anyone the Nazis deemed inferior, including homosexuals, gypsies, communists, and so many others from the far reaches of Europe. Their suffering was beyond description. The romantic needs of those that remained free were insignificant. But yet she couldn't help but feel entitled to some happiness. She had done her duty and beyond. She had silently killed so many who had tried to capture Jewish families hidden in France. She'd killed French collaborators who had denounced or exposed them for personal gain. The traitors wailed the most, begging for their lives as Madeleine came down on them with vengeance. She afforded them their pleas and then executed them for their crimes. Evil knows no nationality. Harm the innocent and suffer the consequences.

Madeleine stood up and paced as much as her cramped surroundings allowed. She would have been happy to sit in the sunshine and wait for the broadcast but couldn't stand being more than a few feet from the radio. Its antennae were already set and she didn't want to have to move them. She knew that once the invasion came, news would travel in an unstoppable wave. She knew France would then come alive again. The warriors of France would rise up and fight in one last desperate surge to drive the enemy from their soil and regain their independence from tyranny once again.

Madeleine froze as the crackle of the radio signal broke into words.

"The dog ate the cheese, the dog ate the cheese." She lurched towards the radio, her face inches from the speaker, "the dog ate the cheese." She did not have to hear it a third time, she leaped to her feet, laughing and crying at the same time. That was her signal. The one she had chosen, remembering a little dog that she and her brother had brought home from the beach one day, begging their parents to let them keep him. He could not have been a worse pet for a restaurant family. The damn thing ate everything he could find. She smiled, remembering her father's response, which was to feed the dog so that he got so fat he couldn't jump up on the counter or tables anymore. It all hit her at once. She would see her parents and Jack again.

Madeleine laughed. "Don't spend all your energy on the Germans, Jack Teach," she whispered as she sat down to control the roar of her emotions. She needed time to think.

Madeleine walked out of the little shed and into the late afternoon sunshine. It would be time to move soon. Word would come when the allies landed. She would stop as many Germans as she could from getting to the fighting. In the confusion she could operate with greater speed. Now they would see what the Angel of Death could do out of the shadows and into the light. Her hands shook as she fumbled with a packet of cigarettes and lit one in celebration. She knew that if she survived the fighting she would remember this day her whole life. She hoped that was a long time. She wanted nothing more to do with excitement and danger. She wanted love, family, and a home, all of the things that she had been fighting for. She wished that she could share her joy with her parents. It would help bring closure to the endless nightmare that had begun with the death of her brother. Her promise to him would be fulfilled when France was free, and that day was coming.

CHAPTER **TWENTY-SIX**

In the basement of a nondescript home in the town of Nieul, a small group of *Maquis* fighters listened to their instructions via the BBC. Their leader, a man known only to his men as Richard, listened intently to the broadcast. He nodded his head as he committed the information to memory. It confirmed what he already knew. A huge convoy of SS trucks was moving north towards the invasion area and he was to proceed to a site north of the town of Siorac along the Limoge River and delay them with explosives.

He looked at his group of men. Few of them were even close to manhood. Most of them looked to be boys of sixteen or so, and much too anxious to get into the fight against the enemy. Hell, these 'men' had barely been out of short pants when the Germans first came. He was originally German, but also a Jew. His own parents had been denounced even though they had successfully hidden in the city of Toulouse. A neighbor and supposed friend had alerted the authorities to their location and religious heritage. Richard's revenge had been swift. He had taken action quickly but he killed the bastard slowly. He took no joy in it but revenge needed to be carried out in a manner that ensured the traitor understood his crime. The man would denounce no others. As Richard had slowly tortured him to death, his screams had given him little solace. Perhaps getting the Nazis out of France would help. Then he could turn his attention to finding his parents who had been sent to concentration camps in Germany, torn from the life of affluence they had enjoyed in Germany prior to the rise of anti-Semitism.

Richard looked around the room and tried to formulate a plan to attack the convoy. He was extensively trained in sabotage and had access to a large cache of explosives. Unfortunately, the boys clustered around him had no training, nor the time for it. He decided that their role would be a supportive one, not offensive. They would follow his orders eagerly, without question, but he was not going to send these green kids into the jaws of the *Das Reich* division. They truly were animals and would burn these kids alive if they took them prisoner. *Das Reich* was regrouping near Toulouse and it was known that when the invasion came they would be activated, charging into battle as fresh and seasoned troops. They were tough fighters who would chew up and spit out his boys without breaking stride. Regardless, he planned to blow as many of the bastards to hell as he could. The Nazis had taken so much from his family. First his sister had disappeared, and then his parents. He prayed that the invasion was the beginning of the end. It had to be. His goal was to defeat the Nazis and end their crimes. He relished the opportunity to strike at the SS. They were the embodiment of Nazi beliefs.

Richard lit a cigarette and listened to the banter of the boys. Resources must have been thin for him to be saddled with this lot. He wasn't even sure they knew why they hated the Germans, and that was a dangerous thing. Had they personally suffered at the hands of the soldiers out here, away from anything of great strategic importance? He was confident that they had been schooled in hating the Germans as an occupying force, but personal experience was the best and cruelest teacher. He had no way of knowing how they would react under fire if it came to that. Caution was the only antidote for his concern. Nothing would be done in the open; he would use them as observers and execute his plan carefully.

CHAPTER **TWENTY-SEVEN**

John Trunce sat in a large airplane hanger among his buddies as they listened to their platoon leaders explain the situation. The atmosphere in the room was charged with a mixture of excitement and resignation. Most of the men had seen combat in Italy. They were over questioning their personal courage in combat but were apprehensive. This was going to be the most important operation of the war. Everyone knew it. General Eisenhower had delivered a personal written message to each and every man concerning the importance of his mission. There was no mistaking it.

"This is it. No more false alarms; we go. Get together with your stick and remember your drop zone. If you get separated, find friends and we'll regroup later. Good luck, boys. We finally get to get into this thing and get it over with," a young airborne officer explained. He seemed barely older than they were, a boy leading boys. To an outsider it might have seemed that way but their confidence and long months of training gave them an air of confidence in themselves and their units. A blade any more finely honed might start to crumble and break. They were ready.

John felt relieved and anxious at the same time. He looked around as his friends readied their gear. Nobody was goofing around now. They were all business. They had long ago stopped being kids, when they were barely out of high school. They had been molded into professional soldiers.

John felt more like a pack mule than a deadly fighting man as he waddled towards the door of the transport plane. At the last second some idiot deciding that they needed to carry more gear strapped to their bodies in leg bags. He moved towards the metal steps descending from the side of the plane and heaved himself up into the doorway. A guy behind him gave him a push helping him through. His gear weighed more than he did. What a relief it would be to get that stuff off him once he hit the ground. They didn't expect him to hump that crap all over France, did they? Once in the doorway he picked up his static cord clip and slid it down to his position in line and found a seat along the side. Every face reflected the emotions that were spinning through their minds. The one thing that was missing was banter among the guys. A subtle change had come over everyone. This was the real thing.

He'd been in going on two years. It seemed like forever since he'd seen his family. He reminded himself that he had volunteered for the paratroops. He was with the best and that helped him calm his anxieties. He knew he and his buddies were the best of the best. Nobody messed with them. He relished the memory, remembering how they had literally run their regular army physical training instructors into the ground. He was hard and as fully trained as he could be. He knew better than to believe the rumors that they would be fighting anything less than Hitler's best. The Germans had been at war for five years. Those boys wouldn't break and run. He expected to be going up against hardened veterans fighting to protect the honor of their homeland.

It didn't seem like they had been in the air that long when John started to hear the flack exploding in the distance. His real fear was getting hit by it and going down without getting out. They would be jumping pretty low, which meant they made an excellent target. The plane started to get buffeted about and was pitching around as the pilot tried to avoid the worst of it. He kept his eyes focused on the jump light. Soon it would turn green and they'd be out. As much as he liked flying, with this much antiaircraft fire, it would be best to be on the ground as soon as possible.

The first signal light came up, telling the men to assemble into their stick. As one the men stood, turning to check the gear of the man in front of them. The plane heaved and dropped altitude as a shell burst nearby. Men held on to whatever was at hand. The urge to move forward and jump was palpable; the open doorway looking like it was a mile away to the men in the back of the line. The green light snapped on and the men moved to the door without hesitation, jumping out one by one. John went out and was caught in the prop blast, propelled out and down. His chute opened up immediately and he oriented himself. As he looked up he saw countless planes dropping men. He winced when a shell hit one, exploding into pieces. The poor bastards. Tracers from the ground flew all around. He wrestled his rifle from where he had strapped it to his body. Every direction he looked he saw explosions and ground fire. He felt like he was in the middle of a fireworks display of gigantic proportions. The display of firepower was overwhelming. He looked down and saw darkness directly below him. Maybe he would get lucky and not land in front of a German machine gun nest, he thought ruefully.

Ready to shoot back at anything on the ground he twisted around as far as his harness would allow, trying to get at least a glance in every direction. He drifted down and away from where he saw ground fire. He tried to see if he could make anything out that looked remotely like his drop zone. All he saw was a swamp. Just like he'd been told, the Germans had flooded the low areas once the invasion began. They had plenty of time to train and prepare for this, John reminded himself.

"Shit, I'm going to get wet," he said aloud and came to a sloppy stop, his parachute billowing out in front of him as it came to rest in the muck.

"Welcome to France, Johnny," he murmured, shaking his head. This was not his drop zone. He detached himself and looked around for any friendly faces. He rolled and crawled his way towards the nearest solid ground, staying low in the mess of mud and decaying vegetation. Swamps are for duck hunting, he thought, careful to keep the muzzle of his rifle covered and out of the muck. He didn't much care if he was muddy, but his weapon was everything. He couldn't do much damage to the enemy with a plugged up rifle. He made it to the edge and crouched down, looking around for movement. He saw a couple more chutes that landed on what looked like solid ground. He adjusted his helmet and moved towards them and the war.

CHAPTER **TWENTY-EIGHT**

"Normandy, not Bordeaux? I see. I will move my men in the direction of Caen immediately, Field Marshal. We should bring all *Panzers* to bear and push the enemy back into the sea. I must admit, sir, that you were correct," General Lammerding said into his phone. He listed to Field Marshal Rommel's instructions. A great deal of what the Field Marshal demanded depended on Hitler's permission. Hitler had taken it upon himself to require his personal consent regarding a broad range of tactical decisions. The time it took for Hitler to authorize an order could cripple counter attacks and create indecision. Many in the German High Command were paralyzed by the need to seek his permission.

"Yes, Field Marshal, I understand," Lammerding said, placing his phone back onto the cradle. "Well, it has come," he whispered, picking the phone back up.

"Kampfe, Lammerding. Invasion in Normandy. Yes, Normandy. Prepare the shipment and see to it immediately. I have a division to move." Without waiting for a reply, he dropped the phone back down and called his orderly.

"Klein! Get my officers together and coordinate a rail movement of our equipment. We must be ready to move now with all dispatch."

Klein responded instantly, leaving the room for the phone on his own desk.

Lammerding paced back towards the windows of his ornate office. The first of the morning light was coming in through the windows. He now knew where to send his men and armor. He had been preparing to do so for weeks. The trains had been readied for some time. He planned to be able to move as quickly as possible once the word came through. All he needed was a destination.

The long guessing game was now over. He had his orders and his own priorities. He could afford no more time to think about his gold. He trusted Kampfe and knew that the gold was in the best hands possible. He turned and strode purposely from his office, wondering whether he or some allied general would be calling it home in the next few weeks.

CHAPTER **TWENTY-NINE**

"I must have some help with the train," SOE operative Brian McDermott said to a middle aged Frenchman standing in the storage room of a small *tebac,* a combination corner store and newspaper stand. The war years had not been kind to the shabby little store, and there were few items on the shelves, the effect of severe rationing. However, McDermott knew that the owner, Monsieur Pernod, in addition to being a Resistance leader, had a variety of items for sale that weren't readily displayed. After all, he was a merchant. Who could better understand the value of things in short supply but available on the black market?

"I can spare no men. They are already off with the *Maquis*, assisting with the invasion."

McDermott shook his head, "We can save hundreds of lives, but we need to disable the flat cars. I have all of the necessary supplies but I cannot do it alone."

"Explosives?"

"Non, monsieur, paste," McDermott said smiling.

"Paste? How will you stop train cars with paste?"

"Help me and I'll show you."

"Will it be dangerous?"

"This far away, I doubt Jerry will be watching very hard. Most of the rail attacks come when the trains are underway. This will be different. We will be able to get to the cars long before they go on their way. We will disable them. If we are successful more than 300 tanks, 1400 additional vehicles and 15,000 men will have to go by road! Time is everything. The longer it takes Jerry to regroup and counterattack, the further inland we get and the more men and armor we can throw back at them if they try. I must have help!"

Pernod smoked his cigarette and looked at McDermott. There was no mistake; he was measuring the man as surely as if he were being fitted for a suit. McDermott held his eyes and watched as Pernod came to some silent personal decision.

"Then I can offer you help."

Pernod motioned to a young girl sitting quietly in the corner. She was school aged at best, but she didn't hesitate for an instant.

"Marie, go and find your sister."

McDermott watched the girl walk out of the room. Her sister must be a messenger. He hoped so; there was little time and no telling when the trains would leave, carrying death and destruction towards men who were fighting for their lives already. He needed help fast.

Shortly, a slightly older girl, who had to be Marie's sister, came into the room. The sisters stood next to their father, waiting patiently for him to speak.

"Here is your help, it is the best I can do."

"These girls? McDermott asked incredulously. They are children. Even young men would be better!"

Both girls instantly took offense. The change in them was dramatic. Their dark eyes burned with passion and their spines straightened as if they were ready to attack.

"We can do anything some silly boys can do," the elder girl spat furiously. "We have been helping for years now. We are brave and have seen more Germans than you have. We won't cry like some lost little boy looking for his mother if things get scary. They are always scary when you are smuggling messages or guns. We know of the rumors of the *L'ange de la mort,* she is a woman and a sister in the Resistance. She would kill you like swatting a gnat. We are daughters of France, and I don't care if you think we're old enough or not! The English of all people should remember the bravery of the young women of France when they are determined to drive invaders from their native land. You English have not lived with these bastards pawing at you, like some toy for them to abuse at will. I have smiled enough. I have kept my head down long enough. I have seen my friends sent away to work in their slave camps and factories long enough! The invasion has come. When I get the chance, I will kill Germans. Watch me!"

McDermott stepped back under the onslaught. It was if the girl grew in stature as she unleashed her diatribe, her tongue lashing raised to a crescendo that was almost a roar. The look in the eyes of the girls was frightening in its intensity. He had offended them deeply. The older girl was shaking with fury. Suddenly his mind understood her reference to Joan of Arc, who at seventeen had led French troops in battles to rid her homeland of the occupying English. He knew he had made a serious misjudgment. He had to correct it or all was lost.

"I am sorry. I did not know. I don't always understand how things have been. My family lives under the bombs in London. My brother is on the bottom of the channel in his Spitfire. I spoke stupidly. I only know what must be done."

"*Oui, monsieur* and what is it we will do?" The younger girl asked gently, the fury receding as McDermott explained himself. The sudden pain on his face communicated more than his words ever could.

"We're going to drain the oil out of the axles of three hundred flat cars and replace it with my special paste."

"That will work?" the girls' father said raising his eyebrows in amazement.

"Oh, it will work. You see, the paste works like oil for a little while, and then it hardens like cement. Those cars will seize up and be useless. Jerry will have to offload his nasty hardware and move it up the road. Other chaps and ladies," he said with a nod to the girls, "will make their life hell all the way to the front."

The girls and their father beamed. McDermott made what would undoubtedly be an incredibly dangerous mission sound like a monumental schoolboy's prank.

"The only thing I haven't worked out is what to do with the oil. It can't be drained onto the ground, it would be noticed. We must collect it and dispose of it."

"I know exactly how to dispose of the oil," Pernod said.

"How?"

"It will be sold."

McDermott smiled at the wonderful irony of it all. They would not only steal Jerry's oil, but they would add insult to injury by profiting from it. He had more than a little bit of rogue in him. He had been perfect for SOE, a natural grifter. He knew Pernod would make a tidy profit selling the oil to his friends and neighbors. Why not? The Pernods were the ones putting themselves at risk. A little compensation for the deed wouldn't hurt anyone.

"You are a man after my own heart. We must begin at once. We will need a truck and a plan to get into the rail yard."

"That shouldn't be too difficult. With the invasion all eyes are focused up north," the Frenchman said.

"Let's hope so. Or, our trip to the station may be shortened a bit," McDermott replied.

The tough little Pernod family nodded in unison, clearly understanding the immensity of the danger they faced.

McDermott and the two girls crouched at the end of the fence surrounding the rail yard where there was a long line of flat bed rail cars loaded with tanks and artillery. Loading had apparently stopped for the day and each piece was covered with tarps in an attempt to mask what was underneath. McDermott sucked in his breath and was awed at the sheer volume of equipment that could be brought to bear by the *Das Reich* Division. The tanks alone would wreck untold havoc on ground troops as they advanced ahead of the armor being down loaded on the beaches. He already knew serious miscalculations had been made concerning allied armor. Nobody had anticipated the nearly impenetrable hedgerows of Normandy. For generations farmers had built up the bramble and tree barriers on top of rows of earth. They served to separate and define individual fields. Tanks without infantry cover were vulnerable to attack from rocket propelled grenades. With every hedgerow a new hiding place, determined pockets of infantry could bring *Panzerfausts* up to shoot grenades at the allied tanks. If the Germans could combine their infantry and armor against the unsupported Allied infantry, their defense would be brutal. His mission, and that of so many others, was to cripple the French road and railway systems keeping the German reinforcements with their massive and heavily armored tanks from getting to the invasion area for as long as possible.

McDermott looked over at his companions. If the two sisters were frightened they certainly didn't show it. For the first time he began to believe that they might just pull it off. They decided to work as a team and hid a small truck nearby that held the paste and empty tanks into which they could store the oil removed from the train axles. They observed the sentries making perimeter sweeps at three hour intervals.

McDermott motioned to the girls to move and the three of them ran doubled over to the train, ducking under the side of the lead car and setting to work. They moved with machine-like efficiency. McDermott was trained specifically for the task and it had become routine for him. As the gear oil had to be routinely replaced, the bolts that allowed for drainage loosened easily. Once the oil was drained into a large wine bottle, they squirted in McDermott's paste like icing piped onto a cake. Several times they stopped and listened for activity. Nothing stirred. The Germans would not have expected any significant Resistance activity this far south.

The three worked through the night with no incident, moving away from the cars when the sentries came by. Clearly all attention was directed to the fighting in the north, a small mercy given the nature of their undertaking.

With the sun starting to rise, McDermott and the girls parted ways back at the *tebac* with a promise to get together for a meal when France was free and the war was over. They were bonded together by the danger they had shared. It was an unbreakable bond that ensured that they would never forget one another.

As McDermott walked away he felt a strong sense of accomplishment for what one man and a couple of French schoolgirls had achieved. He would never take the young for granted again. He was downright cheerful in his ignorance, not knowing that he and the girls had set a series of events in motion that would ultimately claim the lives of hundreds of innocent civilians but would save the lives of many more.

CHAPTER **THIRTY**

"All of the flat cars?" General Lammerding screamed into the phone.

"Fix them immediately. We have been ordered to the front and we have 300 tanks to move now!" As Lammerding listened his face turned from a look of rage to one of utter disbelief.

"General, the flat cars have been disabled. Some kind of paste was put into the axles and the oil has been removed. It solidified into some unknown kind of cement. They will have to be replaced. It is beyond my control." Colonel Victor Rashmeir calmly spoke into the phone. He was Gestapo and had been sent to investigate the incident along with countless others taking place throughout the region and all over France.

"How am I to get to the front?" Lammerding said, having remembered that it was never prudent to scream at a highly ranked Gestapo officer repeatedly.

"You have tanks and trucks, drive them north."

Lammerding was shaking his head, "That will take days, and we'll be exposed to the *Maquis* groups all along the way. My troops will be harassed from the moment we set out."

"Perhaps increased security might have been prudent, *Herr* General," Rashmeier said evenly, with just a hint of contempt. He knew he had Lammerding. He'd had enough yelling from the General for one day.

"Fine. These terrorists will pay, I'll tell you that Colonel."

"Yes, I believe those are your standing orders General, and I am told that to date you have not hesitated to carry them out," Rashmeire added.

Lammerding hung up the phone without further comment. "Damn it!" He thought. I need to move a division of men, armor and equipment to Normandy by road! He yelled for his aide.

"Klein, get Major Kampfe on the phone," Lammerding bellowed. "And I want all of my officers here within the hour. I don't care where they are or what they're doing; we're moving by 1200 hours!"

Lammerding hated to split up his troops and equipment, but it made the best sense to get the convoy moving. He would now have to move the tanks by road and that meant using up precious fuel. Armor needed petrol. It wasn't bazookas or bombs that hamstrung him, it was the vast amount of petrol those tanks drank up when you moved them anywhere. He shook his head again, not for the last time that day. The Allies had chosen the most heavily fortified region to invade. He had spent time in Normandy, familiarizing himself with the fortifications and terrain. It was a fortress, "Fortress Europe" as it came to be known. Why throw yourselves up against that? Bordeaux was much less heavily defended. Just as Germany had simply driven around the Maginot line facing Germany in Northeastern France, the Allies could have skirted the huge guns and fortified positions in the north and split the country in two, fanning out in all directions, cutting off huge sections of German troops from supplies and reinforcements. It was a time-tested strategy. He scoffed; it seemed more of a Russian move just to throw oneself at the enemy relentlessly to see if he would break. It was of little consequence now. Normandy it was. He was ordered to proceed to Caen, stop the advance and launch a counterattack.

Major Kampfe watched as several small but heavy boxes were loaded onto the back of a transport truck by a small group of men. Although the boxes were marked "records" and should have been much lighter, none of the men so much as commented on that fact to their superior officer. Standing next to Kampfe was a lieutenant just recently minted out of the Hitler youth and rabid to please the dashing Kampfe whose reputation preceded him.

"Lieutenant, these records must not fall into enemy hands, not at all costs. They are vital secrets to the war effort and will be instrumental in our eventual defeat of the enemy. Take them immediately to the railhead here at Limoges where you will take them to our agent for transport. This information is for your ears only. This convoy is to appear routine. Understood?"

"*Jawohl,* Major!" The eager officer said as he leaped into the passenger seat of the staff car that was to lead the procession.

A couple of guards accompanied the procession but that was it. Best to hide in plain sight, Kampfe mused as the procession pulled out of the compound. Nothing was certain, he reminded himself. Surviving to spend the gold would be something of a miracle. At least it gave him added incentive not to be stupid at this stage of the game.

Kampfe watched as the small convoy turned onto the main road and out of sight. He hoped that it would be able to slip by unnoticed, as it was largely heading in a direction that wouldn't attract any undue attention. The Lieutenant had been given a letter signed by General Lammerding directing that all assistance be afforded the convoy. Kampfe knew the signature of an SS General should get the convoy through and the gold on a train bound for Zurich without incident. He knew that anything could happen, but at least the gold was heading away from the front and towards safety. He would have accompanied it but knew that a ranking officer would ordinarily not have been sent on a routine errand. That was exactly what he wanted the convoy to appear to be, routine.

CHAPTER **THIRTY-ONE**

Madeleine made her way north, traveling mostly by train when she could without attracting attention. She knew this region well. It was where her cousin lived and where she'd spent many August months in an attempt to escape the heat of the south and the blasting Mediterranean sun. She longed to stop and enjoy a little normalcy with her cousin Gabrielle. She had not written these long months, which had now turned to years. That would simply have been impossible, and would have put Gabrielle and her small family at risk. Madeleine did not resent the fact that Gabrielle and her small town had all but avoided the hardships of war. In fact, Madeleine drew solace from the fact that there were towns throughout the country that had escaped notice. It was near these areas of inactivity that she routinely hid.

On the few occasions that she stopped in a shop or to quietly listen at a café for news, she did so under the pretense of traveling. Her "work" had taken her all over France and her familiarity with the local towns, their industries and the customs of their inhabitants all lent to her skill at avoiding notice. Bulky drab clothing and a set of ugly glasses helped as well. She usually traveled as a student studying to be a teacher. Her mother taught at a local teacher training college. Madeleine smiled now, grateful for the fact that her mother taught languages. Her mother had passed on a knack for picking them up to both of her children. She had always liked English. It was difficult to learn but her mother taught her religiously from her infancy. Crib languages were what she came to understand the term was. The accent was something else. Her English was heavily accented with the raw French accent of Provence. She knew it was one of the reasons the SOE accepted her. She had simply answered an advertisement in a London paper.

You have to love the British. Only they would follow the ordinary conventions of advertising for spies. She had applied immediately once she made it to England.

During the interview process, she had been cautious not to appear too eager or rabid for revenge. Each interview became increasingly secret as she was considered for the work.

Madeleine had always been a prudent person. Her brother had inherited her father's more carefree and happy personality. Even the loss of a leg had not driven out his *joie de vivre*. When he returned to her mother after being wounded during the first war, her mother had told Madeleine from a young age that a leg does not make a man. When she was older her mother had whispered to Madeleine over a couple of glasses of wine that in all the important departments her father was very much a man. Madeleine had been a little shocked but pleased that her usually reserved mother shared that intimate detail with her. Jack was like her father in some respects. He had the same carefree, almost reckless attitude towards life. He simply didn't seem to get overly concerned about the day-to-day stresses of life. On the other hand, he showed great attention to detail concerning his missions and felt personally responsible for the lives of the people under his command. She was in constant danger of discovery. She knew that if captured she would die a slow and painful death. The Gestapo and SS had made it quite clear that any suspect meeting her description was to be turned over to their tender care immediately. She knew enough about rape; and simulated torture had given her a taste of what to expect if captured.

Madeleine shuddered again at the memory of how her rape at the hands of a drunken SS officer had led her down this road. Each kill seemed to cleanse her of his crime momentarily until her hate returned. It was her love for Jack that proved to her that she could enjoy physical love to the extent that she had even after her rapist's brutality. During her time in England she had a few wartime trysts. She was convinced that she would die once she was back in France and engaging the enemy. The men she chose had each been interesting in their own way. She would be damned if she let the cruel, deliberate violence of her attack be her only sexual experience before she died.

As Madeleine expected, her invasion mission was exceedingly dangerous. She was ordered to travel to the Limoges region and target a general commanding an entire SS Division. General Lammerding was her target. Although, in past wars high-ranking officers had been exempt from assassination, the atmosphere of this war trumped playing by the rules. Hitler had directed more than one assassination attempt on Winston Churchill and other leaders with no success. Some of Hitler's own generals had made more than one attempt on his life.

Political assassination was quite different from Madeleine's mission, which was purely military. Lammerding commanded a vital reinforcement division. Anything that could be done to harass, delay, or disrupt reserves and keep them out of the fight for as long as possible saved countless lives. Madeleine's information was that the invasion had been anything but easy. The casualty rate on both sides was huge and the terrain an advantage to the defending army. Each piece of land was taken at great cost. Madeleine knew that getting to the general would be almost impossible. She would have to be invisible to get near him. Her usual method was to take out her targets when they were at their most vulnerable. That meant when they least suspected attack. It was something altogether different to go into the lion's den and pull out one of his teeth while he was wide-awake and hungry. A division of the most ruthless and experienced soldiers in the German army was guarding Lammerding. If she was caught there would be no trip to Berlin for interrogation. Her abuse and torture was assured. She knew she would be raped until there was nothing left of her and then hung for public display. No, they would have to kill her and when they tried, many Germans would die with her.

As Madeleine saw it she had two choices. One was to kill the general when he was exposed outdoors or near a window or entryway. For that she needed a sniper rifle with a decent scope and lots of luck. The other way was to sneak into his headquarters, wait for an opportunity and kill him quietly. The first method would cause much more commotion if the division was underway. She was good with a rifle, but hitting a moving target at distance and getting a kill shot sounded like something for an exceptional marksman. The military had many proficient in that specialty. She had confidence in her abilities but if she missed she would not get another chance. There was no intelligence on when or how the division would move. The scenario carried with it too many variables. Lammerding might travel by train or in an armored vehicle. Once he was in the combat zone, she would stick out like a sore thumb trying to move through enemy lines. Under those conditions he would be heavily guarded. Her decision was to stick to what she did best: get in, lay in wait, and strike. She decided to take him in his headquarters and disappear. She could gain access disguised as a cleaner or a cook or some other domestic servant. She needed to control the situation as much as possible to ensure success and her own safety to a degree. She couldn't chase the man all over France and hope for an opportunity to present itself. She made her decision.

Stenger and Willi drove at a leisurely pace in a small *Kuebelwagen*, the German version of the American jeep. The top was down and there were no windows. The sun was shining and the day was pleasant. Like its American counterpart, the *Kuebelwagen* could go anywhere, just not too quickly. Given their meandering pace and frequent stops to eat and refresh themselves with a beer or two, they were clearly in no great hurry as they slowly passed through the countryside.

"Horst, the invasion is on. Why are we still headed towards Limoges? The Division undoubtedly will be deployed to the front. Nobody is going to care about missing gold anymore," Willi said.

"We have a new investigation, it seems. Some plucky Resistance group up there switched the oil out of Lammerding's flat cars and replaced it with paste," Stenger said smiling.

"Now that is gutsy. I like it. Anyone killed in the process?"

"No violence, no deaths."

"Now that is something. It's beautiful and creative. It'll be interesting to look into."

"Even if we catch someone, I guarantee I'm not turning

them over to the SS or Gestapo. This investigation should see us through to the end, Willi."

"Now I'm happy. I wasn't looking forward to asking any *Das Reich* lunatics about missing gold. Everyone knows they were plundering the countryside. Funny how no gold ever seemed to make its way to Berlin. I suppose sending a couple of old cops was supposed to scare them into compliance."

"Some bureaucrat's notion of a good idea," Stenger yawned.

"Yeah, and as usual, someone hundreds of miles away tucked into a safe comfy bunker with a one-way ticket to Zurich in his pocket," Willi answered. "So, where do we start the investigation?"

"At the top: with General Lammerding."

"He'll be fun. I bet he's a regular kitten, Horsty." Both men laughed at the absurd comment.

"Wear your earplugs, Willi. I guarantee he's going to be a screamer."

CHAPTER **THIRTY-TWO**

Madeleine waited in a basement utility closet while the General's headquarters bustled overhead. At home with the dust and the spiders, she thought. She had come in hours ago under cover of darkness and managed to slip in through a tiny basement window. Living on the run kept you thin. It had been a tight squeeze but it gave her the added satisfaction of knowing that the Germans would not consider the narrow slit of a window a means of entry. Her plan was simple. Wait and listen, and then act. She had been able to determine which office was the General's by listening to the traffic and conversation overhead. It was on the first floor and near the back of the building. She would wait until the General was alone. Make her way upstairs carrying a bucket like a domestic servant. She would then slip inside his door under the guise of cleaning the attached bathroom and shoot him, escaping through the back door and into the maze of streets. It was what she knew best: get in and get out. She was worried that she might run out of time and the General would be on his way. She had discovered that the division train had been compromised and that travel would be by road. Now that was sabotage of the highest order! Madeleine knew that 300 tanks and thousands of men would take a long time to get to Normandy by the narrow congested roads of the region. They were full of soldiers and supplies sprinting for the front. The ensuing bottlenecks would slow every unit down, not just *Das Reich*. The General Staff must just be wild over it, she thought and smiled picturing the chaos in her mind. Her concern was that she didn't know when the General would leave the *chateau* and join his troops in the field.

"Likes his mansions doesn't he, Horsty?" Willi said,

looking up at the imposing *chateau* while the two stood at the entryway to Lammerding's command center.

"Might as well be comfortable after months at the Russian front," Stenger commented.

The two men walked up the stairs and towards a young officer manning the phones in the spacious foyer.

"Major Stenger to see General Lammerding," Stenger said showing his credentials.

"Oh yes, Major. The terrorist investigation. The General's been expecting you. I'll take you to him."

As predicted, the general was a sight to behold. His face was florid and looked like it would burst under his tirade. Stenger and Willi watched as he pounded his fist on the giant oak desk commandeered from the rightful inhabitants of the *chateau*. Stenger knew without asking that this blowhard was a lunatic. His connections had gotten him his command. He was one of Hitler's favorites and that meant the chances were that he was unstable at best. Stenger thought how different this man was from his friend, Field Marshal Rommel. No telling what Erwin was up to. They certainly didn't move in the same circles. All Stenger knew was that first and foremost, Rommel was a fighter. He didn't think there would be any easy surrender for him. Stenger lamented the fact that Germany wasn't led by a man like Rommel. Had that been the case from the beginning of the war things would be quite different now. Hitler fancied himself a master tactician, but he was not; Rommel was.

"Catch them, Stenger. I'll hang them from every lamppost in town. We'll teach the scum to target *Das Reich*. We'll leave them to rot as a warning," Lammerding said; spit flying from his mouth as he bellowed, leaning over the desk.

"Of course, general," Stenger said making a mental note never to turn a suspect over to a ranting lunatic like Lammerding.

"We'll start at the crime scene and move out from there. Someone must have seen something," Stenger promised.

"Then get to it, soldier! I want blood."

Stenger and Willi threw the General a military salute as they walked quickly from the room closing the door behind them.

Both men made eye contact as they paused briefly outside of the door to the General's office. Stenger rolled his eyes as Willi turned to whisper a comment into his ear. As he turned, Willi caught sight of a young woman carrying a bucket towards the back of the building. Her back was turned and she moved steadily away, neither fast nor slow. Willi moved towards the woman, his comment dying on his lips. Stenger put his hand to his pistol as Willi exploded down the hall. Everything seemed to slow down as the woman spun around and reached into the bucket she was carrying. An electric wave of recognition hit Stenger. The Angel of Death! The General was her target. Killing him would hamper a counterattack.

Stenger was about to yell when he saw Willi grab the woman's gun hand before she could disengage it from the bucket. He saw the woman register recognition just as Willi's other hand snapped a quick jab into her chin. Willi was a light heavy weight; she went down like a limp noodle.

"Horst," Willi said looking up. There was a pleading look on his face. He was frozen with indecision. Stenger holstered his pistol and scooped Madeleine up in his arms, taking charge.

"Willi, I'm going out the back door. Go get the car and meet me around back," Stenger said in a commanding tone, having made the decision for both of them.

Stenger moved decisively and carried Madeleine out the back door of the *chateau* into a small, unused courtyard. The main drive circled around the back and there was additional parking for deliveries and guests. Thankfully there was no one in the immediate area.

Stenger glanced around nervously, searching his mind for a logical excuse that would explain why he was holding a young woman in his arms behind the bustling division headquarters. Before he could conjure one up, Willi pulled up in the *Kuebelwagen.* He jumped out and opened the back door, closing it behind Stenger as he piled into the back seat with Madeleine. Stenger sat close, holding her upright by placing her head on his shoulder. Willi slid into the driver's seat and immediately drove away from the building in the direction they had come and away from the town center. Madeleine's breathing was even and regular. Stenger searched her as he would any other suspect. He found a second weapon strapped to the inside of her thigh, along with two flexible blades. His fingers felt the hem of her garments and he found several capsules. Two were smaller than the rest and were marked with an L. He knew they were lethal cyanide tablets. Once bitten through death arrived in less than 15 seconds. Stenger shook his head as he flung them out the window. He took the handcuffs he'd carried in civilian life and placed them securely on her wrists and behind her back. Willi glanced over the front seat. He nodded in confirmation.

"That's her, Horst. Can our luck be any worse? We've captured the most dangerous Resistance fighter in all of Europe and we can't get rid of her."

"You read my mind, Willi. I am not going to turn her over to that jowly bastard Lammerding. I'd never sleep again. She's an enemy of the Nazis. She's not my enemy."

"We can't turn her loose," Willi said.

"No you're right. Her days of Nazi hunting are over."

"She hurt, Horsty? I just popped her a little," Willi said glancing nervously over his shoulder.

"She'll be fine, except I'm sure she'll be madder than hell when she wakes up."

"Where to?"

"Check the map. Pick me a small town with a police station. We're commandeering it until we can figure out what to do next."

CHAPTER **THIRTY-THREE**

Madeleine rubbed her chin and paced in her small holding cell. She was more angry with herself than frightened. She wondered why she hadn't already been turned over to the Gestapo or the SS. Perhaps that was yet to come. She had come to in the back of the *Kubelwagen,* groggy and disoriented. Her jaw hurt but wasn't broken. Little by little she recognized Willi. The other man must have been his partner. She was confused. Regardless, her first priority was escape. She remembered the incident back at the *chateau*. She was glad that she didn't have to shoot Willi, although she had intended to. The reflex would have been automatic, however unfortunate the consequences.

"I think we need to talk, *mademoiselle*," Stenger said as he carried a cup of coffee and a packet of cigarettes into the room, speaking in French.

"How about you talk, I'll listen," Madeline said sarcastically, her eyes never leaving his.

"If you think I want to question you about your former activities, you're wrong." Stenger said, tossing the cigarettes through the bars to Madeleine. He placed a small stool near the cell and set the coffee on it.

Madeleine slowly opened the cigarettes and smelled them. She also stuck her finger into the coffee and carefully tasted it. Stenger tossed her a box of matches and Madeleine lit a cigarette.

"What, no knockout drugs or poison, Major?" She smiled. It was an honest smile and the radiance of her beauty intensified.

"I am not an assassin," Stenger said with a hint of condemnation.

Madeleine nodded, sparing them both any feeble attempt at denial.

"So, will it be the Gestapo or the SS for me, Major?"

"Neither. That is what I want to talk to you about."

Madeleine was clearly surprised. She reached through the bars and took the cup of coffee and took a large swallow.

"God, I hate wartime coffee. Granted its real, but of poor quality. I thank you all the same."

"My plan is simple, *mademoiselle*. The invasion is rapidly advancing. I think France will be free very soon."

"So, I stay here until the allies waltz into town?" She was surprised at the frank assessment Stenger had so easily admitted.

"No. When the time is right the three of us surrender to the first allied forces that arrive in the area. You will remain here with us on the condition that you do not try to leave."

"That's it?"

"No, not entirely. I need your word that your killing days are over."

"How do you know that you can trust me?" She asked, considering the enormous implications of what Stenger was suggesting.

"Because you won't be giving your word to me, it will be to Willi. You each have each spared the other's life and that means everything to a soldier."

Madeleine knew that Stenger was right. She felt a sense of relief as she realized that there was an excellent chance that she'd survive the war. She had missed her chance with Lammerding. Well, too bad. One miss out of countless kills. Perhaps it was fate. That possibility had to be seriously considered, given the present circumstances. What were the odds that she would cross paths with these particular policemen ever again, much less during the chaos of war? If she agreed maybe she would live to find Jack Teach and see the war end.

"So, where's Willi?" she asked casually, leaning back and exhaling.

"You have made a wise decision. You obviously have much to live for. Certainly you have a family and loved ones waiting for you at the end of this horrible mess. Willi's in the kitchen," Stenger said withdrawing a key from his pocket and opening the cell door. "Let's go find him."

CHAPTER **THIRTY-FOUR**

Major Kampfe watched from his staff car as his men exchanged fire with a pair of Resistance fighters they had stumbled across. His orders had been to seek out and kill all Resistance groups. He scoured the countryside in an effort to try to compromise Resistance sabotage missions before they could be brought to bear on his division. General Lammmerding had been furious when his train was rendered useless. It had been his express directive to kill anyone suspected of terrorist activity. To Kampfe these *Maquis* fighters were an insult to a soldier such as himself and the men under his command. War was fought between armies, not peasants suddenly emboldened by an invasion. He would gladly eradicate these scum. He had no compunction against it in the least. Dead saboteurs didn't necessitate any additional consideration. He left them to rot as they fell.

Kampfe sighed as he watched the action. The terrorists had been cornered in a small outbuilding, having been surprised at a roadblock. There was a man and a woman, interestingly enough. His patience was waning and the cocktail hour approaching. He glanced angrily at his watch. He flung open the car door and got out, his patience exhausted.

"What is the hold up?" Kampfe shouted to no one in particular.

"Major, one terrorist dead, one surrounded," a platoon sergeant reported saluting.

"Toss in grenades and blow the bastard to hell! Stop fooling around."

"The men think it's the woman, sir."

"The woman? Can't the fearsome *Das Reich* overpower one woman!"

"Well, every time we get close she hits somebody. Two are dead and three wounded. She's one hell of a shot sir."

"A good shot? Intriguing, she must be highly trained. We might have ourselves a big fish here, Sergeant. Tell the boys to back off a little. We'll make her use up her ammo and take her then."

"Sir!" The sergeant saluted and ran back to the fight.

A prize indeed, Kampfe thought. He whispered to himself, "the Angel of Death? It can't be." Kampfe was SS and there wasn't an SS officer in France that hadn't heard about the shadowy assassin. Nobody could give much detail about her appearance. Must be military trained, he decided. I am going to catch this woman, and we shall soon find out who she is.

SOE agent Violet Szabo crouched behind a door in the ramshackle building, squeezing off kill shots and mentally counting how much ammunition she had left. She pushed a strand of blond hair away from her face and sighted her pale blue eyes on the next target. She squeezed the trigger, seeing the shot hit in her mind's eye before it left her weapon. The bullet struck a soldier directly between the eyes. He immediately slumped. The war was over for him. He had foolishly raised his head and exposed himself to fire. She cursed her lack of ammunition, confident in her marksmanship. She had been parachuted back into France in anticipation of the invasion. How stupid it had been to run into this patrol. She and her fellow agent were armed to the teeth. If the vehicle had been searched they would have been shot.

Violet heard the sounds of men encircling her. It seemed that they had wisely decided to wait her out. She smiled grimly, willing her enemies forward. She was the best shot in the SOE and she knew it. It had driven her fellow male agents mad. Finally she earned their respect, and her skill was openly celebrated.

She glanced down at the wound in her leg and could feel her energy and consciousness fading as the blood freely flowed out. The bullet had passed through and missed a major artery, but it bled profusely. She couldn't afford to apply a tourniquet; she was out of time. I'm going to die anyway, she thought. Maybe they'll recognize me for something other than a local *Maquis* and not kill me straight away. She didn't have the option of escape. Her wound saw to that. Her head swam and her eyes rolled back in her head. Her last thoughts were of the beautiful little daughter she had left behind in her native England. With her father already killed fighting the Germans, and now her mother, the girl would be orphaned. How sad it was that she would be left to fend for herself in a world that might allow the madness of war to rise again. The gun slipped from her hands as her head swam and she slumped to the ground. As her eyes closed she saw the soldiers moving carefully forward.

Kampfe stood over Szabo and directed his men to search her and place her in the back of his car. If she was going to survive she would need immediate medical care. A medic applied a tourniquet as Kampfe considered his prisoner. She was certainly beautiful enough, he mused, and there was plenty of fight in her. It was a pity that she would be turned over for questioning and probable internment in a concentration camp. He admired her courage. He personally had nothing against the British people. In his mind they were of pure race, and their historical ties to Germany and her royalty went back through countless generations.

"We'll take her for interrogation. We'll know her secrets soon enough," Kampfe said as he stepped quickly towards his vehicle dismissing Szabo's fate from his mind.

As Kampfe and his small detachment tore off in a cloud of dust a young boy, no more than twelve years old, watched from the branches of a distant tree. When the hated soldiers were gone he carefully climbed down. If he fell, how would word get to his father? A person important to the Resistance had been taken. His father must be warned. He silently dropped the last few feet to the ground and disappeared into the brush, ghosting his way towards home.

CHAPTER **THIRTY-FIVE**

"Do you know who I am?" Kampfe screamed as he looked down the barrels of several *Maquis* guns, in part angry with himself for falling into the hands of the Resistance.

"Yes. You are a Nazi war criminal and you will be treated as such," a burly, middle-aged man curtly responded.

Kampfe was about to let fly with another tirade when he felt a gag thrust over his head and into his mouth. His arms were roughly tied behind his back. He glanced over and saw Lieutenant Gerlach, his junior officer, receiving the same treatment. The remainder of Kampfe's detail lay dead on the ground. The *Maquis* ambush had been successful and well executed. It had taken place along an area of road that should have been safe for travel.

Kampfe and Gerlach were pushed into the back of a small, nondescript sedan. The German staff car was pushed off the road and hastily covered with brush. The dead soldiers were dragged off the road and their bodies hidden. Kampfe's captors realized that it wouldn't be long before the officer was missed. Their plan was to hold the two officers in the event that they were needed as hostages. Things were happening so quickly now that decisions were made hastily and their consequences or advantages dealt with later. Right now, the SS was rampaging against the *Maquis* throughout the region. A ranking officer like Kampfe might just give them some leverage.

As a final precaution, Kampfe and Gerlach were blindfolded. There was little discussion as the car drove on. Initially, the prisoners were thrust down in the back seat.

During the car ride, Gerlach managed to right himself for a brief moment, trying to orient himself as best he could. Just as the vehicle turned, a rough hand from the front seat pushed him back down and out of sight. The man's hand brushed Gerlach's blindfold and pushed it down allowing him a quick glimpse. He saw a road sign! Ouradour sur Glane. The car continued past the intersection with the road leading to Ouradour sur Glane. There was no comment among the Resistance members as they passed. The town was of no interest to anyone. There was no local *Maquis* organization in town for the men to deliver their prisoners to. They were headed towards Tulle. Many of the inhabitants of Tulle had some involvement with the Resistance. They were organized and well suited to hold the German officers until their utility as hostages had been determined. In the event they were of no use, they would be shot. Years of Nazi murder and cruelty had sealed their fate.

CHAPTER THIRTY-SIX

Richard and his "boy scouts," as he called them crouched in the thick brambles at the side of the road and surveyed the territory. It was an important route and the fastest way towards the fighting from the South. Richard trusted in the predictability of German behavior. That meant that, being efficient and precise, they would take the most direct route. Richard's information was reliable. It had come directly from a British agent operating clandestinely in the area for many months. The agent told Richard that an SS Division would be coming by road as their rail options had been personally compromised by the agent. Richard knew better than to ask for specifics but the agent volunteered that the convoy was huge. It was an entire division of men, tanks, and equipment. Richard wanted to do as much damage as possible and slow the convoy down and allow time to make preparations further north. He wanted to harass these bastards all the way to Normandy like hornets incessantly stinging a bear. The Germans would arrive at the battle anything but rested and fresh. He glanced at the young boys.

"Do not attack any Germans that you see on the road. The convoy we're after won't be coming all at once. We cannot attract attention to this area. I'm not after a couple of cars and men, I want to take out tanks. Familiarize yourselves with the road. The purpose of our mission is to observe so that we can plan appropriately. We will come back and place enough explosives around here tonight to make them curse the day they declared war on France."

The eager expressions on the faces of the boys were heartening but also alarming. Richard didn't want any slip-ups. Prior to the mission he had passed out a few grenades and each boy was armed with a rifle. He had no choice. They couldn't go into the field unarmed. He didn't like it, but under the circumstances it was the best anyone could do.

In the distance Richard heard the distinctive sound of a truck approaching. He peered out of the undergrowth and saw three vehicles. The middle vehicle was a medium sized truck covered with a tarp. Two other smaller cars sat both in front and behind it. There was only a small detachment of men. The convoy certainly didn't look too important, and it didn't seem to be in any particular hurry. It would be foolish to attack this group. That would only attract attention and ruin their chances for a larger score later. This was not the part of the convoy that was expected.

"Let this one pass," he hissed, glancing down the row of eager faces. He motioned them back. "It's not the big one we want."

Richard could see the tension build in the boys. They were bursting with adrenaline. Just as the lead vehicle approached, one of the youngest boys leaped up and darted out into the road, clutching a grenade.

"No," Richard yelled. It was too late. Like lemmings the other boys ran out, firing wildly. A German soldier in the lead car calmly rose in his seat and opened up with a machine gun like he was swatting at a fly. The first boy tossed his grenade into the car in front of the truck. It exploded, igniting the gas tank. The flaming vehicle lazily rolled to the side of the road and burned, oily black smoke billowing into the sky. Richard ran towards the front of the convoy and tossed his own grenade into the cab of the truck. The soldiers in the cab scrambled to find the explosive. The passenger was grabbing at it in an attempt to toss it out when it detonated in a blinding flash, ripping the men inside apart with shrapnel driven by the force of the concussion.

Immediately the driver of the second car slammed on his brakes. Richard spun and fired through the windshield, killing the soldier in the front passenger seat. The driver fired back, scrambling from the vehicle. He backed away into the underbrush as Richard dove back into the ditch at the side of the road to avoid his fire. Richard fired repeatedly at the retreating soldier, not knowing whether he hit the man or not. Without a radio the German would have to walk to find help. With *Maquis* groups marauding all over the countryside he would keep off the road if he had any sense.

After a short time Richard raised his head over the top of the ditch. He looked around, nothing but dead boys and men. He stood up to take stock of what had happened.

Richard walked quickly toward the front of the convoy. There were dead bodies strewn around. The boys were dead. Their bodies ripped apart by machine gun fire and the concussive blasts from the grenades. They hadn't even lived long enough to learn how to fight, he thought as he shook his head. He quickly pulled the boys' bodies out of sight and under the cover of the dense undergrowth along side the road. He was confident that the surviving German soldier was long gone. He cared less for the German dead and turned to see what was in the truck. He open the tarp and reached in to slide a box towards him as he stood on the road. He could barely move it. He leaped up into the bed of the truck to get a better grip. He saw that all of the boxes were marked "records" and bore the standard SS insignia.

"Records?" He muttered aloud. "Not unless they're written on stone tablets."

He shoved the corner of a trench knife into a crack in the wooden lid of the nearest box. He pried up carefully. The contents glowed as the sunlight danced on the bars of gold neatly stacked inside.

"My god," he barely breathed. "Gold?" He saw the insignia of the SS stamped into one of the bars and lifted it up reverently to inspect it. He was astounded. "Somebody is going to miss this," he said to himself. War or no war, he stood transfixed as visions of wealth darted through his mind.

Coming to his senses, Richard stood up without hesitation and jumped back down out of the truck. He made his way over to one of the dead soldiers and found a small shovel. He had few options. He had made up his mind immediately to hide as much of the gold as possible.

Working furiously Richard managed to move the heavy

boxes and hide them a good distance from the side of the road. Thankfully the soil was loose and he had little trouble digging a sufficient number of holes. He worked in a near panic, expecting to hear the arrival of more vehicles at any moment. The sweat poured off of him as he dug furiously.

Once the boxes were buried, each in its own shallow hole, Richard spread leaf litter and branches to cover their location. His rough estimate was that there was at least 600 kilos of gold. His mind raced with ideas. The one he kept coming back to was that this was German gold. He knew it would never replace the family the Nazis had taken from him, but he wasn't about to share it with anyone. If he survived the war his plan was to wait and return for it. He would be patient and claim it for himself. As he finished he took his bearings. One good rain and all evidence of his digging would be washed away as the soil compacted. Even if they came looking for it there was a lot of ground to cover. He had carried the boxes a good way into the forest and on a diagonal path. He was counting on the notion that the Germans would think a second vehicle had cleared out the contents of the truck. His aching back told him that that theory might be believed. With little hesitation Richard decided that the war was over for him. He made his way towards the south, and Spain.

CHAPTER **THIRTY-SEVEN**

"Major Diekmann, wake up, sir. I have the General on the phone," a young soldier said, carefully shaking his Major's shoulder. Diekmann groaned and tried to roll over. The soldier wrinkled his nose as the smell of stale alcohol and a very late night rose up from the crumpled Diekmann.

"Major," the soldier almost shouted. "The General!"

Diekmann's eyes slammed open. All at once clues as to who he was and where he was came rushing through his hangover and into his mind.

"The General? I'm on leave. We don't move out for two days."

"He is fit to be tied, Major. He is screaming much more than talking."

Diekmann suddenly focused on an emotion rattling around in his fuzzy, alcohol-clouded mind. He had less respect for Lammerding than some of the other command officers. He was damned if he was going to be jerked around by that blow hard. Diekmann had his own connections on the General Staff.

"Diekmann," he muttered into the phone his orderly handed him, holding his head in his other hand.

"Where the hell have you been, Diekmann? I have been calling for hours!

"I am on leave, sir, and have been here all morning." Diekmann's orderly handed him a cup of coffee. As he drank from the cup he listened to the General keep up his rant. Knowing that he wasn't expected to speak he placed his hand over the receiver.

"Claus, did the General call before?"

"No sir, the phone service had been interrupted. This was the first call that came through."

"Some sweetener in your coffee, sir?" Claus held out a flask of the powerful local brandy and poured some into the major's coffee. He had been with Diekmann long enough to know it was best to maintain the man's blood alcohol level. He was mean enough even when drinking.

"You are a good man, Claus," Diekmann said gesturing with his cup. He put his ear back to the phone, noticing the pitch of the General's voice drop a bit."

"You there, Diekmann?"

"Yes."

"Kampfe is missing and so is our gold."

"What! How did you let that happen?" Diekmann shouted.

"Remember who you're talking to, Major," Lammerding shot back.

"That really won't matter if this is discovered, General, now will it?" Diekmann shouted back.

"Just get dressed. We need answers."

The phone was slammed down in Diekmann's ear. Kampfe taken, he thought. That was his most immediate concern. Kampfe was his friend and comrade. He was instantly worried. Find Kampfe and maybe we find the gold, he considered. Either way he knew the best way to get to the bottom of the disappearance: start shooting people and see who talks. He gulped down his coffee and yelled for another cup as he pulled on his pants and boots.

"Nice way to finish my leave," he muttered, the brandy starting to take the edge off his blasting headache. Time to shoot some terrorists, he thought to himself. Maybe this day won't be so bad after all.

CHAPTER THIRTY-EIGHT

Kampfe and Gerlach sat in the basement of a small farmhouse. Their hands and feet were bound. Kampfe and Gerlach spoke in whispers.

"We might as well try to escape, Victor. It is highly unlikely that our lives would be exchanged for Resistance prisoners," Kampfe said plainly. To Gerlach's surprise, Kampfe was massaging his wrists. He had managed to wriggle out of the knots securing his hands.

"How did you do that?" came Gerlach's incredulous reply.

"These men are amateurs at best. When my hands were being bound they should have checked them more closely. It took awhile but they're free now." Kampfe grunted as he worked on the ropes securing his feet. Once free he crawled over to Gerlach and undid his bonds.

"The longer we wait, the greater the likelihood that there will be no exchange. This war is quickly moving to the north. There is little to gain from concentrating on terrorist activity once our reinforcements arrive at the front. The move begins today. The convoy will need refueling along the way and I'm sure it will be harassed. That's when the terrorists will strike." Kampfe said, slowly standing trying to work circulation back into his limbs.

Gerlach nodded slowly, "Do you have a plan, sir?"

"Next time someone comes in, we jump them. We will loosely secure our ropes. Once the man or men enter the room we strike. Most importantly, the less sound we make, the better. We can't be sure how many men remain upstairs. These are not soldiers. They have never seen real combat as we have. They will hesitate, that I promise you. Then we overpower and disarm them quickly. We'll make our way upstairs and escape. Surprise is often the best weapon of all. My guess is that they will bring some kind of evening meal. You can generally rely on the French to feed you, even if you are the enemy. We go then. Remember, we still control this part of the country. Once we get out we obtain weapons and flee."

"How many men do you think are guarding us?"

"I have been listening for arrivals and departures in the home above. I think there are at best three or four men up there. Once we get up the stairs, we go in separate directions. Confusion will be our best ally."

Three men sat at a table directly above the German officers.

"It's quiet down there. What do you think they're doing?"

"Sitting and waiting like us," another of the men answered.

"I think they should be shot. They're SS; you know what they've been doing around here."

"We've been given specific instructions to hold them. We should be able to do that. Two unarmed men, tied hand and foot. How hard can that be? What do you want to do, shoot them while they're tied up?" If they are to be shot it won't be on your say so, Philip."

The first man simply grunted. He was nervous and not accustomed to holding German officers prisoner. He knew if they were discovered, the penalty would be swift. He had seen more than one Frenchman put against the wall and shot. Everyone knew the risks. He had been involved in Resistance activities for some time but always from the shadows. Their actions had been emboldened by the invasion. Things were becoming much more like open warfare, and that was new territory for him. He was a small town maintenance worker, not a soldier. Neither of the men had any combat experience. They were brave but untested in battle.

"Since you're so worried, you and Charles can go down and check on them."

Both men got up and picked up the shotguns leaning against a wall adjacent to the small table they were sitting around. They was a loud scraping of chairs and eventually heavy footsteps as they walked down the narrow staircase into the cellar. The men proceeded through the doorway and saw the two soldiers leaning against opposite walls. The two walked further into the room.

"Check his legs," Philippe said gesturing to the first man.

Kampfe watched as the first man leaned down and reached out to check the ropes at his feet. The cellar was dark and the man wanted to do a hands-on inspection. As soon as the man's head was in range, Kampfe struck. He swung the rope that had previously bound his hands around the man's neck. Gerlach acted just as swiftly. Kampfe knew Gerlach was nervous but so was he. Kampfe pulled his man down, tightening the rope. The man gurgled and clawed desperately at the rope but his efforts were useless. Kampfe glanced over at Gerlach doing the same thing to his man, abruptly twisting the man's head, breaking his neck. It was over quickly. It had only taken a couple of minutes to finish the job. Kampfe motioned to the weapons and put a finger to his lips. Both men checked the shotguns for ammunition and walked up the stairs as if they were the two men returning. They paused at the top of the stairs and burst into the room both pointing their shotguns at the man sitting at the table, his face erupting in surprise and fear.

"Get up," Kampfe hissed. "One sound and I'll cut you in half."

The man raised his hands and stood up slowly, his shaking legs barely able to hold him up. Kampfe roughly grabbed him from behind and shoved him towards the cellar. At the top of the stairs Kampfe pushed the man as hard as he could down the staircase. The man twisted and struck his head savagely against the wall, falling in a heap at the bottom. Kampfe handed his shotgun to Gerlach and calmly walked down into the cellar. He stood over the unconscious man, reached down and casually gave the man's neck a vicious twist. Kampfe didn't bother to check his pulse, having heard the satisfying crunch of the man's bones. Kampfe walked back up the stairs and into the kitchen.

"I assume we won't be troubled by the last man, Major," Gerlach smirked.

"No, he died for France," Kampfe said contemptuously.

"He should have left the fighting to the soldiers. Now, we need to get out of here and find some transportation."

Kampfe peered out from behind the curtains covering one of the windows that faced the street. There was little activity. They might have a chance, he thought.

"There's a farm truck parked a short way down the street, and a second vehicle on the other side. You take the truck and I'll try the car. If we're seen, get in and get the hell out of here and find help. I'll do the same. Get word to the troops as quickly as possible."

"I don't want to run out on you, sir."

"Nor me you, Victor, but fate is calling the shots," he grimaced.

"It has been a pleasure to serve with you, Major."

"Me too, Victor. Just remember, *Das Reich* hasn't been in this new fight yet. Wait until the Americans and British get a taste of our *Panzers*," Kampfe smiled encouragingly, clasping the junior officer on the back.

"Let's go, Victor," Kampfe said as the two men moved steadily out the door and towards the two vehicles.

Kampfe crossed to the car and looked inside: no keys. Just as he did so a man exiting the café saw him and turned to shout back inside. Damn, Kampfe thought, Resistance everywhere. He turned to run across the street just as several men ran out of the café. He fired a barrel at the cluster of men and saw one go down. He heard a truck fire up and saw Gerlach stick his head out the window.

"Go Victor, now!" Kampfe yelled, turning as a bullet struck him. He returned fire, the shotgun now empty. He contemptuously threw the weapon at the men, slowly advancing. Seeing him unarmed, they opened fire as one, killing Kampfe instantly. In the rear view mirror Victor saw what happened and careened down the road. He had a sizable head start on the men, unsure whether they would follow or not. He drove at breakneck speed, desperate to find a patrol.

The group of men stood around Kampfe's body, uncertain what to do.

"Should we give chase?" One man asked.

"No. I think we need to clear out and wait for the Germans to come. There's no time to chase that man and get ready."

"Should we wait for orders?"

"Don't ask me."

"What do we do?" A third man said nervously, his knuckles white on the stock of his rifle.

"We certainly don't wait around here to get shot. Put that pig's body in the back. We'll dump him down the ravine and join up with the others," the men's defacto leader decided.

Kampfe's body was tossed into the back of a truck and covered with a tarp and some loose hay. Most of the men had a wild look in their eyes as they drove quickly out of town. Combat was upon them, whether they were looking for it or not.

CHAPTER **THIRTY-NINE**

General Lammerding sat comfortably in a small café in the town of Tulle. He was drinking wine and eating pastry. How foolish it had been for the terrorists to attack the garrison stationed in town. It had simply been a matter of a counter attack. His seasoned combat troops had retaken the town, losing only three men.

The owner of the café glanced nervously out the window as groups of men were paraded by at gunpoint. He had stayed out of the fighting the night before when the *Maquis* had taken the German garrison. They executed more than sixty German soldiers in their orgy of violence. He had known that the Germans would retaliate. They couldn't allow defeat at the hands of a Resistance force. The repercussions would be intolerable. Unfortunately, the *Maquis* leaders were impatient and acted rashly. He pictured the worst as the General calmly sipped his wine. There was something about his casual air that was frightening. A young soldier entered the room and approached the General.

"Well Sergeant, have the criminals been executed? Remember, I want at least two for every man killed by this rabble. How dare they strike at *Das Reich*."

"All but the last group, sir, but there's a problem."

"And…."

"We've run out of rope, sir. Perhaps we could cut some down and reuse the rope."

"No, I want a clear warning left, Sergeant. Leave them up there for their friends and families to contemplate. They will learn the penalty for killing my men. Sixty of Germany's finest, shot like cattle."

"Shall we shoot the rest, sir?"

The general sipped his wine pondering the fate of the

remaining suspects, casually nibbling on a piece of raspberry tart. Many others had been killed by his troops. He had other things to do and was confident that there would be no more trouble here.

"This is quite excellent, *monsieur*," Lammerding said to the café owner standing nearby, his face ashen with shock, too paralyzed by fear to respond. Lammerding had the café to himself. "No Sergeant, release them with strict orders to leave the carcasses where they are. Any man or woman cutting one of the swine down will be killed. I think we've made our point."

Lammerding stood and counted out a few Reich marks and set them on the table. He followed the sergeant out of the café and into the street. He sat in the back seat without looking around and motioned for the driver to proceed.

Once the café owner was certain the General wasn't coming back, he ventured outside. He broke down into tears as he wrung his hands and wandered among the townspeople outside in the street now the Germans had moved on. There were men hanging from almost every light post. Some were smaller, obviously young men and boys. Wails of anguish broke out all over as people discovered the fate of their loved ones. In all, ninety-nine people had been hung. The sheer number of bodies was incredible. The café owner recognized many that had nothing to do with Resistance activities. They must just have been conveniently available. He sat down on the curb and put his face in his hands and prayed. He knew that it would have been better to wait, but people were rabid with a desire for revenge after so many years of abuse. It had been a mistake. These men were not soldiers. Did they really think they could take on hardened combat troops and win? He wondered silently if this was happening all over France. He hoped that if it was, others were faring better. He knew harassing the enemy was important, but at what cost?

"How can this be?" he whispered. How can this be?"

CHAPTER **FORTY**

Diekmann walked around the torched truck and staff car. The occupants were burned beyond recognition, the skin on the bodies charred and twisted. He held a handkerchief to his nose and mouth against the roast pig smell rising off the corpses. He saw the insignia of his division on the lapel of a young officer. The man had died with one hand on the door handle, the other still clutching a pistol. He walked to the back of the truck and threw open the canvas and saw that the back was empty. He nodded certain that the true contents of the records boxes had been discovered and removed.

"I want some prisoners brought here to mark and bury these bodies. Anyone not in a German uniform can be tossed into an unmarked grave. This officer and his men will be collected later once the invasion is repelled. We cannot spare the time now."

Diekmann jumped back into his staff car and motioned the driver ahead. His teeth were clenched in rage as his thoughts focused on the lost gold and the building wrath of his General. He knew he needed information and he knew just how to get it.

Diekmann arrived at Division Headquarters to find Lieutenant Gerlach covered in dust from the road, drinking a large glass of schnapps and recounting his escape to a group of junior officers. He had returned to camp minutes before Diekmann had returned from finding the burned out vehicles.

"You're sure Kampfe was killed, Victor?" Diekmann asked him in an even voice, keeping his anger at bay, drinking his own large schnapps. The liquor kept his anger piqued and fueled him for the violence he was planning.

"Five or six of them fired into his body at point blank

range, *Herr* Major," Lieutenant Gerlach said, looking down at the table. He could scarcely believe he was alive after his ordeal. He was a soldier accustomed to combat, not waiting to be shot while tied up.

"Your captors were killed?"

"Yes sir."

Diekmann grimaced. He needed a plan, and quickly.

"No idea where you were taken?"

"I cannot be positive, but I did see a sign. It read Oradour sur Glane. That's the best I could do, sir. I caught a quick glimpse of it, but only for a second. I can't say if we ended up there or elsewhere. They could have driven us around in circles to disorient us. They were clearly amateurs, Major. I wasn't watching road signs when I drove out of town. All I could concentrate on was getting away. The Major's orders sir."

"Don't worry, Victor, it's not your fault. We cannot predict the actions of these animals with any certainty. We can only eradicate them when they are located."

"Now get yourself cleaned up. We're going to visit our friends in the little town of Oradour. By the end of the day they'll wish they had gotten off as lightly as the good people of Tuelle!"

"I might be able to recognize a few of them, Major."

"Don't worry, Victor. I'm sure the rest of the criminals have fled. The people will know who they are. Some persuasion will loosen their lips if they don't cooperate." The expression on Diekmann's face wasn't angry; there was a cold glee emanating from him. It was terrifying.

"Yes General...Ouradour sur Glane, I'm quite certain," Diekmann said into the phone. He wasn't about to go into any great detail. He was satisfied the town was their best lead. In fact, it was their only lead, and would have to do.

"Get our gold, Diekmann. I don't care what it takes!" Lammerding shouted as he hung up.

"Oh, I will general, I will!" Diekmann said as he placed the receiver back onto its cradle. He walked over to his dresser and carefully filled his hip flask from his stock of brandy. Now prepared for the day's festivities, he walked smartly from the room.

CHAPTER **FORTY-ONE**

Gabrielle looked out the window as she put the last of the dishes away from lunch. Antoinette was taking a nap in the next room and Gabrielle was planning to sit down and take a little rest herself. She looked at the wall clock: it was around 2:00 pm. Suddenly several trucks rolled by, carrying troops headed towards the town center. They must be going to the front, she thought until she saw them stop in the village square and troops jump out.

"What is this?" She muttered. "German troops in the town?" She dried her hands on a dishtowel and walked to the front door opening it. She looked out to see soldiers going from door to door. People were being herded into the street, young and old alike. From where she was she could see the shock and questions on their faces. Nothing like this had happened in Ouradour during all the years of the war. She was still trying to figure out what was going on when a soldier walked up.

"Everyone is to assemble at the village square for a document check," he demanded in broken French.

"But my daughter is sleeping," She replied.

"Bring the brat immediately," he yelled, clearly not anticipating any response.

Gabrielle felt a tingle of fear dance along her spine as she rushed back to get Antoinette. She was filled with indecision. Perhaps here at the edge of town she might be able to sneak away with her daughter. Should she? She had no idea what to do, never having personally encountered a German soldier before.

As she scooped her up, Antoinette groaned and whimpered. She really had a hard time waking. Maybe she'd sleep through the document check. On the way out the door Gabrielle grabbed their papers. Once outside she glanced around and saw that there were roadblocks set up all around town. There would be no easy escape. She made up her mind and proceeded to the village square. A few older people were being dragged from their homes and pushed out into the street. She felt another twinge of alarm but there was nothing she could do about it. As she approached the square she saw the Mayor talking with a German officer gesticulating and nodding clearly trying to comply.

"Mayor, I want thirty hostages to question," Diekmann said coldly. "The rest will be separated and confined. The women and children in the church and the men in those garages," he said, gesturing around casually and waiting for his interpreter to translate. His patience was non-existent and having to wait for the interpreter wasn't helping his mood.

"Forgive me, Major, but I thought this was a document check, but I will be a hostage if necessary," the Mayor said. He glanced around as a few other men joined him volunteering. Some were older and had looked down the barrel of German guns before, years ago in the trenches.

"We are looking for hidden weapons, Mayor!"

"We have no weapons, Major, except for a few shotguns for birds and rabbits."

"There are terrorists in this town, Mayor! Perhaps you are one of them," Diekmann answered, clearly enjoying his power over the man.

"Oh no, Major. We are not *Maquis*. We are a quiet little town. We have caused no problems for Germany," the Mayor said, a hint of panic entering his voice.

"Move, Mayor," Diekmann said, gesturing to a group of men walking towards a nearby garage.

Diekmann followed the group to the old wooden garage watching as forty some odd men were corralled inside. The doors were left open and the men inside faced out towards the street. Diekmann placed men around the exterior to ensure they stayed inside. In several other places through out the town men were herded into similar buildings. No one complained aloud. They simply followed the German's directives in their confusion. The men whispered among themselves. Most of them were convinced that after a short period of inconvenience the soldiers would see that there were no weapons or Resistance members in the town and then they would be released.

Antoinette woke up as the women and children were marched down towards the church. The younger children wore wooden clogs that drummed as they made their way down the cobble-stoned street. The sound was eerie. After a short while some of the soldiers encouraged the children to sing. The children's schoolteachers walked with them and led the children in song. Perhaps this would all end soon, they hoped.

It seemed that just about everyone was accounted for, Gabrielle thought. Amidst the singing some of the children whispered to their mothers as they walked. The women tried to reassure the children that it would only be a short while before they would be released and that the Germans were just checking them to make sure they were who they said they were. The children thought that odd, not understanding the adult need for something so silly.

Gabrielle listened and prayed that that was the truth. She held Antoinette and whispered assurances to her that everything would be all right. There were close to two hundred children in their procession, and as many women, both young and old. Nobody was exempt. Even the infirm had been forced from their homes. With their usual efficiency the Germans had cleared out everyone in the town.

Once they arrived at the church they were ordered to go inside and sit in the pews. The church was old and made of local fieldstone and wood. The church was the center of the town. Generations of townsfolk had been christened within its walls and buried in its graveyard. It was a symbol of the town's past and its future. Gabrielle began to allow herself some hope. What could possibly happen to them inside of a church? It was God's sanctuary. Gabrielle watched as several soldiers were dispatched around the building to secure it and prevent escape. It was a small church and not everyone could get a seat. Once the doors were closed the women began to speak excitedly among themselves.

"What is happening?" One young mother asked Gabrielle as she sat her children down in a pew and stood protectively in front of them.

"I have no idea. How did you get here?" Gabrielle asked, knowing that the woman lived on a small farm just outside of town.

"They stopped and rounded everyone up on the outskirts and a little way out. I think most everyone is here."

"I hope not," Gabrielle whispered, "I hope not. I don't know what's happening but I won't feel safe until the soldiers leave."

"They're probably on high alert because of the invasion," the woman answered.

"High alert? Here? Nothing ever happens here. I doubt any allied soldiers will ever come here. We'll find out we've been liberated when we read it in the paper," Gabrielle said, trying to lighten the mood a little and give herself some confidence while she was at it.

A young man crouched in the weeds, several hundred yards from the town. He was picking mushrooms in the forest to go with the trout he had taken out of the Glane River that morning. He and his family ate pretty well despite the occupation. They were country folk and grew or gathered most of their food anyway. He was just about to cross the meadow into the town when he saw the trucks arrive. He instinctively crouched down to avoid being seen. He had never seen so many soldiers at once. It was a rare occasion when one came into town. There were no *Maquis* here, he thought, remembering the unspoken position of the village to stay out of the fighting. Something was wrong. I had better stay here and watch, he decided. His mother and younger sister were at home and his father was away at market and wouldn't be home for at least two days. The soldiers almost always targeted the men and he was now sixteen. The safest thing for him was to lay low and wait for the Germans to leave. He was confident that the soldiers would leave his mother and sister alone. He hadn't heard anything suggesting that they would harm women and children indiscriminately.

"I think if we just cooperate everything will be fine." Gabrielle heard one of the more outspoken women say. There was a general chorus of agreement.

"They have always left us alone before. They will not find any weapons or contraband here. Does anyone know of any *Maquis* activity? I don't. They'll find nothing and leave just as quickly as they came," another voice encouraged.

Gabrielle was silent. She moved around and tried to see through the small windows of the old church. There were German soldiers everywhere. She saw a truck with a machine gun in the back. Nobody was going anywhere. They were helpless. Besides, what could they do with no weapons and their children to protect?

CHAPTER **FORTY-TWO**

In the center of the town, Diekmann stood in front of a garage into which many of the town's men had been forced.

"I could care less about guns," Diekmann hissed. "Members of your town ambushed a convoy and removed something of great importance to me. They took an SS Major hostage and killed him! He was a hero of the Reich, and my friend! I want names or I will start shooting!"

"We have no Resistance here. I can't tell you something that I know nothing about," the Mayor pleaded.

"I will get answers!' Diekmann shouted, furious that he was being delayed. He had four hours to find the gold, collect it, and get to Limoges. He grabbed his flask from his jacket that he had taken off under the relentless sun. He took a large drink from it and tossed it back into the vehicle.

"No activity, I see. I too can be unreasonable!" Diekmann sneered through his teeth. He drew his pistol and motioned to the soldiers nearest the garage doors to move away. The men inside moved back as the soldier manning the machine gun directly in front of them cranked back the gun's arming mechanism. Diekmann gestured to one of his captains. The officer drew his side arm and fired a shot into the sky.

The machine gun that had been aimed directly at the men trapped in the garage opened up. The gunner lay on the ground and fired randomly, hitting the men trapped inside repeatedly in the thighs and shins. He had been ordered to maim as many as possible first. The men tried to scatter but there was no way out as the bullets ripped into their lower bodies. Many were struck in the chest and neck as they fell to the ground.

Diekmann raised his hand and the shooting stopped. The

injured men on the ground groaned in pain. Diekmann raised his pistol and walked up to the Mayor writhing on the ground.

"Well, *Monsieur le Maire*, how about now? I will be blunt. I am looking for stolen gold. SS gold," he said, standing over the wounded man. It is here in this town. Your people ambushed my friend, Major Kampfe, took him, and stole our gold. Now I do not want excuses. I know you understand more of what I am saying than you let on. Now talk!"

"Mercy Major, we have no gold," he wailed raising his hands in a pleading motion. Like he was shooting an old dog, Diekmann raised his pistol and casually fired a shot into his head, killing him instantly as his pleading hands dropped lifelessly to his side.

An older man was quietly calling for his wife. Diekmann casually stepped over the Mayor's corpse. He stood over the old man and cupped a hand to his ear, feigning as if he was trying to hear the man's pleas. The soldiers laughed, and then abruptly Diekmann tired of the sport and shot the helpless man in the eye.

"There now, he doesn't need his wife anymore. Who wants to tell me about stolen gold? I'll shoot you one by one until I get it."

Several men shouted denying any gold. Others were bleeding too profusely to respond. They simply prayed and waited to die.

Diekmann screamed, "Burn them!"

Soldiers covered the wounded men in straw and doused them with gasoline. Most of the dying men were trapped in the tangle of bodies and were beyond resisting.

"Just hold up your hand if you remember anything about my gold!" Diekmann addressed them like a teacher asking students for an answer in elementary school. He chuckled at his own absurdity as the tinder-dry straw smoked and caught fire. It spread instantly throughout the old wooden building. As the inferno raged he motioned for the doors to be closed and stomped off to check on the other men.

Moments before the shooting began, Gabrielle was pushed back as three soldiers carried in an odd looking bundle. It was about the size of a hay bale and had what looked like fuses sticking out from it. Once it was deposited in the vestibule of the church two soldiers lit the fuses. The soldiers backed out, training their guns on the women and children as they left. The object started to smoke and the women in the church pushed back towards the nave. Several tried to go out a side door. A shot rang out in the distance and the true horror of what was happening struck the women. Screams erupted simultaneously as women and children broke in every direction. Gabrielle grabbed her daughter up off the floor and moved to the far side of the church away from the mass of women trying to escape. The door burst into splinters as a machine gun opened up, firing directly into the women trying to drag their children away from the stream of fire. Many were hit and Gabrielle saw several children's lifeless eyes staring out from their ruined little bodies. Others screamed at their mothers and grandmothers who died, leaving their children to their fate. Smoke from the bundle filled the church and random gunfire continued from outside.

Diekmann walked up to the church and watched the first of the smoke billow out from the windows.

"No, no, too slow!" He walked over to one of the enlisted men and took a grenade from his belt. "Like this," he laughed and lobbed a grenade through a window at the side of the church. Several others took his queue and lobbed in others. Flashes and flesh rending explosions tore from inside the church.

"There," said Diekmann. "Make sure it burns. I want this town turned into rubble," he said as he walked briskly off, as if on a routine inspection of his troops. Some of the older soldiers from the regiment seemed to be enjoying themselves and laughed at the newly conscripted Alsatian soldiers, whose eyes were wide with panic. They were from a part of France that adjoined Germany. They had been forced into this madness.

"What, no stomach for war? Show these animals that they should fear *Das Reich*," an older sergeant bellowed as he pushed two stunned men towards the church. They stood in frozen disbelief as they listened to the screams of dying women and children from within.

Gabrielle saw the first grenade fly through the far window and explode, tossing the bodies of children and women aside like so much confetti. She pulled Antoinette to the ground. The child was screaming in terror, calling for her father and for her mother to make it stop. Gabrielle looked around wildly for some escape. The interior had caught fire along with several people, completely engulfed in flames as they ran into one another. There was no escape. Gabrielle sank to her knees sobbing at the horror. Hell could be no worse.

"Mommy and Daddy love you, Antoinette *ma cherie*," Gabrielle whispered into her daughter's ear, kissing her fiercely.

Sensing something in her mother's voice, little Antoinette cried. "Don't leave me Mama, don't leave me."

Gabrielle reached around behind Antoinette's small head, firmly gripping her chin, her hand draped by the child's blond curls. "Never, my darling, never!" As soon as she spoke Gabrielle violently jerked Antoinette's head around, snapping her neck. Gabrielle let out a savage wail, every part of her screaming out in anguish. There was nothing human in it as it tore from the depths of her soul. Without hesitation, Gabrielle stood and walked towards the nearest machine gun fire. With Antoinette in her arms she fixed her eyes on the ancient crucifix hanging behind the altar. It was untouched by the violence erupting all around. She stepped forward towards her death, trusting in the sacrifice made for her soul so long ago by the man who gave his life for love.

CHAPTER **FORTY-THREE**

Madeleine had been feeling out of sorts and nervous all afternoon. Stenger and Willi sensed it right away. They said nothing, but the tension in the small police station was growing. Suddenly a wave of fear hit her. She clutched her stomach and sank down onto a cot. She had a strong intuition. All of the women in her mother's family had it. Something was wrong, terribly wrong. Madeleine felt it physically. She knew that she wasn't sick. Her emotion was grief, and she was struck by it as intensely as she had been upon the death of her brother. There was no mistake; she had lived with her grief for more than three years. She was wild to get out to find out what had happened.

"Stenger! Help!" She screamed instinctively. Stenger and Willi were through the door in an instant.

Stenger saw Madeleine's face contorted in fear. He had seen fear too many times to be mistaken. He went directly to her, Willi close behind. Without hesitation Madeleine threw herself into his arms.

"Something horrible has happened to my family," she cried into his chest. He held her gently as huge sobs shook her body. Stenger looked over at Willi and caught his eye. He had been right. There was more human compassion and love in the woman he held than he had suspected. He pushed aside his amazement and held her in her torment. It was as real as if she had witnessed a loved one's horrible death.

"I must go to my parents," Madeleine pleaded, torn between thoughts that Jack had been killed or her mother or father.

"Where are your parents? The time for secrets is past now, *mademoiselle*. I will call the police station there and have them run a routine check."

Madeleine thought quickly. Stenger was right. This was her first step in regaining some trust in the world. If she could not feel trust for this man, then to whom could she?

"La Ciotat. We own a small restaurant, Chez Toche."

"Toche. That is a strong name," Stenger said in a reassuring tone.

Madeleine began to regain her composure as Willi left the room to place a call to the small police station in La Ciotat.

Minutes later, Willi's call went through. Glad I'm calling south, he thought, considering the chaos and cut phone lines up north closer to the front.

"Chez Toche on *Le Boulevard de la Republique* is open for business. One Jean-Pierre and Claire Toche are offering a *daube de boeuf* and *potage de Pommes-de-terre* on the board today. They are safe and sound, *mademoiselle*."

"You may call me Madeleine. I am Madeleine Toche. I am an officer in the British army, a special operations division. Thank you, Willi. At least I know my parents are safe. It makes me feel a little better, but I can feel that something is wrong."

"Saying it only confirms what I know, *mademoiselle*. I suspected all along that you were with the SOE. Their agents are the best, but it changes nothing. We will all surrender to the British or Americans. Willi and I have both done it before."

"The Great War?"

"Willi and I were at the Marne, among other delightful locations."

"My father's left leg is still there," Madeleine replied casually, her initial panic having somewhat subsided. Her thoughts turned to Jack. She knew there was no phone call that could be made to check on him. She would have to wait. She racked her mind and tried to think of other family. None of them were in harm's way, and most likely not involved in the Resistance.

"Did you hear that, Willi? The Marne," Stenger said turning.

"Then we're almost family," Willi said, smiling. " Did your father ever tell you about it?"

"He told me many things after my brother died. He was

killed in the first days of fighting up north."

"Lots of painful memories there," Stenger said. "My generation was used as cannon fodder. Mostly by foolish officers fighting a modern war with conventional tactics."

"My father says the same thing, and that your sacrifice has been forgotten."

"One million causalities at Verdun. I guess that wasn't enough for the world," Stenger said his voice trailing off, sitting down heavily.

No one spoke, but it was clear that they had cast aside any remaining barriers between them. Souls had been laid bare. Madeleine was now bound beyond her word. Stenger knew she would never do anything to put her parents in danger.

"An SOE agent? No wonder you took me so easily, Madeleine. But much more importantly, your family owns a restaurant. Can you cook?" Horsty here is pretty good with boot leather, but I'm tired of that," Willi said, smiling.

"You just show me a kitchen, Willi," she answered as she stood.

CHAPTER **FORTY-FOUR**

Field Marshal Erwin Rommel's face was pained as he read the scant details in a report concerning a cursory investigation of the destruction of Oradour sur Glane. It was a two-page document intentionally devoid of any meaningful detail. Not a man prone to intense outward displays of emotion, he paused as he finished reading the document and lowered his head and slowly shook it from side to side. The report was conclusive enough to tell him what he needed to know, that an SS division had razed a town and murdered its entire population. He swung around in his chair and looked out the window of his office and contemplated the disaster unfolding as Germany tried to defend against the invasion. His hands were securely tied. Any meaningful command decisions had to go through Hitler's office. All of Rommel's efforts to station armor near the front in preparation for invasion had been largely ignored. The tragedy of this town was a direct result of that stupidity. The farther away your armor is, the more time, fuel, and resources it took to bring it to bear. He had argued that the longer the road to the front, the more opportunity for the Resistance to attack. Rommel knew that unless the invasion became a stalemate, Germany's chance to negotiate reasonable terms of peace with the Allies would be lost. Without negotiated peace, they would crush Germany into oblivion.

The Field Marshal stood up and began to pace. He wondered whether Germany would be permitted to exist as a nation after this. Some officers took the more direct approach by trying to assassinate Hitler. He had not participated in any of that. His duty was to his men and the defense of Germany. Things had been much easier in the beginning of this war, he mused. He thought of the heady days in command of the seventh *Panzer*, his beloved "Ghost Division," spearheading through France like a blazing meteor gobbling up and casting aside military resistance wherever he encountered it. Sometimes he had been so far ahead of the rest of the German army that even command headquarters didn't know where he was. Hence the name,"Ghost." This was his second war leading men into battle by example, and, sometimes, by reckless bravery. He had the privilege of serving with men of monumental courage and determination. This abomination could not go unanswered. A country has a right to defend itself. When combatants fight they know they risk death. The women and children of Ouradour were not combatants.

Rommel made a decision. Although not technically his responsibility, he knew that an investigation had to be completed. He wanted there to be examples of propriety and adherence to the rules of war followed by German officers when future generations considered the whole bloody mess of this war. He was not going to be said to have turned a blind eye. His troops did not engage in such conduct. He could not fathom how any man could condone such savagery. He walked out into the adjoining office where his aides and staff officers were located and called an aide aside.

"Find out where Major Horst Stenger is located. He is military police. Once you have him located, place a call to him immediately. Contact me as soon as you have found him."

Rommel walked back into his office and collected the papers on his desk. It was time to move. He commanded from the front and expected his officers to do the same. The fight was right down the road along with his duty. If his old friend and comrade in arms, Horst Stenger, couldn't get to the bottom of what happened in Ouradour, no one could. Horst was brave and smart. He had a tenacity that when unleashed was inspiring. Rommel had commanded him in the first war. Stenger had proven himself beyond measure. Horst would find out what happened and produce a report for Berlin that would also bear Rommel's name. One last act of decency, even if he knew in his heart no one would be punished.

Stenger's face blanched as he listened to his old

commander over the phone.

"Horst, I'm not sure what happened over there, but I do know that over eight hundred civilians were massacred," Rommel said quietly into the phone.

"General, I don't know what to say except that I will find out."

"Thank you, my old friend and comrade. Of course, remember that they're SS and highly unlikely to take kindly to your involvement."

"Is this widely known yet?"

"It's out there enough so that *Das Reich* and that fool Lammerding will tread lightly. I'm sure that Lammerding will blame some subordinate, claiming he had no direct knowledge of it. I just want names and their personal actions. I have dispatched a courier to give you the appropriate orders. You should have them in your hands before the end of the day. Now I'm off to the front. I trust your decisions more than my own sometimes, Horst."

"Is there anything but war for us, Erwin?" Stenger asked, speaking to a friend who he sensed he might never see again.

"I think not for me, Horst. Make sure there is for you and Willi. You two are the best soldiers I have ever known." With that Rommel slowly set down the receiver and abruptly walked out of his office.

Stenger walked back to the kitchen of the small police station and found Madeleine and Willi playing cards and filling the little room with cigarette smoke. They both looked up, sensing something wrong.

"What's happened, Major?" Madeleine asked, her face suddenly serious.

"That was Field Marshal Erwin Rommel calling me about some police work," Stenger replied.

"Did it concern me?" Madeleine asked simply.

"No, Madeleine. All I seem to have left is my word and I have given it."

Madeleine nodded. Her hopes had not been misplaced. She desperately wanted her war to be over and was content to sit it out in the comfort of the little police station and wait for the

British. She was after all a British agent and she had some back pay coming.

"What do you need from me?" Willi said, concern on his face. Stenger could never hide anything from Willi. They read each other's emotions openly.

"Just stay here for now, Willi. I'm taking a trip. Strictly police business. I am afraid it is bad business."

"I thought we were out of that now," Willi said with a sad smile, trying to lighten the mood a little bit."

"This is a direct request from General Rommel. He needs a report on some SS activity," Stenger said, skirting the truth. He had not failed to notice the flash of interest in Madeleine's eyes as he mentioned the SS.

"Remember, *mademoiselle,* you are retired," Stenger said, giving Madeleine a meaningful glance.

"Of course," Madeleine smiled demurely, slightly inclining her head.

Stenger looked at Madeleine. She was so beautiful, in the way that only daughters of the Mediterranean can be. The years of killing and running hadn't harmed her savage beauty. In the last few days he had learned more about her and concluded that his decision to spare her might have been one of the best decisions of his life. There was no bloodthirstiness in her.

CHAPTER **FORTY-FIVE**

Stenger rode with a small detachment of regular army troops past the small road sign marking the entrance to the doomed town of Ouradour. Their vehicle pulled up to a roadblock staffed by some SS troops.

"May I help you, Major?" the soldier asked, having made no move to have the truck blocking further access to the town moved.

"Yes, you can move that truck and let me through."

"Can't sir. My orders are to allow no one in without permission from General Lammerding."

"How about permission from his senior officer Field Marshall Erwin Rommel?" Stenger said handing over an enclosed case holding one of several copies of his orders signed by the Field Marshall.

"I, I don't know if..." the soldier said, clearly confused.

"See this insignia, corporal? Military police. I am giving you a direct order. If you do not follow it I will have you shot on the spot. Perhaps I'll order one of those fellows to do it." Stenger had allowed his voice to build until he was shouting. He had stood up in the vehicle and unbuttoned the flap covering his side arm. The corporal's eyes had grown to the size of saucers as he shrunk in the face of Stenger's barrage.

"Move that truck," the corporal stammered as he hastened to distance himself from Stenger and his pistol.

Stenger intentionally glared at the corporal as they passed and the men proceeded into the town. As they entered the outskirts Stenger's driver slowed. It wasn't long before the men in the vehicle grew silent as they surveyed the damage. It seemed as if every building had been demolished and then set on fire. Stenger's face was grim as he directed the driver to stop in the village square.

"Spread out, I want pictures and notes taken. We will meet back in an hour." Stenger said, exiting the vehicle.

The men moved cautiously, as if on hallowed ground. It was clear that something evil had taken place. Stenger didn't have to walk far before he saw signs that a crime scene had been compromised. Heavy equipment had been used to move earth and, presumably, bodies. There was evidence in every building he looked into of arson and cremation. In their haste, charred body parts had been overlooked as they had been hastily collected and most likely shoved into communal graves. An untrained eye might have missed the pieces of human bone scattered everywhere. To Stenger it represented an unmistakable trail of evidence. It looked like a bone yard.

Walking out from the perimeter of the town, Stenger approached the remnants of a small church and looked inside. He saw more than one child's clog that had not been completely engulfed by the flames and explosions that had ravaged the church. He saw blood cooked by the intense heat into the porous stone floor of the building. Tears stood in his eyes as he realized the true magnitude of the barbarity that had obliterated the people of the small town. He had seen carnage in war, and as a detective in civilian life. He had seen dead children, both as casualties of war and as victims of the worst of crimes. He knew instinctively that hundreds of women and children had died in the most horrible manner imaginable within the confines of a house of God. The evidence was beyond dispute. He raised his own camera and began to take pictures, having to stop periodically to wipe tears from his eyes so that he could do his work and record the shadows that remained of an unspeakable act that demanded justice. He knew that his report would be read with the usual degree of efficiency and then no significant action would be taken. Stenger shook his head silently, horrified that such a crime would go unpunished and the victims forgotten. He was not so calloused by war that his humanity was corrupted. In truth it was the one thing that saw him through his first war, killing to keep himself and his friends alive. Humanity drove him to pursue a life of service and to hunt down those that preyed on innocence.

Once he finished, Stenger went back to the church for one last look. He was about to make the hardest decision of his life, and he wanted to be as close to God and the victims of the town as possible. As he looked inside his eyes caught sight of a small, smoke damaged crucifix nailed up in a recessed area that had escaped the brunt of the damage. The small figure of Christ seemed to be looking at him silently, imploring the decision that took root in his mind. The German high command might never seek to punish the guilty, but he knew somebody who would, a champion so fierce that nothing could keep her from getting revenge.

CHAPTER FORTY-SIX

Madeleine sat silently looking at the photographs Stenger quietly set down in front of her as he explained the situation. Willi silently examined the floor as the enormity of the crime settled upon them.

"You are sure this is Oradour sur Glane, Major Stenger?" Madeleine said in a steady, even tone. There was neither pain nor anger in her voice, only the cold distant promise of retribution.

"Yes, Ms. Toche," Stenger said, adopting a little formality as he felt the transformation begin in Madeleine. She had been showing signs of trust and happiness. It was clear that a friendship was developing between them.

"Everyone?"

"If they were in town."

"My cousin and her four year old daughter then?"

"I have no way to know, I am sorry."

Madeleine nodded almost imperceptibly, acknowledging her belief in Stenger's compassion. She remembered mentioning to Stenger that she had family in the region days before the tragedy occurred.

"I appreciate you telling me. It is a demonstration of trust and I cannot tell you how I have lacked an ability to trust for so long. Had this information come to me before I was captured I would have killed every officer responsible and every soldier under their command that I could find. I am bound by my oath although every tiny piece of me is screaming for revenge. I cannot explain it, Major. It lives inside me and its strength is terrible to resist."

"What I am about to say I will deny if ever questioned. I am a soldier and a police officer. I trust in the law and justice but that is impossible here. Something must be done, something I cannot do," Stenger said, his eyes locking on hers.

Madeleine watched Stenger walk over to a beat up old cupboard over the sink. He reached in and took out a small bundle and placed it on the table along with a box of ammunition. He unwrapped the contents and handed them over to Madeleine. She silently accepted her pistol and silencer, remembering another man she held in the highest regard hand her a similar pistol years ago in another kitchen. Willi watched, a sadness crossing his face as the realization of what was happening set in.

"Willi, I gave my word to you," Madeleine said giving him the final say.

"When you go, keep your head down, soldier. *Das Reich* are animals," he said as he stood and walked out of the room, gently placing his hand on her shoulder in affirmation as he passed.

Without another word Madeleine stood, tucking the pistol under her clothing.

"Any idea where and who, Major?" Madeleine asked as if ordering a cup of coffee on the terrace of some quaint café.

"I believe a Major Diekmann was in command. By now they should be in Normandy, possibly around Caen." Stenger said without hesitation.

"We will meet again, Major."

"Yes, we will *mademoiselle.* I know of a lovely little restaurant just off the beach in La Ciotat," Stenger said, a grim little smile playing on the corner of his lips his internal struggle rending him inside. He hoped he was right.

"You and Willi keep your heads down too," Madeleine said and left the room without further preamble.

Stenger waited and Willi walked back into the room shortly after she left.

"We never really caught her, did we, Horsty?" Willi said placing a bottle of cognac and two coffee cups on the table.

"You can't catch the night, Willi. You can't catch the night," Stenger almost whispered, holding his cup up as Willi poured.

CHAPTER **FORTY-SEVEN**

John Trunce looked at the little scrap of map he had and knew he was lost. He was roughly where he was supposed to be, but the fight was behind him. Not only was he behind enemy lines, he was behind the enemy. He needed to find the fight, and then get back through and find the American army, if he could. That would be step one; he'd find his company after that.

Madeleine walked into a small hotel in a village approximately thirty miles from the front. She traveled more openly under the auspices of returning home from employment in the south. There was little likelihood that anyone had time to look for the Angel of Death with the decisive campaign of the war being waged in Normandy. She had covered a great deal of distance with little or no concrete idea of where or how she would find *Das Reich*, much less Major Diekmann. He was first on the list. Her plan was to move towards the first allied army she could find and get word to London. The SOE would know where *Das Reich* was, and then she would. The fact that she would have to cross both the German and Allied lines didn't faze her. She knew she could pick an easier area on the edge of the fighting and make her way through. All she knew at this point was to make her way towards Carentan. It was pivotal strategically for both sides. She knew that if she tried to travel straight North she would be heading towards the more heavily reinforced German areas. She avoided Resistance groups along the way. She had operated alone for this long; she didn't want to get sidetracked or captured. It was best this way. She could tell from the demeanor of the civilians she encountered and spoke with where the battle was headed. No one knew for sure, and by no means had the French declared victory. Most people just prayed that their town would be spared as the two

Goliaths pounded one another. Her cover story was always the same, she was waiting to meet a relative leaving a town in the path of battle. It got her closer with each day. Her plan was simple and familiar. She would locate Diekmann's regiment, then the man himself, and put a bullet in his eye. She knew she couldn't kill them all in the midst of a pitched battle. She would find him when he came off the line. He was a Major, after all, and would be directing battle as orders came down from command. Northern France was a vast area to be looking for one man, but she knew that if his division was engaged he would be there and she would find him.

Madeleine had eaten a good meal and was able to find a room in a small family hotel. Most people were moving away from the battle. The proprietors were much like her family. Once you've poured your love into a business, leaving it behind is unthinkable. The family was as resolute as hers would be. When the battle came, they would lock the front door, put a 'closed' sign in the window and retreat to the basement until the storm passed.

She was no farther than thirty miles away from Carentan and knew that she was approaching the rear of the German army. The closer she got the more immediate she felt the need for something more powerful than two small caliber pistols. She had trained with everything the SOE provided. She wanted to avoid open combat, but she knew it was a possibility. She would be conspicuous in any event and intended to keep to the shadows as much as possible. If she could find a German MP-34 machine pistol she would be content with that. It had massive firepower and could take out a platoon of men in seconds. Her plan was to kill an SS soldier and "borrow" his.

John Trunce hid among the brambles of a hedgerow as a small German patrol walked by. They were moving quietly, speaking in whispers. They were disciplined and experienced troops. He waited to see if they were indeed alone, scanning the area in all directions for stragglers or a rear guard. He had been trained in ambush and had killed several men during action in Italy. Once the men passed he stepped from his hiding place and shot them in rapid succession. He moved quickly over to investigate.

The three were dead and he checked them for anything that might let him know more precisely where he was. He stripped the men of their weapons and slung one of the machine guns and some extra ammo over his shoulder. He also found grenades and what turned out to be an old road map. It was crude, but he was glad to have it. He knew that he was somewhere near Carentan, having spotted a road sign earlier. Knowing where he was, all he had to do now was decide where he was going. He pulled the dead soldiers off the road and under the cover of the hedgerows that seemed to be everywhere. He had hardened since the excitement of his first taste of combat in Italy. Even then, as scared as he and his buddies had been he always was able to temper that fear with confidence. He knew it made his chances of survival and doing his duty that much more likely. A soldier without fear gets people killed, but then so does a soldier who is paralyzed by fear. He was something in between, a good soldier.

Madeleine woke up in the middle of the night. There were still many hours before dawn. She decided it was time to move cross-country, find the front, and then try to skirt it. She gave no consideration to waiting until the country was liberated. She could not take the chance that Diekmann would be captured or be withdrawn to where she couldn't reach him. She left the hotel, having paid for her lodging the previous evening. She walked out of the town and headed north across the first field she found.

Madeleine kept up a steady pace, eager to cover as much ground as possible under the cover of darkness. She kept to the edge of the hedgerows and trees so that she could quickly take cover if necessary. The sounds of the day's earlier battle were sporadic now, as if there had been some unspoken agreement to cease-fire until the sun came up and the killing could begin again the next morning. From time to time there was a brief exchange of gunfire as scouting patrols ran into one another. She knew she wouldn't be able to move well during the day with the heavy shelling and continuous exchanges of gunfire.

After many hours of steady walking Madeleine started to see the evidence of small skirmishes. There were dead soldiers in small groups from both sides. She saw the insignia of American troops for the first time.

As Madeleine came closer to a small hamlet she heard the sound of German voices. Her plan required avoiding all combatants if possible. She moved quickly into a hedgerow and burrowed down into the damp leaves and twigs. She was glad that it was early summer. The ground was wet and the leaves made no noise as she pulled them over herself. She watched as the patrol came by. These were soldiers of the German regular army and seemed less cautious than a squad hellbent on ambushing the enemy. They were green troops, and by the careless way they walked and spoke, they simply did not seem to know any better. She was a veteran of the ambush. She had killed more than one Gestapo officer by remaining hidden before the kill. It was remarkable how her profession so easily relied on the simplest traits of human nature. Once her targets were discovered and the alarm raised, the soldiers scattered in every direction out from the killing ground to find the killer. No one thought to search the immediate area. Soldiers weren't trained as assassins.

As she lay in the dark Madeleine reminded herself that now was the time to be more cautious than ever. She could hear the old German's whisper in her ear, "there will come a time when passion, and not duty calls on you to kill. That is dangerous territory. Driven by passion you may kill indiscriminately, and that leads to a place from which you can never fully return."

Madeleine stood and moved out from under the brambles and watched the road for some time before she continued down it. Eventually she would have to go around the more fortified and entrenched positions. She considered finding some more protected hiding place to wait for the battle to proceed past her. Every instinct told her that mobility kept her options open. Suddenly she saw a figure step fully into the road fifty yards ahead of her. She crouched down automatically and moved her body, crablike, towards the hedgerow. The figure started to move carefully in her direction. Had she been spotted? She believed not; she had been in the shadows when she'd first seen the movement. She eased her pistol from the pocket of the dark sweater she wore and carefully screwed the silencer into place. The man was moving cautiously, stopping every so often to look all around him. He had the feel of someone with combat experience expecting an ambush. It was a dangerous but necessary game. Once the battle began it was right in your neighborhood, the immediate hundred feet around you. All the best planning and training went out the window and things became very personal.

Madeleine carefully turned her head, never taking her eyes off the man. It was too dark to make out his uniform. Without warning the man crouched, crossed over to her side of the road and proceeded directly towards her. Every nerve in her body tingled as a wave of adrenaline passed through her, spreading electrically out from her core. She quieted her mind and slowly pulled the pistol up the length of her torso, keeping it in the dark shadow of her profile. She held it next to her face as the man crept forward. He must have sensed something, as he seemed to hesitate and peer into the hole of shadows in which she hid. He waited for what seemed like an eternity. Madeleine was not used to being hunted. She instinctively knew that the soldier could feel a presence. She had only one weapon upon which she could rely, born of training and endless dark nights alone with her fears, her thoughts, her uncertainty and the endless waiting. There was no one to share her thoughts with to help shoulder the burden she carried, no one to ease her mind through the bond of companionship. She was alone. Some people found the courage to act through the strength of those around them. She had only herself and her cold lonely courage.

"There is somebody out there, Johnny," Trunce mouthed to himself without making a sound, his eyes darting around nervously. His mouth felt like dust but his hands were damp. This was not good. He'd never find a friendly face in this place, he thought. He had been clambering around for several days now. He was way off the grid but every time he tried to get closer to the fighting another German patrol would blunder by. What was he thinking? That he could just run to the front and skip over to the other side? With all these damn hedgerows there were hundreds of little battles everywhere. There was no defined front. Well, what did he expect? He reminded himself, I'm Airborne, and we're always surrounded! He just wished that he could be surrounded with a few buddies. He couldn't do shit on his own except an ambush here and there. He could do that just fine but he was trained to fight in a team. Tonight he was a goddamn guerrilla and he was sure there was another bush fighter out there just down the road! He had a signaling device in his breast pocket, a little metal toy that made a clicking sound. One click was supposed to be answered by two. There was no way he was going to click that damn thing until he knew what the hell was waiting in the dark. He lowered his body to the ground and began to crawl with his weapon held diagonally in front of him. He swished back and forth as he pulled himself ahead, snake like into the gloom. Man, it was dark but there were pockets of cave dark along the sides of the road. His night vision was good but Dracula couldn't have seen anything in there. He paused and listened for a cough, the rustle of fabric, the sound of a safety disengaging, anything. He started to think that he might have been imagining things.

"You had better speak English," a voice whispered as a round metal object was pressed carefully into his ear. A thousand thoughts raced through his mind.

"82nd Airborne, on your side, I hope."

"Keep your eyes ahead and tell me if anyone is on the road."

"Not that I can see."

"Now, slowly turn your head and look behind you. I will not be looking away. If you move abruptly, you die. You will not hear the shot."

Trunce knew better than to try anything. There was something chilling in the voice as it spoke. It didn't carry threat; it carried certainty. He would die if he didn't do exactly as he was told.

"Clear."

"Leave your weapon and stand up slowly and move back onto the road."

Trunce stood carefully and walked a few paces backwards into the road. He strained to see back into the darkness and saw a small figure rising up from the ground, a pistol and silencer pointed at his chest.

"You are cautious, I will give you that, Airborne. Now, any chance you have a cigarette?" Madeleine said stepping out from the darkness.

Trunce could barely believe his eyes. He felt his body uncoil and relax. She looked hardly older than he was. He could tell from the way she stood and the outline of her body that she was very much a woman, though.

"I have a pack in my pocket. May I get them?"

"Get two," Madeleine said suddenly lowering her gun. "Let's both have one."

Trunce had a thousand questions but instinctively knew that now was not the time to start asking them. He lit two cigarettes and handed one to Madeleine. When she stepped closer to take it he could see the features of her face and the hard grace of her body. She reminded him of a cat. She was a frightening mixture of beauty and implicit threat.

"*Merci*," Madeleine said and tasted the tobacco. She relaxed as she blew the smoke out and she looked at Trunce.

"May I pick up my weapon, ma'am?" He asked.

"Of course. We may yet need to kill a few Germans."

"French Resistance?" John asked, unable to bridle his curiosity.

"British Intelligence, SOE."

"Well, that explains it then."

"Explains what?"

"Why you were better than me back there."

"You were pretty good yourself. I am trained to wait. Sometimes it seems forever. But forever has come in the form of the United States Airborne."

"At your service," John said with a slow salute. "May I ask what you are trained to do?" John asked casually.

"To kill Germans."

"Then we have something in common already," John laughed quietly.

Madeleine couldn't help but chuckle at the insanity of it all.

They were two young people who could have just as easily stepped out of a dance hall for a quick smoke and a chat. She found herself liking the young soldier immediately. He had a calm, easy way about him. He hadn't shown any fear and seemed to care less that she was a woman. At least he had the sense not to comment on it. Maybe he was being deferential, but in her heart she didn't think so. The man simply had an ability to go with the moment, to adapt and improvise. She was sure there weren't many like him. Not so young and attractive anyway. She had to admit to herself that he was handsome in an open, natural way. He was lean but broad shouldered and held himself with the kind of casual grace that cannot be learned. It was the mark of being at home within one's own skin.

"I need to find my unit," Trunce said.

"That will do for me also. I must get word to the British command. I need some information."

"Then what?"

"Then I go back in and kill a few SS," Madeleine said casually.

"Back in? So the war won't yet be over for you either."

"My war has been a long one, but I have one more duty to perform before I can lay down my weapons and pick up a spoon."

"You don't seem much like a housewife. You must be a cook then."

"I am nobody's wife, not yet," she replied meaningfully.

"Courting someone?" Trunce said, accentuating his Missouri drawl.

"Oh yes, we've courted," she replied wistfully, a secret smile playing on her lips, obviously misunderstanding the meaning of the word. John caught it too and felt himself blush and smile simultaneously.

Madeleine realized her mistake and laughed too. "Courting means dating, not the other?"

"Yes, although sometimes there's some pretty close dating."

The two paused briefly and surveyed the road.

"I hope you have a better idea of where we are than I do," Trunce admitted.

"We are between Caen and Carentan."

"Carentan was one of our objectives. I am way off. My plane was hit and the pilot struggled with the controls for a long time. There was so much confusion that my stick didn't make it out all at once. I barely did."

"And the plane?"

"I don't know. Many planes were hit. I got out, that's all I know. I hope the pilots made it," Trunce said uncertainly.

"The Germans have much to answer for. There are so many dead. My brother among them."

"I am sorry to hear that. I have a brother too. He's younger, though. I can't imagine your loss."

"We had best be moving. It will be light soon and we won't be able to move as easily."

"Lead the way. By the way, may I ask your name?"

"Madeleine, and yours?"

"John," he said holding out his hand. She took it. He was amazed at the firmness of her small hand's grip. There was nothing delicate about her, he thought, but he kept stealing a glance here and there. She was a beauty, but not in a doll-like way. She was ethereal, as if formed from the most dark and terrible things of the earth into a thing of splendid radiance. He knew that he'd come across someone special. Without a second thought he knew he'd die to protect her.

The two set out, moving quietly now. When they spoke it was in whispers. There was a discipline between them. They moved as one. They both were happy to be with another person. Especially one so highly trained.

As they walked, night thinned and the first glow of the sun peeked over the horizon. The shadows became weaker and their need for stealth increased.

"Where do you think you are going?" A harsh German voice bellowed through the pre-dawn silence.

Madeleine and Trunce quickly found cover and crept forward. The voice had come from around a bend in the road.

"This one looks like Resistance," another taunting German voice broke in.

Madeleine peered over the trunk of a fallen log and saw a squad of German soldiers surrounding a small wagon. A family sat on the wagon as the four soldiers roughly dug through a haphazard heap of their belongings. Madeleine saw one of the soldiers, dirty from battle, pulling a young woman from the cart, the girl's mother struggling to hold onto her.

"*Non*," the father cried out.

"Shut up, you," another soldier yelled and smashed his rifle butt into the man's face, crushing his nose, blood spurting out as it ruptured.

John raised his rifle to fire and Madeleine quickly put her hand up in front of his face. She motioned for him to flank around the side. Placing her mouth on his ear she whispered, "Wait. Fire only if you need to." He nodded his understanding as Madeleine crawled silently around the other side of the group, her silenced pistol held slightly raised in front of her. Trunce moved to flank from the other side, careful not to create a crossfire with Madeline's position. What he saw next he would remember for the rest of his life.

Without breaking her forward movement, Madeleine came out from the brush immediately behind and to the right of the cart. She raised her silenced pistol and shot the two soldiers nearest her. John saw a hole sprout between the eyes of each man in rapid succession. She then simply walked forward without haste and put two bullets in the side of the soldier's head as he was trying to pull the girl off to the side. She shot the fourth as she casually stepped over the body of the third man. He had hesitated, fumbling with his rifle, and that mistake cost him everything. Trunce had seen killing and done it himself in battle. But he had never seen it done as effortlessly and surgically as now. The look on Madeleine's face held no animation, her black eyes fixed on each man as she struck. In that instant John knew how lucky he had been last night. She would have killed him without any hesitation. An enormous respect for her solidified in his mind, along with a healthy measure of fear. She was no ordinary agent reporting on troop movements, she was death itself.

The woman holding her husband's head on the cart was

paralyzed with fear. Madeleine had moved over to the terrified girl who had watched her abductor simply melt away to her side as Madeline's bullets tore into his brain.

Madeleine lowered her pistol and slowly put her arm around the girl's shoulder. She led her back to her parents. The father looked through the blood that ran down his face and whispered, "*Merci, merci.*"

"*Partez maintenant*!" Madeleine said gesturing down the road with her head.

"*Est- vous, L'ange de la mort*?" The young woman asked as she passed.

"*Je suis une fille de France,*" Madeleine answered with a quick nod in affirmation. She had gone a long time without any praise or recognition for her dangerous work.

The two women smiled grimly, pride showing behind their eyes, it was an emotion Madeleine had not seen on the streets of her country for too long. It was the pride of the undefeated, knowing France would be free again. As the cart proceeded past the corpses of the Germans, the little family did not even afford the dead a glance. The soldiers were only so much dirt beneath the hooves of their horse.

As the cart passed, John walked out from his position. Madeleine had already started to drag one of the bodies to the side of the road and into the brush. John did the same and soon they had covered the soldiers and made a perfunctory search of their persons. Madeleine watched the respect Trunce gave the dead. He did not riffle through their pockets looking for valuables. Two of the men had watches that he left on their wrists.

"No plunder for the victor?" Madeline asked breaking their silence.

"Not mine to take," he said simply.

Madeleine shook her head in agreement and walked over to the middle of the road.

"Remind me not to make you angry," John said, catching her eye. She smiled firmly in return.

"Do you see the insignia on those lapels? Those are SS *Panzer;* they are experienced soldiers. Two of them had ribbons from the Russian winter war. They are hard men, and animals. They raped their way across Russia and liked it. The Russians will exact their revenge for themselves. I will do it for the French."

"*Panzer* means tanks. Things are going to get complicated," John said as the rumbling of artillery began in the distance.

"The middle of a tank battle is a bad place to be," Madeleine said, stating the obvious.

"Tanks support infantry and vice-versa. If we're not blown to pieces we might find friendly forces," John replied.

"Then let's go find them," Madeleine said striding off towards the cannon fire.

"Here we go," John muttered, turning to follow.

As they approached the battle, Madeleine and John increased their pace. Gone was the time for stealth, as any soldiers they encountered now would be in combat. Madeleine carried the German machine gun John had taken the previous day. If they had to fight, her pistol would be of limited use. The shells screamed overhead and the ground shook as they hit the earth.

The sound of a machine gun's constant staccato was just in front of them as they left the road and made their way up the side of a small hill. Walking on the road this close to the battle would be suicide. Both armies would have fortified positions, expecting armor or troop transport along any passable road. There would be no way through that route. At the crest of the hill smoke from the battle and the screams of the wounded rose up from below. In every direction there were entrenchments of German soldiers facing the opposite direction.

"We need to punch a hole through somewhere. It might as well be here," John said, checking his ammunition.

"See you on the other side of that field," Madeleine responded as they both stood and fired into the two entrenchments in front of them. John emptied his rifle into the machine gunner and his belt man as Madeleine fired short bursts into another. John knew he was seeing fire discipline of the highest magnitude as she advanced. Suddenly a shell screamed out of the sky and landed directly to her side. She was blasted away from it, as if torn off her feet by a giant hand. John yelled and ran to her side. He grabbed her by one arm and threw her over his back as he scrambled for cover. He ran with her to the nearest machine gun nest and dove into it with her over his shoulder. Bullets came from every direction as the Germans realized that they'd been attacked from the rear. The advancing Allied soldiers were also firing on their position. John grabbed the German machine gun and fired immediately on the German position to his right. They were stuck between shooting to keep the advancing soldiers at bay and this new threat from their left. John walked the heavy caliber bullets up the ground and into their flank. He then immediately swung the gun around and fired into the position to his left. As he did so, he felt a bullet rip through his left shoulder, leaving a deep gouge. As he began to turn, Madeleine threw herself into the back of the trench and fired into a group of soldiers directly behind them. A few were killed and the others threw themselves to the ground or behind whatever cover they could find. They were completely surrounded. Bullets hit the dirt and sand bags all around them. Madeleine and John caught one another's eyes for the briefest instant, communicating a fierce commitment.

Bullets slammed into their sandbagged position from all directions. John tossed his two grenades towards the German line to their right and left. The air was charged with the overwhelming odor of gunpowder and explosives and the air was a mixture of heavy smoke and dirt that hung dispersed like a screen over the battlefield. Men were dying and screaming all around them as Madeleine and John fought for their lives.

In rapid succession two German stick grenades, called potato mashers after their shape, landed behind John. Madeleine was on each instantly, flinging them back at the Germans one after the other. John was amazed at her presence of mind and cool demeanor under fire. There was more fight in her than a squad of men, he thought. While he poured bullets into the enemy, Madeleine conserved her ammunition, exposing herself to fire for the briefest instant while she mechanically and unerringly killed each target. It was a frightening thing to see, a raw display of discipline and sheer guts under fire. It was like watching a marksman plink ducks in the shooting gallery back at the Patience County Fair. Together they were pure warriors without fear or caution. They fought flat out.

Suddenly John ducked down and tore off his paratrooper jacket. He tossed it so that it laid over the front of the nest.

"Flash!" He heard yelled from the edge of the trees nearby. How he heard it over the crash of gunfire and explosions he didn't know.

"Thunder!" He yelled over and over bringing the machine gun to bear again on both flanks. Madeleine and he had created a weak point in the line and he could see flashes of American uniforms from behind trees and brushes. Without warning two men threw themselves into his fox hole and joined Madeleine firing from behind. Even in the heat of battle the two men were shocked to see a stunningly beautiful woman firing into the enemy and killing them right and left. They joined in her fire and poured it onto the enemy position.

Soon other soldiers moved up as the German line retreated. Madeleine heard the metal upon metal squeak of tank tracks and saw the American star on the side of several tanks crashing ahead of the advancing soldiers. Madeleine slid down to the bottom of the trench as the firing moved away and the Germans retreated.

"Welcome to France," she breathed heavily as she reached out to accept a cigarette from John.

"Nice welcome. Is everyone here as hospitable as you?" one of the other soldiers laughed.

"Not to Germans, they've been here long enough." She stood up and moved away from the trench and past the astonished faces of American soldiers as they ran past her towards the fighting.

"Hey buddy, who the hell is that? French Resistance?" The second soldier asked.

"Nope, British Intelligence," John said, clearly enjoying his chance to shock the two men. He smiled as he looked at the incredulous expression on the men's faces. He stood up and wiped the sweat and dirt from his eyes as he caught up to Madeleine.

"Last thing I remember was flying through the air,"

Madeline said putting her hand on John's shoulder. "Thank you."

"We're even on that score. You were great back there. I would pick you every time over three good men. I thought we were done for."

"We have the singular distinction of having two enemies fire on us at once," Madeleine said.

"I think we should try to avoid that in the future."

"Yes John, I think we should."

CHAPTER **FORTY-EIGHT**

"Teach, you're familiar with Caen. What's our best plan for deployment along these sectors?" General Montgomery asked Jack as several men stood around a map table hastily set up not far from the front as British armor rolled towards Caen. They stood inside a large canvas tent that served as the British temporary command center.

"There's high ground towards the back that we have to take quickly, sir. We don't want this thing to turn into a siege. We know we have *Panzer* resistance and my latest reports tell me that in addition to determined infantry, we are up against the *Das Reich* division. They have a solid reputation for nastiness, sir. They barely got away from the Russian front, and then only in pieces. Things became very unholy there, sir. They will make us pay for every inch we get."

Montgomery listened carefully as Teach spoke. It was clear that Jack knew what he was talking about. Montgomery was either loved or hated by the various allied commanders, but he was always respected. He had bravado and courage that inspired his men. This too was his second war, too, having seen significant action during the last war during which he was so severely wounded that a detail actually dug his grave in anticipation of his death. 'Monty' was credited for expelling the Axis armies from North Africa and was more than happy to face Rommel, his old nemesis, once again.

Jack stepped away from the table as Montgomery left to take a phone call. Jack pushed aside the tent flap and lit a cigarette, looking south as he often did when he thought of Madeleine. There had been no contact except a US military inquiry that had gone through channels requesting information for a field operative.

It wasn't highly classified. It simply requested the last known position of *Das Reich*, the same division that waited for them near Caen. There had been some reports of massive retaliation against the Resistance by the SS. But what would the Americans have to do with that?

Jack had been informed personally about the tragedies at Oradour sur Glane and Tuelle. He was confident that Madeleine wouldn't have been in either place and certainly wouldn't have waited around for capture. Other agents hadn't fared as well. He had received news that Violet Szabo had been captured and sent to a concentration camp. The Resistance had dealt with the Germans responsible in a messy, stupid way. Many mistakes had occurred, on both sides. The German defenses, however fierce, were disorganized and the command structure in some disarray. He could only surmise that Berlin was interfering and frustrating the ability of her commanders on the ground to make quick and effective decisions.

It was well into July, and Montgomery, along with his detractors, thought they should have secured Caen long before now. Teach was frustrated with the lack of progress but several factors including the weather and the ferocity of German Resistance had delayed things. To him, every inch of French soil liberated meant that Madeleine would soon be out of a job. SOE was now assisting with intelligence and ground experience wherever it was useful. Madeleine was part of SOE's "F" section, F standing for France. For his part Jack had been redeployed to Montgomery's staff. He couldn't have asked for a better posting and was told that he had earned it. He would experience first hand the victory England so richly deserved. In addition he had spent a great deal of time in occupied France and knew these areas intimately.

Jack dropped his cigarette and ground it out under his boot. He pushed his thoughts of Madeleine as far back in his mind as possible. He had to concentrate. His personal life would have to wait just as it did for so many other men and women on both sides. The German's weren't going to hand Caen over with their compliments. Yet who knows? He smiled, thinking maybe it was

Madeleine coming at them from the other direction. Somebody was in for one hell of a surprise if Madeleine was after them. A couple of passing soldiers gave him an odd look as he chuckled out loud at the absurdity of the notion.

CHAPTER FORTY-NINE

Madeleine and John sat across from one another in a mess tent just a few hours after breaking through to the American lines. Madeleine relished the strong black coffee and the endless stream of cigarettes and complimentary looks the young American soldiers gave her. John watched all of the attention with a crooked smile on the side of his mouth. If they only knew, he thought. Madeleine flirted a little with the men. They were mostly boys like him from farm families or hardworking city dwellers. They had all lived through the depression and many of their families had barely scraped through. They were used to hard work and treated women with deference. They were glad to share a few moments in the company of a woman as beautiful as she. Madeleine kept them at bay, letting slip that her boyfriend was an officer in the British Military fighting along the same front as they.

After they rested, John introduced Madeleine to his company commander. He had developed a rapport with the officer and told him the full story including Madeleine's attachment with British military intelligence. The commander raised his eyebrows more than once when John described the way Madeleine dispatched the SS soldiers intending to rape the French girl they had encountered.

"SOE, Toche? Tough as nails, the SOE I've heard of," Captain Franklin said as if stating a fact cast in stone. Whatever you need, give me the word. I've already lost too many good men to these SS bastards. Go kill all of their God damn officers for me!"

"I will see to it with pleasure, Captain. I thank you for your service to France."

Madeleine had said the magic words. Franklin saluted her,

a look of stoic pride spreading on his face. He turned and walked out of the mess tent.

"That, John, is a soldier. I already know without asking, he would lead every charge if he could."

"And then some," John answered.

Captain Franklin contacted division headquarters to determine the intelligence on *Das Reich*. Word had come shortly thereafter that the *Panzer* division was reinforcing Caen against Montgomery. The inquiry was fairly routine. The location of the enemy was pretty common knowledge. The enemy was everywhere the Allies wanted to go.

"John, I need one more favor from you before I leave," Madeleine asked.

"Anything, Madeleine," John answered, suddenly remembering that she had to leave. He felt genuinely sorry to see her go. They had shared an instant bond. Friendships like that come once in a lifetime, if you're lucky.

"I need a sniper rifle and adequate ammunition for it. Some kind of case to transport it in would be preferable. I could wait for one from England but that will take too long."

"I'll find you one on one condition."

"What?"

"Write to me later on after you get home. I get letters from home, but they're few and far between."

"Only if you write to me," Madeline said with obvious pleasure.

The lanky paratrooper could tell she liked him, too. Their bond and trust was forged in battle.

John left the tent and found his commanding officer going over some requisition forms near a supply tent.

"Sir, I need to find a sniper rifle for the field agent."

"Go back to ordinance and have one issued on my orders. Just make sure there's no damn paperwork. I see one more damn requisition form and I will take a unit and go commandeer what we need myself," Captain Franklin said, only partially joking.

"That's it, sir?" John said with some surprise.

"You are a hell of a soldier, Trunce. I take for granted what you told me about the SOE agent is true. She is a damn killer. It would be far better to have her out there doing her job than on a boat back to England. Quite frankly, I don't think she's going back until whatever job she has left to do is finished. By the way, sergeant Trunce, I need a new lieutenant around here. You're hired." He strode forward and pinned the lieutenant's bars on Trunce before he could utter a word. "By the way, that's part of the deal too, Trunce, you keep those bars or no rifle. Now get going. I have work to do."

John turned and left before his Captain could change his mind. Jesus, that man was rough and tumble. He was an inspiring leader. Things were a little different in the Airborne. The man just made a decision and didn't agonize over it. There was something to be learned from that and John intended to.

John returned and found Madeleine packing a small sack with a couple of canteens and food rations she'd rounded up.

"With the compliments of the 82nd Airborne," John said handing over the sniper rifle.

"New shiny bars, John?" Madeleine teased, touching his lapel, accidentally brushing against him for a moment.

"I keep the bars, you get the rifle," John said, stepping back slightly and turning his head so that she couldn't see him blush. It's going to take some getting used to having a friend and combat buddy that looks like she does, he thought.

If Madeleine noticed she didn't let on. She hefted the rifle and walked a few paces to a small table. She expertly detached the telescopic sight. Next she broke the rifle down to its constituent parts and then reassembled it in a series of fluid exacting motions. A couple of paratroopers off to the side watched her, their mouths open in surprise.

"I guess I don't have to ask you if you know how to shoot one of those," John said smiling.

"No, I was trained by the best. I am better at close range with a light pistol but I'll need a bit more persuasion than that. There is an agent I know of who is much better than I with any weapon. She is the best shot in the SOE, a British girl not much older than I. Of course the best snipers in the world are women.

There are many hundreds of female snipers in the Red Army. Some have more than two hundred kills. I have that from an infallible source, the man who trained me."

"He must be a formidable man."

"Oddly enough, a German Jew. He was a German war hero in the first war. They rewarded him by throwing his family into a concentration camp and trying to do the same to him."

"He escaped, I take it."

"He killed many of his countrymen escaping. He is a lost soul and the most dangerous man either of us is likely to ever know. I feel sad for him. When the war is over he will have nowhere to go and probably no one to go home to."

"War isn't just armies and battles is it, Madeleine?"

"No, John, it's about politics, power, and the elite. It is about people like you and me torn from our loved ones and our lives when all we want to do is live a good life. That's all I want. I want a husband who loves me, some children and a little restaurant to call home."

Madeleine picked up the rifle and the small bag.

"You keep your head down, John. We will meet again some sunny day *en Provence*!" Madeleine said with a flourish and walked out of the tent.

John waited a moment, not wanting to follow her like some puppy dog. But finally he couldn't help but step out and look for her. It had only been a couple of minutes but she had vanished into the wind.

"The British will be coming again soon, Major Diekmann," Lieutenant Boche said, looking through field glasses at the preparations the British were making below in the lower part of the city of Caen. The town had seen fierce fighting as the Germans tried to hold onto it. Diekmann and his men were dug in on the high ground on the far side of Caen. The strategic importance of the town was too great to simply abandon it to the allied advance. His orders were "to die in Caen". When the German High Command regrouped for a counter attack a major crossroads like Caen would be of vital importance. It represented one of many stepping-stones to Paris and, ultimately, the heart of Germany.

"Let them come. We'll show them more of the same. We have more armor arriving and will give them a nasty surprise, Diekmann answered.

"How was Paris?" Boche said casually, not taking his eyes from the glasses.

"You mean the obligatory inquiry? Nothing much happened. I expect that nothing will. Everything is tied to the outcome of the war and they weren't about to pull a field commander from the front. The General intervened as well, I am sure. Perhaps they realize that if we have any chance in this war that we must show no mercy. The Fuhrer now has rockets falling on London and there are new weapons being deployed. There are only war crimes trials for the conquered. I appreciate your being unavailable for the inquiry."

"I am glad, Major. Those people were terrorists and terrorist sympathizers."

"Well, I am going to check our forward positions, Lieutenant," Diekmann said as he stepped out from behind their entrenched position.

Several hundred yards away in a blind constructed of brambles and field grasses, Madeleine watched the small building that had been fortified by surrounding it with sand bags. Earlier she had been much closer to the building armed only with her pistol and field glasses, having hidden the sniper rifle for later retrieval. She had lain hidden for hours watching the German officers preparing for battle. She was close enough to identify that the division was *Das Reich* and by process of elimination she had picked out the more senior officers. One in particular, a major, seemed to be constantly on the move. There was a violent, bullying air about him. He matched the description that she had been able to obtain through Resistance contacts. It had to be Diekmann. Regardless, she saw every man in the regiment as a criminal. If she shot the wrong pig by mistake she could live with it. Madeleine considered the enormity of the additional evidence.

There had been a few very lucky survivors of Oradour sur Glane. They recounted their terrifying ordeals once the Germans were gone as they returned to the ruin of their village. It had been almost completely decimated. None of the buildings were inhabitable, even the one that the German's had occupied, drinking the contents of the owner's wine cellar in an impromptu celebration, as he lay dead in a hole somewhere. The next day his home, too, was torched.

One woman had escaped the church through a back window, along with a young mother and her baby. The three had been machine-gunned, but the older woman had survived by crawling away to hide in a nearby field. Miraculously, some wounded men had escaped. As the barn they were in was set ablaze they were able to crawl away and hide. Diekmann and his *der Fuhrer* regiment had gone on a looting and killing orgy. Bodies were found down the well at the center of town. Madeleine needed no further proof. Diekmann would never see a courts marshal. She was going to send him straight to a higher authority for judgment.

"I see you, Diekmann," She whispered. She moved over to the rifle, nestled in a makeshift cradle to steady her shot. With a few minor adjustments she readied the scope and rechecked the distance and wind velocity. She positioned herself behind the rifle and saw Diekmann standing alone. She put the cross hairs of the telescopic sight on the side of his head. The arrogant fool refused to wear a helmet. That can be dangerous, she thought coldly. Diekmann seemed oblivious to the malice that radiated from her. She felt her heart beat and regulated her breathing. The finger of her right hand curled evenly around the trigger. She released her breath slowly and between heartbeats squeezed the trigger. The heavy grain bullet ripped apart Diekmann's head long before the report of the rifle was heard. She was so far away that little sound reached the German troops. Diekmann collapsed as every muscle in his body simultaneously relaxed. It was almost a minute before anyone noticed his inert body on the ground. Men took cover when the gun's report reached their ears. He was clearly dead and it was several minutes before lieutenant Boche crawled over and inspected Diekmann's body. He looked down at what was left of the man's head, the eyes vacant and cloudy.

"Move the Major's body and cover it for burial," he told two attending soldiers. He looked in the direction the shot must have come from and was puzzled. If the sniper was an advance scout he would have continued firing as a signal for a British advance. Neither happened. Diekmann had been singled out and assassinated. A cold chill ran down his spine as he considered what that meant. There was a killer out there that had specifically targeted Diekmann. For all he knew maybe the sniper had been sent from Berlin in an attempt to put an end to the ramifications of the business at Oradour sur Glane. The general himself may have ordered the killing. Equally disturbing was the notion that someone else was retaliating. If that was so, it might never end. Was he next? He scanned the horizon and knew that he needed some kind of answer. He assembled a squad of three men and piled into a vehicle with a mounted machine gun in case the British decided it was time to start the war again and attack.

Not far away, Captain Teach stood among several officers preparing to signal the British advance against Caen. The men looked at each other as they scanned the horizon with their binoculars looking for the shooter.

"That didn't come from our side, lads. The sound was from Jerry's flank. I don't remember sending a scouting party over there, it would be bloody suicide at this point. Maybe some *Maquis* is taking pot shots at the Hun."

"That was no potshot, Harry," Teach said, addressing his fellow officer. If the shooter is who I think it is, there is a dead German in hell right now."

The men looked at Teach. His face glowed with something they couldn't label.

"Not one of your old crew, eh Jack?"

"You know I can't tell you that, old boy," Jack said with a jovial pat to the man's back. "If I did, I'd have to kill you."

The assembled men chuckled, as they broke apart to attend to their duties.

"Soon, Madeleine," Jack whispered aloud as he walked towards the command tent.

A short while later Lieutenant Boche was summoned over by one of his men.

"I think we found the weapon, Lieutenant," a young soldier said, pointing to the sniper rifle laying where it had been fired. "It took us a while to get close. We weren't sure the shooter had moved on. The man must have some talent to make a head shot from this distance."

Boche walked over and looked down at the rifle still cradled in the shooting stand. The bolt had been removed, rendering the weapon useless without repair. He walked over and reached down and picked up a small hat that was carefully laid next to the weapon. It was a tiny scrap of a thing but he recognized it for what it was immediately. The killer had left behind a tiny baby's bonnet charred and discolored with smoke. Inside the bonnet was a small piece of bread. His insides turned to ice as he remembered the screams of the children of Oradour. He remembered hearing that one of the soldiers had thrown a live baby into the oven of the local bakery. Their ghosts sought vengeance and this was the beginning. Boche turned and walked away, trying to banish the memories from his mind. But the sound of hundreds of tiny feet marching in wooden clogs drummed accusingly in his head.

CHAPTER **FIFTY**

Madeleine was sitting in Colonel Maurice Buckmaster's office. He was head of F section and responsible for the SOE activities in occupied France. He had been the man who had originally interviewed her over tea and scones. Those days seemed a lifetime away. The Colonel was a much more relaxed man now that his directive in the war had been accomplished.

Madeleine received years of back pay as an ensign and used some of it to put herself up in the Ritz hotel and to purchase some new clothes. She smiled at the memory of the British women as they watched her make her way through the expensive shop making several purchases, her confidence adding a layer of sophistication and depth to her already stunning good looks.

Buckmaster returned her smile. She looked chic and stylish in clothes tailored to fit her. She had gone to Harrods and received a full beauty treatment and was turning heads in the street wherever she went. There was a porcelain quality to her skin, complementing her fine bone structure and features that had taken on a more sensual look than the twenty year old girl his section had sent to France as a killer. He found himself having to break eye contact with her often. Funny after all he had endured that he would feel like a schoolboy in the presence of one of his own operatives.

"I don't suppose I can talk you into undertaking another mission, Madeleine. Germany is far from defeated and a person with your talents can be very useful."

"No, Colonel. I am finished. I have completed my assignment and leave the rest of the fighting to the soldiers. France will be completely free very soon. Once the south is liberated, I will return to La Ciotat and my family."

"You have served your country and the cause of freedom with utter distinction. There will be medals and honors for you once this is all done." Buckmaster slowly poured the tea in the formal manner that gave him such pleasure. It was the simple things that reminded him that Britain had endured her people and traditions, her backbone. He was just bursting with patriotic pride these days. Many agents had been lost to the war, some perished in battle, and others suffered a slower death in concentration camps. The Germans would have much to atone for and he intended to participate in whatever wartime tribunals were established to punish the atrocities of the Nazis.

"I wonder, Colonel. Assassination hardly ranks in the gentlemanly art of war. I was the hammer of the dirty tricks department. I killed so many."

"Madeleine, every flight that bombs German towns kills hundreds and thousands of civilians. For the most part, all of your targets were military and, I might add, some of the most demented and unholy of men that have ever walked the face of the earth. We are quite sure that our suspicions that these same SS and Gestapo participated in the mass extermination of countless numbers of Jews will be confirmed, along with their more open crimes like those perpetrated at Oradour sur Glane.

"I tried when I could to help get Jewish children out. I remained anonymous as possible. There were many brave young men women risking their lives to do the same without training. All they had was courage and trust in God. Their heroics saved lives. I took lives."

"The Nazis are monsters, Madeleine."

"True enough. I have fulfilled my promise to my brother Yves. France will be free. Now I must return to my parents. They have had no word from me for more than three years."

"You have news of their safety?"

"Yes, the German police officers of whom I spoke verified that they were alive."

"Major Horst Stenger and Captain William Petersen?"

"Yes sir. If you have any influence, please locate them and see that they are afforded privileged status. They are Germany's future and her past. I find that after knowing them I cannot hate the German people, however hard I try. Stenger and Willi saved me in more ways than one. Stenger will be a leader in the rebuilding of Germany. I know it in my heart."

"I have some additional although unconfirmed information about those two." Buckmaster said, tapping a thin file on the table next to the tea service. It seems that hundreds of Jewish refugees have told stories about being aided in escape by men they thought to be masquerading as Gestapo agents. One taller and blond and the other darker, compact like a prizefighter."

Madeleine tried to speak but couldn't, peals of laughter rolling out of her as she looked at Buckmaster. Tears rolled down her cheeks, letting her emotions go unchecked. She felt just marvelous. Buckmaster stared at her a look of utter surprise on his face. This was their stone killer! Eventually he couldn't help it and dissolved himself. His own sleepless nights were becoming a thing of the past. His agents had fulfilled their jobs, as had he. France was free. People passing in the hall must have wondered what was going on in that little room on the second floor of 64 Baker Street, London.

Stenger and Willi stood behind the temporary barbed wire fence along with hundreds of other German POWs awaiting their fate. They were relatively clean, not having been in combat as many of the other captured men had.

A few days earlier they had surrendered to a US patrol, sitting austerely in front of the little police station drinking coffee. The Americans had been relatively cordial believing that they were basically arresting German MPs. Enlisted men everywhere treat MPs with some deference, regardless of which side they're on. Both men turned to watch as a British jeep pulled into the compound. Two officers jumped out and presented some orders to the commanding officer of the makeshift POW camp.

"Major Horst Stenger and Captain William Petersen, front and center," one of the guards called out.

"What's this, Horsty? I don't care whose army this is, it's never good to get your name called out," Willi said out of the side of his mouth.

"We better find out, Willi," Stenger said, equally surprised.

One of the officers marched stiffly up to the fence. Snapped to attention and saluted Stenger as he stepped forward.

"Major Horst Stenger and Captain William Petersen please report!"

"Stenger and Petersen here," Stenger answered.

"Come with us, sir. Somebody in London has ordered your release."

"Who might that be?"

"The directive ordering your release was signed by Winston Churchill."

"I don't believe it," Willi managed to say.

"You must have friends in high places, gentlemen."

"No, an angel on our shoulders," Stenger said, shaking his head and smiling knowingly at Willi.

"You are officially released and are now posted in the service of her Majesty's Navy as civilian employees for the duration of the war."

"Doing what?"

"I don't believe it. You two are going to be night watchmen at the Bullmastiff brewery in Cardiff, Wales. You lucky sods!" The officer proclaimed incredulously.

"I trust the brewery is intact, Lieutenant?" Stenger said, addressing the officer.

"Your planes dropped bombs everywhere else but it was never hit."

Stenger roared with laughter and Willi was shaking and giggling so hard he had to hold onto Stenger.

Willi finally managed, "You see, Horsty, I got you in the brewery business after all!"

CHAPTER **FIFTY-ONE**

Jean-Pierre Toche sat at the kitchen table and went over his restaurant accounts. Things had improved dramatically once the Germans left. The people of La Ciotat were still celebrating and spending money at the restaurant. His stocks of wine and spirits were down, but he grinned, knowing that there would be another round of celebration when Germany was defeated. He mechanically did the books, but his thoughts were far away. He and his wife had not seen nor heard from Madeleine in more than three years. He had long since prepared himself for the worst. Not knowing what had happened to her was very difficult. He had no idea if she was dead or alive. He couldn't allow himself false hope. It was his soldier's way of dealing with grief. War takes the young and leaves the shadows of their parents to pick up the pieces and live bravely on he thought, staring down at his ledgers, seeing them there but focusing on nothing. His eyes misted as the heaviness of grief settled on his shoulders.

Madeleine rode in an American Military Jeep as it drove down the streets of La Ciotat. In the open Jeep, the salty fresh air blew in off the Mediterranean. It filled her and cradled her in its raw embrace. It was then she knew she was home. Everything in the town seemed the same, yet different. There was an excitement in the air. She saw hope and promise on the faces of people that she caught a glimpse of as she passed. Things were so different from when she had stolen away in the dark of night, the blood of her first kill on her hands. It was this place and the bold patriotism of its people, that had sustained her during her times of loneliness.

Suddenly she grabbed the driver's arm, pointing hurriedly to the opposite side of the road. The young soldier slammed on his brakes and skidded to a stop right across the street from a small, orderly restaurant. The Jeep swayed as it came to an abrupt halt. Madeleine had to grab the dash to keep her seat. She sat unable to move as she looked in through the windows of her home. Indecision crept into her thoughts for the first time in years. She was not the same daughter who had left them so many years ago. The innocence of youth had been ripped from her by the terror of war, and by the things she'd seen and done. She caught a movement in the window and knew it was her mother. All hesitation disappeared as she threw herself out of the jeep and ran towards the open door.

"*Maman!*" Madeleine cried as she ran through the front door.

Madeleine's mother stood in shock as Madeleine ran forward. The tray she was carrying clattered to the ground.

"Madeleine!" she yelled and grabbed her daughter, squeezing and kissing her to make sure she was real. Seconds latter Jean-Pierre charged from the back room, stumbling a little with his prosthetic leg. He crashed into his little family and they clung together, tears of joy and laughter shaking them as they held on for dear life.

Later Madeleine and her parents sat around the small family table in the back eating and drinking, stopping only for frequent hugs and kisses when they couldn't hold back.

"You fought with the British, I see," Jean-Pierre said touching the insignia on Madeleine's sleeve."

"I was commissioned and worked for the SOE French division. I was an agent."

"Were you in France with the Resistance?" Madeleine's mother asked without a hint of surprise.

"I worked alone, mother. Always alone," Madeleine said glancing away.

A slow smile grew on Jean-Pierre's face as he began to understand the truth behind his daughter's words.

"You killed Germans, didn't you, Madeleine? You took revenge for Yves and for France," Jean-Pierre said.

"Yes," Madeleine said without hesitation looking directly at her mother.

"*Claire,* I am pleased to introduce you to the most dangerous French woman the world has ever known, *L'ange de la Mort*."

When Madeleine didn't deny the statement the shock on her mother's face slowly changed into a gleam of knowing pride.

"Of course she is, Jean-Pierre. I have often cautioned you not to cross the women in my family. Our blood is both the hottest and the coldest," she said, not missing a beat as she raised her glass to Madeleine.

Major Jack Teach walked down the cobble stone street checking the signs on the various businesses as he passed. It was hot and the sun was beating down on him. He had never been so far south in France. He wished for some bathing shorts and a towel for the beach he could glimpse in the distance. He had asked directions at the train station, in his British Grammar School French. It was just down the road. As he made his way down the road he rubbed an ache in his left shoulder. He still carried a nasty piece of shrapnel he'd picked up courtesy of the retreating German army. He'd been informed that Madeleine was alive through his old posting in Baker Street. He was overjoyed by the information, and immediately requested a long overdue leave. He needed to find her and to fulfill his promise. He refused to think about whom he would find after so many years of separation and war. The same hope he had carried throughout the war drove him forward.

Teach turned a corner and saw a few tables and chairs arranged in the shade of a large plane tree in front of a modest sized building bearing a simple sign, Chez Toche. He dropped his bag in the street and the small slip of paper on which he'd written down the directions fell from his hand as he crossed the street against traffic, ignoring the surprised complaints of a few motorists and pedestrians traveling past.

Madeleine was peeling potatoes and enjoying the feel of the simple task that she had taken for granted day in and day out before the war. The smells of the kitchen and the lightness in her parent's voices pushed the pain and memory of loss away. When she wasn't basking in the joy of her return to life, she thought of Jack. The British were still fighting, and he was as British as they came. She had patience and from the letters she sent and received from John Trunce, she knew the war was coming to an end. She had managed to get a pair of wool socks to him, just in time for spring, his faithful return letter had lightheartedly told her. She smiled at the thought as she froze, slowly raising her eyes up to the window. My instincts never fail me, she thought, and then she saw Jack. He was impossibly tall, trim and fit. His dress uniform strained to hold in his wide shoulders and broad back.

"*Mon dieu,*" she whispered to herself as the memories of his physical being rolled through her. She dropped her paring knife and sped past her parents, setting up place settings in the dining room. They cried out in alarm as she ran past and rushed into the street.

Teach saw Madeleine and swept her up into his arms. Madeleine grabbed the back of his head and pulled him to her mouth. Neither said a word as they urgently kissed, passion slowly giving way to tenderness.

"You have a priest in this town, Madeleine Toche?" Teach said the first to speak.

"Wherever he is, I am confident that you and I could find him, Jack Teach."

"We had best find him right now, or I fear the honeymoon will start here in the street."

Madeleine laughed and they embraced again. Jack whispered into her ear, "There are two people watching us from the doorway. Your parents, I hope."

"Oh yes," Madeleine said turning. "Jack Teach, these are my parents Jean-Pierre and Claire Toche."

Jack walked forward and embraced them both. "You have a remarkable daughter. We plan to marry immediately."

To Jean-Pierre's surprise, Claire spoke first.

"Madeleine has told us so much about you. The church is this way." Madeleine and her mother each took one of Jack's arms as Jean-Pierre stopped only to duck back inside to collect the two servers that were on for the night.

"Madeleine is getting married. We need witnesses," He said with glee, taking in their shocked expressions.

The little group stood in the coolness of the nave as the afternoon sun filtered in through the stained glass, filling the altar with a magical glow. Madeleine looked down and noticed a potato peeling stuck to her shoe and wished briefly for a chance to change into some clothing more befitting the day of her marriage. Jack insisted that he had waited long enough.

Madeleine looked at Jack and the joyous expressions on the faces of her parents. The three people she loved most in the world were together and happy. The joy she felt filled her completely, pushing deep inside the last vestiges of her anger and her hate, its power absolute and cleansing. The same way the venom of her anger and malice had permeated her being after Yves' death and her rape, love burned it all away. She now understood why good triumphs over evil. Love cannot be denied.

Teach was looking into Madeleine's eyes, feeling the glow radiate from them. He was beyond joy with the knowledge that the adventure of their life had only just begun.

After the brief ceremony the family sat around outside in the shade on the steps of the church.

"I must be getting back. We'll have guests soon," Jean-Pierre said.

"Anything I can do to help?" Teach asked.

"I knew he was a good man," Jean-Pierre said, reaching up and clasping him on the shoulder.

"Where will you go for a honeymoon?" Claire asked.

"We haven't thought of that," Madeleine said.

"I have," Jack said. "Do you sail?"

"I was born on the water," Madeleine said teasingly.

"It's true, Jack," Jean-Pierre said. We were out on the sea, hoping the rocking of the boat would move matters along, and out came Madeleine and Yves."

"How about you, Jack?"

"Sail and plunder. Did you not catch the last name? One of my ancestors was a famous pirate. Perhaps you know him by his pirate name."

"*Mon dieu*, it's Blackbeard!" Jean-Pierre whistled.

"Righty-O matey! Blackbeard, Edward Teach, the scourge of the seven seas. Jack laughed slipping his hand around Madeleine as the others broke into laughter.

Madeleine winked at her mother. "Toche women never marry boring men," she said.

Author's Note:

The characters in this novel are largely fictitious, except for those of historical significance. The Das Reich Division of the SS perpetrated the massacre at Oradour sur Glane. The reasons behind the actions of the Nazis and their destruction of Oradour are clouded. There is no definitive answer. I chose to incorporate the theory put forth by Robin Mackness in his nonfiction book, "Massacre and Aftermath" (c) 1988, concerning a possible explanation. That information is referenced on an Ouradour sur Glane website, http:www.mikekemble.com/ww2/oradour.html. Regardless of the reason behind their actions, the Nazi SS Das Reich Division perpetrated an unconscionable act upon the men, women and children of Oradour. It is my fervent hope that the punishment for their crimes is perpetual.

I would like to thank my friends, family and parents for their encouragement and support during the long process of bringing *Cold Lonely Courage* to print. I would like to specifically thank, Ben Oney, my first editor, for his help and direction and Judy Bridges, Redbird Studio, for her critique. Finally, Reagan Rothe and Black Rose Writing, for their belief in my work and for providing me an opportunity to share my characters with the world.